The Life She Wants

J. M. Hewitt is the author of five crime fiction novels. Her work has also been published in three short story anthologies. Her books usually incorporate twentieth and twenty-first century events and far-flung locations, and her novels explore the darker side of human behaviour. In contrast to the sometimes dark content of her books, she lives a very nice life in a seaside town in Suffolk with her dog, Marley.

THE
LIFE SHE
WANTS

J. M. HEWITT

San Diego, California

CANELO US Canelo US
An imprint of Printers Row Publishing Group
9717 Pacific Heights Blvd, San Diego, CA 92121
www.canelobooksus.com

Printers Row Publishing Group is a division of Readerlink Distribution Services, LLC. Canelo US is a registered trademark of Readerlink Distribution Services, LLC.

This edition originally published in the United Kingdom in 2019 by Canelo.

Published in partnership with Canelo.

Correspondence regarding the content of this book should be sent to Canelo US, Editorial Department, at the above address. Author inquiries should be sent to Canelo, Unit 9, 5th Floor, Cargo Works, 1–2 Hatfields, London SE1 9PG, United Kingdom, www.canelo.co.

Publisher: Peter Norton • Associate Publisher: Ana Parker
Art Director: Charles McStravick
Senior Developmental Editor: April Graham
Production Team: Beno Chan, Julie Greene, Rusty von Dyl

Library of Congress Control Number: 2022932402

ISBN: 978-1-6672-0227-3

Printed in India

26 25 24 23 22   1 2 3 4 5

For Joan Daly

With love

Prologue

It was a terrible shock to her body, being plunged into the icy water of the lake. At first, she was numb, sinking lower and lower, the weight of her clothes dragging her down into the freezing depths. Moments later, she gasped, her body demanding air but finding water instead. It burned in her lungs, a deep, screaming, searing pain in her chest.

I'm drowning.

The thought was the only clear thing, the knowledge that this was it, this was the end. She relaxed, drifted for a moment, before her body protested.

She kicked her legs and punched out her arms, something deep inside her instructing her to head up to the surface, to find air so that she could open her mouth and breathe. The rest of it could wait: the cold, the wet, the snow, even her attacker up there on the lake.

Up, up, UP!

The persistent thought was like a chant in her head. She reached out with fingers that were turning blue and grasped the mantra as though it were a rope that could pull her up to the surface.

It was pitch-black in here, in the hole, underneath the water, but a tiny pinprick of light guided her. It was hope instead of hurt that bloomed in her chest now.

One last push. She felt her body engaging every muscle to propel her forward. She could sense that the air that had eluded her so far was within touching distance.

She was already gleeful, teeth showing in joyful gratitude, not caring about the water that seeped into her mouth through her smile. She was ready to burst through the surface of the water and gulp in great breaths. She had made it.

Smash.

She cried out in pain, letting even more water into her mouth as her fingertips came into contact with something solid. Realisation hit her hard, and she clawed at the ice above her head, frantic, her whole body rolling until she wasn't sure if it was the world that was upside down or herself.

A shadow fell, cutting off the light that came from outside and above. It turned her mounting panic into something akin to a survival instinct. She tilted her head back and forced herself to watch through eyes that were stinging painfully.

Through the thick ice she saw boots, legs, the person they belonged to moving steadily over her.

The person who had attacked her.

They were still out there, waiting and watching.

Time – and air – had run out.

She closed her eyes. She felt her breathing slow. Her body was shutting down.

It was over.

Chapter 1

Paula Ellis paused by the window on the first floor of her home and looked outside. Leaves carpeted the tree-lined avenue, the street a kaleidoscope of red and gold. Yellow rose bushes bordered perfectly manicured front lawns. The flowers were thinning out now, their duty done for the summer, but no wilted brown petals littered the grass. Here in suburban heaven, everything was crisp and clean. With a smile, she pulled up the sash and leaned out, breathing deeply.

Autumn. Changes. It was the time of year when Paula always felt the potential for transformation.

She put down the pile of clean washing she had carried upstairs and sat on the windowsill, deep in thought. It was invariably during October that Paula and her husband, Tommy, would begin talking about making alterations in their home life. She imagined finally getting a dog, the same dog they had been talking about for the previous four autumns as the evenings drew in. Somehow, the cold blue sky and the piles of leaves made it easy to imagine them wrapping up and taking family walks in the countryside that bordered their Essex home. Often, the talk would then turn from a puppy to a baby. The conversation was always started and led by Paula, with her pointing out that if they were going to do it, then it should be soon. After

3

all, they were both thirty-five, and Paula didn't want to be a forty-plus-year-old mum at the school gates.

Tommy's face, open and eager when the talk had been of a dog, would shut down. Usually they would then argue. Or he would. She would sit there on the lovely three-piece suite, her head nodding lower and lower, until he had patiently explained all the reasons why it wasn't a good time.

He'd had a lot of reasons to hesitate, the last four years of 'new changes, new life' conversations. He was moving on up in his workplace, having started at the bottom as a foreign exchange junior back when he graduated. He ticked off every box every year, and the rewards came in annually: a car for each of them, Paula finally able to quit her job and practise becoming a stay-at-home mum. Two years ago had come the biggest bonus so far: the five-bedroom, three-storey town house in the new Wickford development of Riverside. Views of the River Crouch out the back, meadows and wooded areas at the front, and just a forty-minute commute to London for Tommy. It was perfect. It was a home too big for two, and Paula had moved in with a sense of positivity and hope for the future.

But that January, just like the ones before, there was a promotion on the table, and once again it wasn't the time to start a family. Inevitably they would leave it there, Tommy full of promises to pick up the conversation again towards Christmas. But the next year there would be another reason, another job that had opened up, another box he had to tick as he rocketed towards the top. Not the best time. Maybe next year.

She appreciated that she didn't understand how hard his work was, not really. After all, she had all the time in the world; all the hours in the day were hers to do with as she wanted. As long as there was a nice dinner on the table for him when he got home.

Paula drummed her fingers on the windowpane. Could this year be different? After all, Tommy had gone as far as he could go, having landed the top job of director of accounting in the summer.

She felt a thrill run through her and she shivered at the fresh realisation. There were no more reasons to delay. *No more excuses.*

She inhaled deeply, the scent of change in the air, and suddenly she couldn't wait for Tommy to get home.

She abandoned the pile of washing, skipping past it and into their master suite. Peering in the mirror, she pulled her hands through her shoulder-length brown hair, teasing it up and pinning it. Quickly, she moved over to her wardrobe and flicked through the hangers.

She would make an effort tonight. After ten years of marriage, it was important to keep things good for her husband, who worked all the hours. She would nip down to the butcher's on the high street and buy a couple of nice steaks for dinner.

Candles and wine; she made a mental note as she pulled out a woollen dress the same shade as the leaves outside. Music and a great dinner, and maybe an early night.

Paula smiled, bathed in hope. Could this be it?

-

'I was only going down to the high street, the local butcher would have been okay,' said Paula as she jostled her shopping into the booth and sat down opposite her best friend, Julie.

Julie appraised Paula's Waitrose bags. 'It wouldn't have been organic, though, would it? And if you're going to start a family, you want only the best. Start as you mean to go on.'

Paula shushed her, glancing around furtively. 'Nobody knows!' She giggled. 'Even Tommy doesn't know yet.'

Julie raised her eyes. 'I don't know why you've waited so long. I mean, why don't you just go ahead and get pregnant anyway? You're married, for Christ's sake!'

Paula said nothing as she picked up the menu. It was an area where she and Julie differed. As soon as Paula had started dating Tommy, well over fifteen years ago now, Julie had spotted his potential, and had warned her friend not to let him slip through the net. After all, she reasoned, how many opportunities came along in a lifetime to get with a man who would never, ever be poor?

For Paula, it had been different. She had seen a good man in Tommy, one who peppered her with kindness and wasn't stifling in his love. She had never needed the annual bonus that his work brought in, nor the big house, nor the two cars, or the once-in-a-lifetime holiday taken every year.

She'd just wanted a man to love, one who would love her back.

Now, she had everything she could possibly want, except for the easiest thing of all — a baby. Tommy was still there, though, and she smiled at the thought of him.

'It's not right, doing something like that behind his back,' she said. 'We have to discuss something as big as starting a family.'

Julie snorted. 'Discuss it long enough, sweetheart, and the decision will be taken out of your hands.' And in case Paula didn't get her meaning, she leaned forward, her ample bosom resting on the tabletop. 'You'll be too old.' She sat back, crossed her arms. 'Maybe that's what he's stalling for.'

Paula rolled her eyes, taking no offence from her best friend's straight talk. 'Shut up, Jules. If he didn't want a family, why would he have bought us a five-bedroom house?'

'For show!' Julie said. 'People like Tommy Ellis need the big house, the flash car. It's all about appearances.' She pointed her finger at Paula. 'Just don't wait another year.'

'I need to lose weight if I'm having a baby. God knows I don't want to be shifting baby weight *and* pre-baby weight afterwards,' Paula said. She slammed the menu closed. 'Salad for me, and a mineral water.'

Julie raised her eyebrows. She said nothing, but it spoke volumes.

'What?' asked Paula.

Julie sighed and shut her own menu. 'Do you ever do anything for yourself?'

'What?' Paula laughed, but at the sight of Julie's face, it trailed off into nothing.

'It's just everything you do or say is for Tommy. I can't remember the last time we did something that wasn't ultimately for him.'

'What do you call this shopping trip?'

'It's not for you, we're here for steaks for Tommy!' Julie said. She took a deep breath, then reached over and covered Paula's hand with her own. 'Just... don't lose yourself. You're a person too, and a pretty damn good one. It shouldn't be all about him.'

Paula wrenched her hand from underneath Julie's. Of *course* it was all about Tommy. He was the important one in their relationship. Without him, they'd have nothing. *She* would have nothing.

'I've been where you are, remember, and nothing you can do will stop whatever's going to happen,' Julie continued.

Paula's blood ran cold. 'But your husband cheated on you! Multiple times!' She stared at Julie. 'Are you saying Tommy's going to do that?'

'No, Christ!' Julie flapped her hand at her friend. 'I just meant—'

'I don't want to talk about it.' With tears threatening, Paula grabbed her bags and stood up. 'I don't want lunch any more, I've lost my appetite.'

Julie's eyes narrowed to tiny slits, and she sat back and crossed her arms. 'Fine. You go. I'm staying. I *am* hungry, and I'm not starving myself for anyone, certainly not a man.'

The words bubbled up and out before Paula could stop them. 'And don't we know it,' she snapped spitefully, tearfully, and turning on her heel, she stalked out of the restaurant.

Chapter 2

In the booth behind Julie and Paula, hidden by the high-backed seat, Anna Masi listened with interest and growing anger. White-hot heat simmered inside her.

How were there women in the world like those two? Women who seemed to have everything – a car, a house, the capacity not to have to work – and yet still were not happy.

Anna appraised her own reflection in the mirrored wall of the coffee shop. She sucked in her cheekbones, angled her face so the harsh lighting bounced off her porcelain image.

'Elfin' was what the magazines called people like her. She embraced the description, wearing her hair short, highlighting it carefully so it had a surfer look to it. William called her his little elf too, even though he was far too old to know about it from the fashion magazines she coveted.

Thinking of William made Anna glance at her watch. Time to go. Time to head back to the old boy, cook him his dinner: pie and chips; no organic meat for him, not like the women whose conversation she'd spent the last half-hour listening to.

As she got off the bus and crossed the street towards William's little terraced house in Ilford, she spotted his neighbour coming out of the house next door. Pausing, she took her beret out of her handbag and pulled it on, pushing her short hair up inside it.

'Afternoon, love,' called Mr Henderson as she strode up the path.

She smiled and gave him a friendly wave before hurriedly inserting her key in the lock. The bags she was clutching slowed her down, though, and Mr Henderson held out a hand.

'Got William's dinner in there, have you?' he asked, craning over the waist-high fence. 'When you going to start looking after me?' He smiled, though it was really a leer.

She gave a barely concealed sigh. The constant battle against men and their proprietorial nature. All the words she really wanted to say to him ran through her head, but she bit them back. If she spoke them, he would tell William that she had been rude to him, and she would lose her job. That couldn't happen. To further help her keep the cascade of abuse inside, she allowed herself to imagine returning to the place that had taken her so long to escape from.

No. She couldn't lose this job, this home. It was everything. It had saved her.

She fixed a smile on her face, bright on the surface, icy cool beneath if one looked hard enough.

'Oh, you,' she said. 'Have a nice day, Mr Henderson.' And she slipped inside before he could delay her further.

Inside the dim, dark hallway, she let the carrier bags drop to the floor as she leaned against the door.

'That you, dear?' called a tremulous voice from the kitchen. 'Come in, I'm just putting the kettle on.'

Anna paused. William hardly ever felt well enough to make a cup of tea. That was why he employed her.

Cautiously, she picked up the carrier bags and moved through to the kitchen.

The first thing she noticed was that he was dressed. And not just in his old T-shirt and pyjama bottoms, but actually dressed, in a shirt and a suit and even a tie! Her gaze went to the doormat, and the pair of shiny black shoes that sat there, the edges crusted with blades of grass. A brown leaf was stuck to the sole of the left shoe.

'William, have you been... outside?' she asked suspiciously.

Unable to hold it in, he beamed at her. 'I have,' he said. He held his arms out wide and turned in a circle, gripping the edge of the worktop as he moved painfully slowly. 'I don't scrub up too bad for an old git, do I?'

Anna felt as unsteady as William looked. He never went outside. Not even into the garden in the spring or summer, and definitely not when it was a cold, wet autumn day like today.

He wobbled, and Anna threw the bags on the old wooden kitchen table and dashed to his side.

'You need to sit down,' she said. 'Come on, I'll finish the tea.'

He allowed himself to be led, and Anna put an arm around his waist, taking almost all of his weight upon her slight frame. In the living room, she lowered him into his chair.

'Did you get my things?' he asked.

She nodded.

'And what did you buy for yourself?' he asked, resting his head back and smiling up at her.

Anna smiled back. 'A dress,' she said, and then, coyly, 'Would you like to see it?'

He raised a liver-spotted hand and patted her arm. 'You know I would.' His eyes gleamed, cobalt-blue chips that pierced her. 'Put it on, I don't want to see it on the hanger.'

Obediently she left the room, grabbing the bags off the table as she went upstairs. In the room that had become her own, she stripped down to her underwear and emptied the bags on the bed. A dress, she had told him, when in fact she had purchased five. Always, when he sent her out on shopping errands, he told her to get something for herself. After a while it had become clear that he never checked his credit card bill or receipts. In fact, when she had been caring for him for just three weeks, he asked her if she would mind taking over the paying of the bills. Anna had obliged, realising very quickly that William had more than enough in his bank accounts to cover any amount that she spent on his card.

She selected one dress and pulled it on. It was a body-hugging woollen winter number that skimmed her thighs. Appraising her reflection, she shook out her hair. For some unknown reason, the women in the coffee shop came to mind.

Neither of them could wear this, she thought with a sense of satisfaction. Definitely not the heavier of the two, but even the other one, the married, spoiled one, was the wrong side of thirty and the wrong side of size 10 to carry off a dress like this.

The husband would want her to, Anna knew that much just from the way the women had been talking about him. And she would try something on, a dress like this, and his eyes would be filled with disappointment. He would suggest something else, maybe a trouser suit, or a maxi dress that hid a multitude of sins.

On a whim, she pulled out her phone, tapped into the Facebook app, and searched for the name she had over-head earlier that day. It was a relatively common name, and she stabbed at the screen, going into the accounts one by one, checking the relationship status to look at the profiles of the wives, seeking the woman she had seen. The right Tommy Ellis came up at last, and his profile picture confirmed everything Anna had thought about him: tall, tanned, and he clearly took care of himself, even if his wife didn't. He had the money to, she thought bitterly.

Scrolling through his photos, it was obvious what sort of world he and his wife lived in. A universe in which it rained money. The house, the five-bedroom one that she had mentioned to her friend; the car, a BMW – of course it would be – flashy and with a personalised number plate. Older pictures of him in rugby kit. And yes, that made sense: people like him always veered towards rugby rather than football. She made a bet with herself that he played squash weekly, and spat a laugh when she came across a post tagged in a squash court in Essex. He was a walking cliché, just like his wife.

But just for a moment she let the screen fade to black, imagined herself living a life with a man who was hand-some and successful, rather than her actual life, taking money from William here and there, living in a terraced house with the old man, doing all the chores that came with looking after a pensioner.

She clicked the phone again, scrolled some more. There were holidays galore. Sunshine, beaches, cocktails. Him always in a crisp white shirt, rarely topless in any of the pictures, actually. She peered more closely, saw he had the potential to be a big man and wondered how hard he worked at keeping his body just this side of good. She grinned spitefully, knowing that when the kids the wife wanted so much came along, both of their frames would go from respectable to a state of let go. Briefly she wondered if that was what had happened to 'Jules', the wife's fat friend.

Intrigued, she hovered over a photo of him with his arms around his wife, then clicked on her profile.

Paula was her name. Her page was public, as was Tommy's. Which it would be; if you had this much money and property and fancy living, you'd want the whole world to know about it.

She wrinkled her nose and scrolled down the page. She blinked at Paula's latest post: the raw steaks laid out on a wooden chopping board, fresh chives, mushrooms tumbled beside them.

Anna's lip curled. She imagined taking a photo of William's uncooked pie and frozen chips.

'Gemma, what're you doing up there?' William's voice drifted up the stairs.

For a split second, as always, the name threw her, before she realised he was talking to her.

It had been an easy mistake, when they first met and she had introduced herself as Anna. He didn't have his hearing aids in, thought she had said her name was Gemma. She had gone to correct him before biting back her words. She wasn't sure why she didn't tell him her real name, but as time went on, and more and more of William's money came her way, she decided that the misunderstanding might not be a bad thing. It was the same reason she always wore a hat outside: beret in winter, cap or sunhat in summer. The less anyone knew about her to be able to identify her, the better.

After all, she didn't plan on staying with William forever.

'Coming!' she called.

Clicking away from Facebook, she looked at herself in the mirror one last time before skipping down the stairs to show William what he had bought for her today.

Chapter 3

Paula stared at the steaks on the chopping board. Blood leaked around the grooves, settling into the wood. Grabbing a piece of kitchen towel, she wiped it up, only for more brown liquid to appear a moment later.

She took a deep breath, disposed of the paper towel and checked her phone again.

It was almost seven o'clock, and there was no Tommy, and no dinner. She hated delays, despised radio silence. As the minutes ticked past, her worry grew. Scenarios were vivid in her head: the train off the rails, a slip from the platform. They ballooned in their intensity, becoming visions of terrorist bombs and personal attacks.

When her worry threatened to overwhelm her, she snatched up the phone and dialled his number. Just as it began to ring, she heard his key in the lock. Hanging up, she moved into the hallway.

'Where have you been?' she asked. 'The steaks have been sitting out forever, and you said you'd ring when you were getting on the train.'

Tommy paused, briefcase satchel halfway off. He glanced at the front door and she wondered if he were considering bolting.

'Jeez, Paula, can't you wait until I actually get in the house before having a go at me?' He smiled as he spoke, but his words cut.

She bit her lip as she walked towards him, wondering how her blind panic over his well-being had emerged as nagging. She hadn't meant her words to be anything other than a normal question. She reached out and stroked his arm, instantly contrite. 'Sorry, baby, but I asked you to ring me so I could get timings right on the dinner.'

Propping his bag against the stair post, he straightened up and scratched his head. 'When?'

'When what?' Swiftly, she picked up the case and hung it on the hook inside the cupboard under the stairs.

'When did you ask me to let you know what time I'd be home?' he asked. Reaching past her, he retrieved his bag. 'I need this, got some work to be getting on with.'

'I asked you when I texted you.' She slipped her hand into his jacket pocket, pulled out his phone and showed him the screen. 'Look, an unread message, from me.'

He grabbed the phone back. 'Bloody hell, Paula! My life is a world of shit all day long at work; is it too much to ask to have a few minutes' peace when I get in before you start attacking me?'

She swallowed hard. 'Sorry, sweetie. You go and sit down, I'll put the steaks on.'

With a nod, he dropped a kiss on the top of her head. 'That sounds like a plan,' he said, and strode into the lounge.

Deflated somewhat, Paula returned to the kitchen and began to prepare the steaks. She thought of her friend from the gym, Alexa, whose husband loved nothing more than cooking for her, and who seemed to text and ring her all the time. She wondered what that might be like, tried to visualise it.

But what did it really matter? Tommy worked all day; Paula stayed at home. The least she could do for him was serve up a decent meal at the end of his more-often-than-not twelve-hour shifts. Plus, their marriage was absolutely fine. So, he didn't cook. Sometimes, when he missed his connecting train, he would wander around Liverpool Street station and come home – albeit late – bearing flowers, or a piece of jewellery, or a slice of cake from that expensive place just outside the upper level. Her worry at his lateness would fade, replaced by a rush of love at his kindness.

She shot a look towards the lounge as she heard the television come on.

She uncorked a bottle of red and poured two glasses. She threw hers back before carefully carrying the other one through and presenting it to him.

–

Later, steaks eaten and wine drunk, Paula looked at Tommy. He had the recliner all the way back, his leg slung over the arm. His tie was loose and his face relaxed for the first time since he had come home.

She chewed on the skin around her thumbnail. It shouldn't be this difficult to start an important conversation with him. He was chilled out right now, with a full stomach, and he'd been warmed by the wine. It should have been easy to slide into the talk she wanted to have with him.

'What's up?' he asked, catching her staring.

She didn't reply straight away; instead, she regarded him critically, noticing how tired he looked. A thought came into her mind for the first time: that if they went ahead and had a baby, she would be raising it pretty much alone. Oh, sure, Tommy would be there, he would be present, in body but not in spirit. He wouldn't have the time to bathe it or change its nappies or even look after it if she wanted to go out with Julie.

She looked on the bright side: the child would be all hers. It would love her more than anything else in the world. She smiled to herself.

'Hun?' he prompted her.

She took a deep breath and dived in. 'I think we need to talk about us,' she said. 'And whether we are actually going to extend "us" into a family.'

He turned his head back towards the television, but she caught the eye roll. A sour ball of hurt replaced the feeling of hope from just a moment ago.

'Tommy?' she said, tentatively.

He sighed. 'Do we have to do this tonight?'

'No…' she said softly. Swallowing, she raised her chin and dared to ask, 'But when *can* we talk about it?'

'I'm just not sure it's the right time,' he replied mildly. 'For a baby, I mean, not to have this conversation.'

And in spite of all her hope, she had known it, that this was exactly the way this conversation would go. She would ask, he would say no, and in less than a minute the baby dream would be shattered until she found the nerve to bring the subject up again.

The ball of hurt in her belly turned to disappointment, raw and stinging inside her.

Try again, she told herself. She took a deep breath. 'Julie said the time is never completely right,' she said softly. 'And if we keep putting it off, the decision will be out of our hands. I'll be too old.'

He looked at her now. 'You've been speaking to Julie about this? Christ, Paula, why do you have to gossip with her about me? Why can't you just talk to me?'

She drew in a breath at his sharp words. The inhalation had the unmistakable shaky quality of a sob. 'I try, but you won't discuss it.'

He held his hands up, a gesture of surrender. 'Listen, it's just work, it's full-on, you know that.' He lowered his hands and reached cautiously into his briefcase. 'You know I appreciate everything you do, and I think you'd be a wonderful mother.'

The feelings of hurt dissipated. Gratified, she leaned forward. 'Do you really believe that?'

He didn't answer; instead, he handed her an envelope, crisp and white, gold letters embossed on the front spelling out her name.

'What's this?' she asked.

'Open it.' He reached out an arm, put his hand on hers. 'I agree we should talk about this baby stuff, we should plan it. And this,' he tapped the envelope, 'is a perfect time and place for that conversation.'

Unable to wait any longer, mollified by the unexpected gift, she carefully opened the envelope.

Tickets.

She put them in her lap, read them carefully, then raised her face to look at him.

'Tommy! A cruise?'

'Yes.' He grinned. 'On the maiden voyage of the *Ruby Spirit*, setting sail from Southampton and heading for Iceland.'

Paula gasped and clutched the tickets to her chest.

'To see the Northern Lights,' he added.

'Oh my God!' she squealed.

'And,' he said, drawing out his words for maximum effect, 'we leave in a week.'

'Good day, intrepid adventurers, and welcome to the maiden voyage of the Ruby Spirit. This is your captain speaking! We will be cruising off at a rate of fifteen knots as we wave goodbye to Southampton and travel down the Solent before we ease into the North Sea, where we will sail up past Ouddorp and Åndalsnes before turning in a north-westerly direction towards Iceland.

'I'm pleased to tell you that a veritable smorgasbord of charming astronomical sights is anticipated in November's cold, crisp night sky. We will be praying to Poseidon for clear skies in which we will be blessed to capture such prominent constellations as Pegasus, Andromeda and Cassiopeia.

'Something that should be seen at least once on your cruise this week is the Leonid meteor shower, which will occur from the second week of November right through to the end of the month. This celestial shower is renowned for its fast-moving meteors, which appear to hang in the sky for several seconds. The shower is due to peak on the seventeenth, when around twenty meteors per hour are expected. And as always, don't forget that the spectacular Northern Lights can appear at any time, so keep watching!'

Chapter 4

Later, as Paula sat on the edge of the bed and applied her moisturiser, she couldn't help but smile as she looked at the tickets, propped up on the mantelpiece in their bedroom. What a turn of events!

She cast her mind back to the baby conversation that had turned into a surprise holiday. He had agreed to a baby. Not in so many words, but he'd said that she'd be a wonderful mother. And that *we should plan it*. She would expect nothing else from Tommy; he was a planner. Every major event of his life was meticulously thought through, all the way from his proposal to her (down on one knee on the white sands of their private beach in Jamaica) to the latest BMW (*weeks* of research into that one) and where to live and what sort of house to buy. Even selecting a bottle of Christmas whisky for his boss (back when he had one, before *he* became the boss) had involved a trip to the most expensive private clubs in London.

Needing to share, Paula grabbed her mobile and rattled off a text to Julie, before she remembered their argument. She deleted it slowly, and the excitement wavered.

We'll be fine, we've had rows before, but I'm not apologising first.

Instead, she flicked onto Facebook, smiled at how many likes her steak post had got. And so it should, with the filters and the placement. She should have put it on

Instagram, tagging all those food critics and top chefs. The new additions on the mantelpiece caught her eye, and with a smile stretching across her face, she took a photo of the tickets and posted the picture on her timeline with the words *Unexpected present from Tommy!* She added a heart emoji, then, satisfied, sent it out to be admired by her many friends.

Her phone lit up, compliments already pouring in. *Tommy is the best!* gushed one friend. *You're SO LUCKY*, said another, and a third, *He's a keeper!*

Finally satisfied, she put the phone down, screwed the lid back on the moisturiser and climbed into bed next to the already snoring Tommy.

'Love you, babe,' she whispered, planting a kiss on his bare shoulder.

Then she reached over and turned out the light.

—

Anna opened the oven door to check on William's pie. It was nearly done, and she turned up the grill to allow the chips to catch up.

She rearranged her apron, making sure it covered the new dress. It wouldn't do to get any food stains on it. She'd wanted to change back into her jeans once she'd modelled it for William, but he insisted she keep it on.

'Your figure looks very lovely in it,' he'd said softly.

Anna was quietly furious. She knew she looked good in it, but it wasn't for William's admiring gaze. She had relented, though; he had bought it after all. She needed to keep him sweet.

'Dinner's ready,' she called. 'Do you want it on your lap or at the table?'

'Table,' he replied, walking slowly into the room. 'And you can sit with me.'

She did as she was told, feeling his eyes on her as she dished up.

Once he had his meal in front of him, Anna took a seat opposite. She never ate with William; in fact, she rarely ate at all. Instead, she sipped at a cold, crisp white wine while William added several teaspoons of sugar to his tea.

'You never said where you went today,' she remarked, glancing at his shirt and tie.

William nodded – grimly, she thought. 'I was reading the newspaper this morning after you went out.' He chewed slowly, swallowing before continuing. 'Another bank collapsed.'

'Really?' She frowned, sure she would have read or heard about something as major as that. 'Which bank?'

He gestured with his fork towards the counter, where a newspaper sat. A piece of meat flew off the fork, narrowly missing her dress and landing on her arm. Trying to disguise her distaste, she flicked it away, before reaching for the newspaper.

It was the *Telegraph*, and it was from 2008. The news story he had read was over a decade old. She said nothing and put the paper back.

'So, I went to the bank; both of my banks, actually,' he said. 'I told them I had worked too hard all my life to lose my money, and I withdrew it.'

Anna put her glass down. 'What do you mean, you withdrew it?'

He shoved another forkful of pie into his mouth, chewing infuriatingly slowly before planting his hands on the table and pushing himself upright. 'Come with me.'

Anna followed him down the hall and up the stairs, her hands outstretched in case he stumbled like he had before. Nearing the top, he wobbled. At the last minute, his hand shot out and gripped the banister. Finally, he led her into his bedroom.

'There,' he said, pointing at a black sports bag that she'd never seen before. 'I figured my money is safer here, where I can keep an eye on it.'

Anna eyed the bag. 'William, how much is in there?'

He pulled a piece of paper from his breast pocket and squinted at it. 'Eighteen thousand pounds,' he said. Carefully, he folded the paper and put it back, then patted his pocket.

'Bloody hell,' she whispered. Suddenly her heart was thudding in her chest.

How did he even get it here? She was sure eighteen grand must weigh more than his frail frame could carry.

'Was it heavy?' she asked.

'The taxi driver helped me,' William replied. 'Nice chap.'

'Did you tell him what was in the bag?' She felt cold suddenly.

He shrugged and turned his smile up a few watts. 'You worry too much, dear.'

She thought, hard and fast. She put a hand on his arm, caressed it gently. 'You're a smart man. I never trust banks either. But you can't just leave it there.' She smiled winningly at him. 'Would you like me to keep it safe for you?'

He flapped his hand at her dismissively. 'No, it's okay. I like having it where I can see it.'

Bored now of his big news, he stumbled over to his bed and sat down, patting the cover with a wrinkled hand. 'Would you like to lie with me a while, Gemma?'

She forced a smile, moved over to him and plumped up his pillows. 'Let me just wash up; give me ten minutes and I'll come and sit with you.'

No matter how many times it happened, she always gave the same answer, and she always said 'sit' when William had said 'lie'. Occasionally he would be fast asleep when she had run out of stalling time, and she hoped today would be one of those times.

'Don't be long,' he called as she left the room.

Anna paused at the door, her eyes lingering on the black sports bag. 'I won't,' she promised.

-

In the kitchen, she drummed her fingers on the table, deep in thought. Eighteen thousand pounds in cash, in a bag on the floor just above her head. Briefly she wondered if William would ever count it, and how much she could sneak out of the bag without him knowing.

Her eyes lit up at the idea, and once again she thought of the woman in the café. She'd bet Paula didn't have eighteen grand at her disposal, no matter how much money Tommy made in his big important job in the City.

She was supposed to be clearing the dishes, and she cocked a head towards the ceiling, listening for sounds from William. All was quiet up there, and she reached for her phone. It opened on Paula's Facebook page, and there was yet another post from the woman.

Unexpected present from Tommy! And the accompanying photo: tickets for a cruise to Iceland.

Anna zoomed in, looked at the date on the ticket. Leaving Southampton in seven days. She placed her phone on the table, careful to avoid the gravy spots from William's messy meal.

A thump from upstairs, followed by slow, shuffling footsteps. She sighed, pushed herself up from the table and began stacking the plates.

'Gemma!' William's voice came from above.

'I'm coming, just clearing the dinner things,' she called back.

As she worked, she caught sight of her reflection in the window. A beautiful girl, an expensive dress, covered by an apron spattered with pieces of the old man's dinner.

She turned away and pulled the apron off over her head. Bundling it up and throwing it on the table, she walked slowly up the stairs towards William.

–

He woke early, like all old people seemed to. Anna hadn't slept, and at close to midnight she'd tried to slip off the bed, but William had heard her, and his big hand had gripped her upper arm and pulled her head back down to the pillow.

He didn't say anything; didn't need to. Reluctantly, she lay by his side, listening to his snores, smelling his scent, a peculiar combination of talc and cooking fat. His hand rested heavily on her thigh, but inch by inch she finally slid out of his grasp and returned to her own bedroom.

She removed her clothes, sniffing gingerly at the woollen dress. Annoyed, she realised it would need to go to the dry cleaner's. William could pay for it, she thought bitterly.

It was six a.m. and still dark when her door creaked open. Always she slept on tenterhooks, knowing that William was prone to wandering, not wanting him to come any closer towards her tiny single bed.

'William?' She pushed her hair back, pulled the cover up to conceal her nakedness. 'It's early. Go back to bed and I'll make some tea.'

In the light from the hallway she looked him up and down. He had dressed – well, half dressed – in a greying vest, navy-blue braces holding up his brown trousers. She looked away, across the room, hoping he didn't see the disgust on her face.

He shook his head and looked down at the faded carpet. 'I have to get on,' he said. 'I've got so much to do.'

Her mouth twisted, bitter and resentful. What exactly did he have to do? Nothing. She, Anna, did everything. William had nothing in his life: no chores, no hobbies, no friends.

'You haven't got to do anything,' she said in what she hoped was a soothing tone. 'Go back to your room. I'll get up soon and sort us out some breakfast.'

'You don't understand,' he said, and his words were soft and low; his eyes, when he raised them to look at her, troubled. 'My son is coming over.'

–

In the darkened lounge, Anna listened as William told her all about his son's imminent visit.

Jason was his name. He lived in Spain, managing some restaurants and bars there. In the time she had been working for William, he had never come to visit. As far

28

as she knew, he didn't call, or write; in fact, the only sign there was a son at all was a Christmas card each year.

'He wants to open another bar, a café bar,' explained William. 'And he wants me to go back to Spain with him.'

'I don't know if you'd like Spain,' she said. 'It'll be too hot for you; you know you don't like the sun.'

His eyes took on a faraway look. 'It might be nice,' he said. 'I'd be useful; I could look after the kids while their parents are at work. Jason says they have bingo games every evening, and take naps every afternoon.' He looked towards the window, at the bitter rain smacking against the pane. 'He needs me, anyway.'

Anna sat deep in thought. Suddenly the pieces clicked together. 'William, are you going to invest in this bar?' she asked, thinking of the bag of money sitting upstairs.

He shrugged, glanced at her. 'I think he could do with a little help from me on that side of it.'

Of course he could do with help. He wanted nothing to do with his father all year round, but now that there was money involved...

'When is he coming?' she asked, her mind racing now.

'Tomorrow,' said William. 'He's got some business here and then we'll probably leave in a week.'

There was more, but he wasn't saying it. She took a deep breath and walked over to him, sat on the arm of his chair and touched his shoulder. William took a deep breath and scrubbed at his nose. 'I don't think he would agree with you being here.'

Anna's body went cold.

'I'm your carer,' she said stiffly.

'Yes, but...' He offered her a watery smile. 'You're more than that, Gemma. So much more.' He planted his hands on the arms of his chair and pushed himself unsteadily up. 'I've got something for you. A little going-away bonus.' He jerked his head at her. 'Come.'

Half of the money, she thought. I'll go quietly for half of the money that's in that bag up there.

It took an age for them to make it up to the bedroom, and Anna stood primly in the door as William lowered himself to the floor beside the bag. He unzipped it, plucked at a pile of money. As he counted it carefully, Anna looked at the bald spot on the back of his head, the scalp baby-pink and flaky, the hair surrounding it fine and white.

Finally, he looked up at her, holding out a thin pile of notes with one hand, his other absently rubbing his chest.

She reached over and took it.

A hundred quid.

One measly hundred fucking pounds.

She straightened up, pulling her shoulders back, and tucked the money in the back pocket of her jeans. 'Come on, let's get you back downstairs and I'll make you a nice cup of tea.' She moved around behind him, hefting him up.

William staggered to his feet and leaned heavily on her.

'Thank you, Gemma,' he said, his voice paper-thin.

She nodded, manoeuvred him in front of her and steered him to the stairs. On the top step, he stopped abruptly and twisted round to look at her.

'You're a good girl, Gemma,' he said.

She stared into his eyes, pale blue pools now, weaker than they had been yesterday, when he had made her wear the dress and parade in front of him. More faded than they had been last night, when he'd clutched at her, leaving the imprints of his fingers in a blue-grey stain on her skin, and made her lie with him.

'I know,' she agreed, even though it wasn't true.

He kept his eyes on her, and they were leaking now. Why was he crying? she wondered. Was it because he was losing his faithful servant who cooked and cleaned and fussed over him? He wouldn't be able to have someone like her in Spain, under the watchful eye of his son. He wouldn't be able to leer at Jason's wife, or make her model new form-fitting clothes for him, or get her to lie next to him on his bed. Or was he weeping because he knew he had been wrong to ask her to do those things?

'I'll miss you,' he said.

'I know,' she said again, and she raised her hands, planting the palms flat against his chest.

She leaned into him at the same time as she wedged her hip against the wall at the top of the stairs. Then, using every ounce of her strength, she pushed him as hard as she could.

–

There was no need to rush. Jason wasn't coming until tomorrow. She had a full day, and potentially a night too, to ensure every last trace of her was removed from this house. She didn't want to stay the night, though, not with William crumpled at the bottom of the stairs.

But she had time, and she reminded herself of this as she hurried back into the bedroom. *Don't rush, take care, don't leave anything that could tell anyone who you are.*

First things first. She fell to her knees beside the black bag, pulling open the zip and breathing in the scent of the money. It smelled like success and escape. It eclipsed the awful smell of William's home, and his old-man odour. It was the aroma of a brand-new life.

She lifted the bag, testing the weight. It was heavy, but she'd been half carrying William around for months. She was used to a dead weight.

She zipped up the bag, stood and moved into her own bedroom. Carefully she pulled all her clothes out of the wardrobe and laid them on the bed. She thought back to when she had arrived here; the weekender bag was all she had. She would need more suitcases for sure. But she had to be careful. She couldn't call a taxi from this address; when Jason came tomorrow and found his father's body, he would no doubt inform the neighbours. They in turn would tell him about her.

She thought of the guy next door, leering old Mr Henderson. At least he too thought her name was Gemma. Nobody would be searching for Anna Masi. *She* had ceased to exist a long time ago.

But regardless of the safety of her fake name, questions would still be asked. If she used a taxi from the house, the driver might come forward, might have CCTV in his cab. No. A taxi firm was out of the question, which meant she would have to take only what she could actually manage to carry to the bus depot or train station.

Unless…

She darted out of the room, into William's bedroom, and pulled open the old-fashioned bureau. In a shoebox he kept blank greetings cards, old now, left over from when he had people to send them to, and the energy and the balance to go out and buy them. She pulled one out, a hare on the front, a relic from a long-ago outing to one of the museums in London. With a faint smile on her lips, she scrawled inside:

Dearest William,

Thank you for everything you did, it was a pleasure working for you. I'll miss you!
Enjoy your new life in sunny Spain!

Love, Gemma

She stood back and scrutinised her work before bending over and adding yesterday's date. Satisfied, she propped the card up on William's bedroom mantelpiece. She reached for the rest of the packet of cards and shoved them in her pocket to put in the bin later.

Perfection. And a brilliant idea.

But she had to get a move on now. It wouldn't do for the son to turn up tomorrow and find the farewell card with yesterday's date on only for nosy old Mr Henderson to catch sight of her today and impart that bit of information to Jason.

Back in her room, she worked quickly, picking out clothes, discarding some, packing others. No time for neatness. No matter now if she left something behind; time was of the essence and there was no room for sentimentality, even though it caught at her as she pulled out the beautiful clothes she had been sneaking away for months. She glanced at the bag of money and smiled as she tossed a dress onto the pile to be binned. She could buy anything she wanted now, replicas of everything she couldn't take with her if she so desired.

The room spun suddenly, and lights floated across her vision. At first she thought it might be excitement, the possibility of potential, until her stomach grumbled loudly and she recognised the feeling as hunger. She sighed, closed the lid of the suitcase. She didn't have time to eat, but a cup of warm water with a slice of lemon should sort her out for a while.

She stepped over the bag of money, a smile still lingering as she rounded the corner of the landing and tripped happily down the stairs. At the bottom, she skirted William's inert body, barely glancing at him as another wave of faintness hit.

She steadied herself against the wall. Something brushed her foot; there was a split second of confusion, then she let out a piercing scream as William's hand clamped tight around her bare ankle.

Chapter 5

Before

I so clearly remember the first time I was touched with kindness and affection. I was at primary school, in the playground, and it was midwinter. Snow had fallen; a magical occurrence in my dark, isolated world. I ran around in it, copied the other kids as they scooped it up and patted it into balls. My hands soon turned numb. Gloves like the other children wore were a luxury that I didn't even know existed. When my fingers became painful, I turned away from the snowballs and sprinted the length of the playground to warm up.

Even at that young age I had learned survival instincts.

But at the far end, the drain had overflowed and it was an ice rink. I went down, hard.

And then, from behind me, a firm pair of arms picked me up, carried me a few yards and set me back down on my feet in the snow.

'Are you okay? You took a tumble there.'

I looked up into the red, smiling face of one of the dinner ladies. I was fascinated by her expression; she looked so… happy. In my little world, nobody smiled like that.

She mistook my awe for shock at having fallen, and without hesitating, she pulled me into her arms and squeezed me close to her chest. At first, my own arms hung loosely by my sides. Then nature, or instinct maybe, kicked in and I raised them, put them around her thick middle, mimicking her pose.

I had never been cuddled before. I had heard about it, seen it, watched other people doing it, but along with comfort and love, I'd never experienced it.

Once I did, I craved it more than anything in the world.

–

I began to act clumsy. After that first, precious hug, I caught on. If I was hurt, or sad, or wounded, people offered comfort. I became an expert at tripping, falling, slipping.

Later, I discovered that if there was visible blood, the comfort I received multiplied.

I started to cut myself.

That first time, I sliced the blade of the scissors along the pad of my forefinger. The pain made me hiss; the sight of the bright red blood that drip-drip-dripped onto the desk was fascinating. The sharp pain dulled to a throb. I held my hand up. The red tracked down my arm.

'Miss?' I called.

She was efficient, scooping up paper towels as she marched to my desk. She wrapped my finger, gripped it tight, 'so it clots and stops bleeding,' she murmured. But I didn't want it to stop. My eyes swam with tears and she put her free arm around me and pulled me close.

We stayed there like that for a while, my small hands digging into her shoulders, until the other kids grew impatient and bored.

I walked to and from school on my own, even at five years old. There was only my mum at home, and in the mornings she didn't function well enough to walk with me. When the final bell rang, it was her busiest time of day, so she didn't walk with me then either.

My home was a thin house in a street filled with other thin houses. They were all joined together, with a gaping black hole between every other home that led to an even thinner back yard. When I came home from school, I fitted my key in the lock, shoved the door open (it swelled and stuck most days) and stood in the hallway, staring up towards the top of the stairs.

There was a room there on the landing, Mummy's room, and if the door was closed I was to wait in the back yard. Today it was closed — it was most days — so I made my way through the narrow hall and into the tiny kitchen. Reaching up, I unlocked the back door and then sat down on the step, still with my coat on.

While I waited for my mum to be finished, I pulled off the plaster that Miss Fairfield had so kindly and tenderly put on my cut. I looked closely at it. Miss Fairfield was right: it had stopped bleeding.

I heard a thump upstairs and looked at the ceiling. She would be done soon. Up on the worktop was a fork left over from last night's dinner, or maybe even the night before. I grabbed it, and with the prongs I dug at the cut on my finger. Soon, blood was seeping out again.

There was talk in the hallway now as my mother said goodbye to her friend. The front door closed and I put the fork back, now with blood on it as well as the dried and crusted clumps of potato.

'Mummy,' I said, as she came into the kitchen.

She looked down at me as though surprised to see me there, and wrapped her dressing gown around her, tying the belt tight across her middle.

'Look, Mummy,' I said. I held up my hand, the blood trickling down to my elbow to drip on the lino floor.

She grabbed it, let it go almost immediately and moved over to the kettle.

'Put a plaster on it,' she said as she reached for the jar of coffee. Her words were long and slow and drawn out as she yawned.

Chapter 6

Paula stood glumly in the kitchen as she poured herself a hefty glass of gin. It was early, too early really; and did she really want to be *that woman*?

With a flick of her wrist she tossed it down the sink and switched on the coffee maker instead.

She should be excited, should be packing suitcases and choosing outfits, but Julie's harsh words were going round and round in her head.

Julie was wrong. Paula wasn't losing herself. She knew *exactly* who she was.

But on the other hand, stranger things happened than a husband cheating. Paula's face grew hot at the thought of Tommy trading her in for a younger model. That was what had happened to Julie. Julie had been lucky in getting half of her ex-husband's fortune. He had been rolling in it, could afford to give it away if it meant a quiet divorce. He had willingly paid her off, despite them having no children.

Paula tipped her head back. Tommy wouldn't do that. If anything happened, he wouldn't be generous. He coveted his bank account and savings and bonds and stocks and shares. She would receive the bare minimum that he could get away with as a settlement.

She pushed herself away from the sink. An insurance policy was what she needed, a way to stay in this lifestyle that she had become so accustomed to. How had it come to this? Once upon a time she'd been a woman who had a science degree, an actual degree that she had earned, and yet she had never used it. Not once had she held a job or career that showed her achievements. The promise of a life of luxury had appealed to her so much that she had simply become Tommy's wife.

Idly, she wondered where her degree certificate was now, and glanced at the wall in the study where the proof of Tommy's qualifications hung.

She couldn't even use her degree now, if she had to find a job for herself. Almost two decades had passed; things would have changed, and she wasn't sure she'd be able to remember anything of what she had learned.

She went up the stairs and drifted into the bathroom.

Insurance policy.

Before she could change her mind, she snatched her birth control pills from the cabinet shelf and very deliberately pushed the remainder of the month's tablets through the foil into the palm of her hand. One by one, she tipped them into the toilet bowl, watched as they bobbed around. And then, because it wasn't how she had planned it, because she had actually wanted this to be a mutual decision, she pulled her gaze away from the toilet.

Closing her eyes, she flushed the pills away, yanking at the lever before she could change her mind.

–

Anna breathed heavily, a second scream caught in her throat. Her feet were bare, and William's too-long nails grazed her skin.

She shook her leg, gripping onto the banister as she kicked out as hard as she could.

'Ooof,' wheezed William as her foot caught him in the neck.

She took advantage of the moment, wheeling backwards, feet skidding on the floorboards. Her back hit the wall, and she slid down it, feeling the sweat on her face, doubly faint now, and not just from hunger any more.

He spoke, but so quietly that she couldn't hear the words. She didn't want to hear them, and she turned her face away so she wouldn't have to watch his lips moving soundlessly or the plea for help in his cloudy eyes.

And as her breathing slowed, she realised that though the fall hadn't killed him, he was in a bad way. He wouldn't live long, but she couldn't leave him like this. He might hang on until tomorrow, when his son arrived. He was strong when he needed to be, when he gripped her wrist to stop her from leaving the bed that he liked her to lie on with him.

At the bottom of the stairs, he moved very slightly, and though it was barely discernible, it galvanised Anna into action. On her hands and knees, she scuttled over to him, gripping his shoulder and turning him fully onto his back.

His eyes opened, blue orbs of confusion that were full of pain.

'You're a filthy old man,' she said, her voice thin and reedy.

He shook his head; it wobbled on his skinny neck as he disputed her statement wordlessly.

She wanted to spit more vitriol at him, but what did it matter? It wouldn't change anything; nothing had been as she had thought in the first place. Her mind drifted back to when she had started this gig, thinking that he would leave everything to her when he passed away, that she would get this house and the contents of his bank accounts and finally, she would have the money to live the sort of life she was destined to. It had all been a pipe dream.

She didn't speak to him again as she covered his mouth with one hand and pinched his nostrils tightly together with her other, pressing down on him with all the strength she could muster.

The confusion cleared; she saw it as the clouds vanished from his eyes. They were blue lasers now, sharp and bright, as they would have been when he was young. His instinct to fight and survive took over, and he bucked his lower body, a sudden surge of strength that nearly threw her sideways. Swearing under her breath, she clambered up and over him, pinning his scrawny bird arms down with her thighs, clamping at his airways once more, careful not to scratch his face, trying not to leave a trace of herself on him.

It didn't take long, but to Anna it felt like hours.

–

Outside the front of the Southampton hotel, Paula wrapped her arms around herself as protection against the cold. She watched as Tommy walked up and down, peering into the road for the taxi that would take them to the cruise ship.

As she waited patiently, thoughts crowded her head. It was a horrible thing she'd done. A terrible, awful thing. She hadn't slept since flushing the birth control pills away, had even thought about calling the doctor's surgery and making up some excuse that she'd lost a pack and needed another prescription.

Awful.

Wicked.

Tommy would be furious if he found out.

Or would he? Her breath quickened. After all, he had booked this holiday in order for them to plan a baby, hadn't he? So, all she had done was get a head start on it. Maybe he didn't need to know what she'd done.

But still. Disappointment in herself hung heavy around her like a cloud. She had done Tommy a disservice, and he deserved better.

It was too late now; they were about to get on the cruise ship. The time to request a repeat prescription had passed.

She shook her head to dispel thoughts of her bad behaviour. As Tommy approached, she turned to him with a bright smile.

'What actually *are* the Northern Lights?' she asked.

'They're electronically charged particles in the atmosphere that interact with each other,' he said. 'Cool, huh?' His face crumpled into a pout. 'I really hope we see them.'

Paula frowned. 'What do you mean? Of course we're going to see them; it's what this whole cruise is about!'

'Yeah, but they're not always there. Thousands of people do this and never see them. It depends on cloud cover. Ideally, we'll need a clear, dark night.' He flashed a smile at her. 'There are lots of other things happening up there, though.' He glanced upwards, into the white sky.

Paula followed his gaze, seeing nothing but clouds. 'Like what?' she asked.

'Meteor showers, new moons, planets in orbit.' He grinned, suddenly animated again as he spoke about his passion. 'The Taurids shower is our best bet. It's really unusual because it consists of two streams of debris.' From his back pocket he pulled a notepad, one that she had never seen before. He flipped through the pages until he found what he was looking for, putting his finger on a paragraph: 'The first stream comes from Asteroid 2004 TG 10, the other one comes from Comet 2P Encke. It's actually been going on since September, but it peaks this week.' Slipping the notebook back in his pocket, he rubbed his gloved hands together, still with that goofy smile on his face.

She stared at him, rather shocked by the foreign language he seemed to be speaking. She had always known he took an interest in the night sky, but had no idea his knowledge ran so deep. When did he learn all of this? And, rather disconcertingly, why didn't she know this about him? She recalled snippets of conversations, comments he had made, comets and stars and space stations… Was it possible he had tried to involve her in his passion over the years and she had dismissed him out of her own lack of interest?

Deflated, Paula pulled her coat tighter around her. It was freezing out here, and it would be worse on the boat. Why were they going on a cruise to the coldest place in Europe instead of a long-haul flight to Jamaica or somewhere equally hot? She'd been all for it when she thought she was going to witness these magical lights, but now there was a chance they wouldn't even see them…

She stamped her feet, looked enviously at Tommy's hiking boots, his feet encased in the insulating socks she had bought him. Why hadn't she bought any for herself?

She watched a couple walk out of the hotel and continue arm in arm down the street. Fleetingly she wished she was wearing the woman's coat, a thick, quilted puffa, instead of the Chanel-inspired one she herself had chosen. Absently she fingered the material. It was beautiful, but far from practical. She had chosen style over function, to look good, to not show her husband up. Just like always.

'Here he is,' said Tommy as the taxi rolled slowly around the curved drive. 'Come on.'

He picked up his case, expecting her to follow him, and she waited while he loaded the case into the boot. He sidestepped her, slipping into the passenger seat of the cab, and she heaved her own case up, struggling under the weight. After a moment, the taxi driver appeared, taking the case from her and flashing her a smile. She thanked him quietly and hurried to join Tommy in the warmth of the cab.

It took only twenty minutes to reach Southampton Dock, and as she stepped out of the car and stared up at the *Ruby Spirit*, Paula forgot the biting cold.

The cruise ship towered over the smaller yachts and sailing boats surrounding it, rising elegantly out of the water. It had a sleek black body with gold lettering and a red trim curving along the passenger rails.

Paula took a step back and shaded her eyes from the weak sun as she tried to count the decks.

'My God,' she whispered. She turned to Tommy, who stood to one side as the taxi driver hauled their bags out of the car. 'It's huge!'

He paid the driver and made his way over, winking as he patted at his crotch. 'Thanks, so I've been told,' he joked.

She wrinkled her nose and turned away from him. 'Don't spoil it,' she muttered.

'What? Come on, you can't say something like that and not expect—'

She shushed him as a porter approached. 'It's not appropriate to say things like that when we're about to board something like this.' She jabbed a finger at the vast ship.

'What the fuck?' Tommy said loudly.

Cringing, Paula moved to stand in front of him and smiled brightly at the porter.

'Can I be of assistance with your luggage?' he said, and Paula dipped her head, grateful that he either hadn't heard Tommy's crudeness or had chosen to ignore it.

'Thank you,' she replied, and nudged Tommy. 'The tickets?'

Still with a face that held traces of his mood, Tommy handed them over.

The porter studied them briefly before turning up the wattage on his smile. 'The Expedition Suite,' he confirmed. 'The *best* suite,' he emphasised.

Inside her chest, Paula's heart swelled. Outwardly, though, she remained calm, as if being in a better-than-first-class cabin was what she was accustomed to.

And that was the way it should be, she thought to herself as she trailed Tommy and the porter down the quayside to the walkway. She had spent years learning how to conduct herself: classy at all times; impeccably dressed, hair styled, face made up, even if she wasn't planning on going anywhere.

And yet Tommy, the man who had worked his way up through the perils of the stock industry, occasionally slipped into someone he'd never been. It saddened her; that her every action was for him and the way he expected her to behave.

'The Expedition Suite,' announced the porter. He stood with one arm behind his back, the other braced on the door handle.

Tommy and Paula came to a stop in the corridor, a moment of expectation built by the porter with professional panache before he swept open the door and gestured for them to enter.

Tommy, finally seeming to remember who he was, stepped back to allow Paula to enter first. She glided past him, barely able to stifle a gasp as she entered the huge open-plan cabin. Beneath her feet, her thin-soled stilettos sank into the plush cream-coloured carpet.

And the light! She looked up to see daylight streaming in through glass double doors, a balcony beyond them. For a moment she imagined sitting out there sipping a cocktail from room service, before remembering that it was winter and it wouldn't be at all pleasant. She moved soundlessly over the floor to the doors, unable to contain a smile at the sight of the open sea.

'And a welcome gift, for sir and madam,' said the porter, making a sweeping gesture to a large hamper on the table by the king-sized bed. 'Do either of you have any questions?'

Paula rearranged her face to an expression of cool collectedness before turning towards him. 'No, it's all very lovely, thank you.' She glanced at Tommy, hoping he caught the meaning in her pointed look, but to her relief, his wallet was already out, and he was pressing a small wad of notes into the porter's hand.

When the door closed behind the man, Paula kicked off her shoes and ran across the room to jump into her husband's arms.

'Oh, Tommy, it's such a beautiful suite!'

He caught her easily, allowing her to wrap her arms and legs around him for just a moment before setting her down none-too-gently on the floor.

'I'm going to look around before we set sail,' he said, pocketing the key card that the porter had left for them.

'Well, give me a second and I'll come with you,' said Paula.

He held a hand up, and didn't smile. 'You settle in here. I'll be back before dinner.'

With that, he was gone from the room without a back-ward glance.

—

The Arctic Suite was one notch down on the price list from the Expedition Suite. It was still plush, still luxurious. Like the Expedition Suite, there was a welcome hamper, though it was slightly smaller and only contained one bottle of champagne instead of two.

Anna Masi thanked the porter, pressed a few of William's ten-pound notes into his hand and closed the door behind him.

Then, finally alone, she looked around the room that would be her home for the next ten days. Six grand was a lot of money to spend on a holiday, but it still left her with just under twelve thousand, having spent the last week in a hotel in Southampton. But after the last year, caring for William, letting him put his hands on her and living in his home smelling of old meat and fried food, she reckoned she'd earned it.

The last few days had been interesting. She had surprised herself the day after she had left the terraced house, waking up and feeling the need to return to the scene of the crime.

She had dressed carefully, concealing her face with a beanie hat and a scarf that covered her nose and mouth, and had taken the train all the way back to Essex. It was the same train she had escaped the house on, having decided against a taxi. Clarity had fought through the panic: what if the son demanded that William's death was looked into? What if the taxi company were contacted and said they'd given her a lift the day *after* the date she'd written in the goodbye card?

In the end she had slipped out of the back door, hauling three bags, struggling under the weight as she slunk off to the station, light-headed and near to collapse once more by the time she staggered onto the train that would take her far, far away from the scene of the crime.

Now, there was no movement from William's house, and it was too cold for Mr Henderson to be skulking around the front. In the café opposite, which she had never visited before, she ordered a coffee and sat in the window, waiting for William's son to put in an appearance.

She was on her second latte when he pulled up. Even though she'd never seen him before, she knew immediately that this was the famous Jason. His all-round tan, the slightly shell-shocked expression on his face worn by those living in sunnier climates all year round who are forced back to wintry Britain. He looked in a rush, and it was with spiteful satisfaction that Anna watched him stamp his feet against the cold as he rapped repeatedly on William's door.

Her heart rate sped up as he bent over and pushed the flap of the letter box to peer inside. And even from across the road she heard his shout, a primitive yell as he straightened up and rammed at the locked door with his big shoulder.

She sipped at her coffee, running her eyes up and down the distraught man's figure. Another rugby player, she mused, treading that fine line between muscular and fat. She wondered which would eventually win.

Finally, the hammering on the door brought Mr Henderson outside. Gestures from Jason, Mr Henderson hurrying back inside his own house to fetch the spare key that Anna hadn't realised he had. Then they were pushing at the door, Mr Henderson clapping his hand over his mouth as it jammed against William's body, Jason shoving his way inside.

The big man dropped to his knees, and the last thing Anna saw before the door swung closed was William's limp arm, the sagging skin mottled a deep red.

She had drained her latte, pulled her hat low and scarf high, and left the coffee shop and the horrible little street and Essex for the last time to the tune of the sirens that blared out as they passed her.

And now here she was, in a room that smelled of fresh paint and newness. Time to begin the next part of her life. A part she had earned.

In the corridor, she heard the soft click as the door to the Expedition Suite closed. She skipped to her own door, put her eye to the peephole and watched as Tommy Ellis marched away from the suite. Her lips curled upwards in a smile. She could easily follow him; even though he had turned the corner out of sight, she had no doubt she would find him in the bar. Taking a step away from the door, she smoothed down her shirt and shook out her short hair, then moved over to the mirror to scrutinise her reflection. Five days of intense tanning in the salon down the road from her hotel had done wonders. She slipped her fitted top off one shoulder and inspected her skin. No tan lines. Just an entire sun-kissed body, golden and thinner than she had ever been.

She staggered slightly and clutched at the wall, wondering if the ship was setting sail already before realising she was light-headed.

But this was no time to eat, and no time to go chasing Tommy either.

No, that could wait. Well-versed in the move she was planning to make, Anna knew that it was imperative she get the wife on board first.

But the wife was enclosed in the cabin next door, and there was plenty of time for all that. Snatching up her bag, Anna gave herself one last look in the mirror before sweeping out of the room and heading in the opposite direction to where Tommy had gone.

–

Paula sat on the edge of the bed and stared out at the sea. This wasn't the way this trip was supposed to begin, Tommy being huffy and weird and disappearing before they'd even set sail.

Automatically she reached for her phone, was halfway through tapping out a text before she remembered she had pissed Julie off, and her best friend wasn't speaking to her. She tipped the phone out of her hand onto the bed.

She knew why Tommy was mad: because she'd chastised him for his stupid dick joke on the quayside. He was worried that the porter had overheard. Not worried that he'd overheard his crassness, but angry that he might have heard Paula telling him off. That was the thing with Tommy, he always worried about the wrong thing.

Had she overreacted?

Probably. She usually did, or so Tommy said anyway.

Maybe she should apologise.

She nodded to herself. She would. He had bought her this lovely holiday and she'd annoyed him before they had even got on the boat. But she wouldn't go after him yet. When his mood was black, he wasn't receptive to hearing her grovel. She would give him time and space to cool off. This was his holiday too, and God knows he deserved it, working all those hours.

But she didn't want to spend however long it took him to calm down stuck in this room. As lovely as it was, she wanted to see what else the ship had to offer. She reached for the brochure next to the hamper and opened it, her eyes immediately landing on what she was seeking. Feeling much better, thoughts of Tommy diminished, she gathered up her bag and key card and left the room.

–

By the time Paula reached the sixth deck, they had set sail. She darted out of one of the heavy doors, gasping as the cold air hit her. She almost turned back, but reminding herself of where she would be in ten minutes did the trick, and she forced herself out onto the open-air deck and over to the edge.

Gripping the white railings, she watched the dock as the ship moved off. A few feet away, a family held their children aloft, gripping the kids' arms in a wave as they cheered. Suddenly sad, Paula dropped her head. It wasn't that it was a monumental moment – they weren't on the *Titanic* or the last Concorde – but this was still a maiden voyage and she shouldn't have been witnessing it alone.

Hitching her bag back onto her shoulder, she hurried back to pull the heavy door open and continued on to her original destination. As the sign for the spa materialised, she smiled with relief. This was her domain; this was something that was always just hers. A place where she felt at home.

In the little wooden changing room, she stripped quickly down to the bikini she had put on before she left her cabin, and grabbed her towel. Conscious of the elastic of her bottoms digging painfully into her thighs, she avoided the mirror on her way out. She made her way over to the lockers, frowning as she peered at them. They all appeared to be locked, and no amount of working her key card against them seemed to activate them. She looked around, realising there was nobody else there, and that this wasn't likely to change. Everyone would be up on deck. She shoved her bag on the top locker and, clutching her towel to her stomach, moved down the narrow hallway towards the sauna.

She could feel the heat even outside the wooden door, and gripping the handle, she pulled it open and slipped inside. She let out a murmur of appreciation as she spread her towel out on the bench in the darkened room and sat down. This was more like it. This was what she had wanted – no, *needed*. Some well-being time, some time just for her, where she didn't have to sit and fret about Julie or Tommy or babies.

She leaned back against the hot wood and closed her eyes. She could almost feel herself drifting off and wondered how appropriate it would be to come here several times a day. She shifted, the bench creaked... and then someone cleared their throat.

Paula sat bolt upright and peered into the gloom. As her eyes adjusted, she felt the heat double in her already flushed face.

Someone else was in here. And... she was *naked*!

Her first instinct was to apologise, to blurt out that she hadn't realised the sauna was occupied, but the sight of the woman in all her unclothed glory stopped her short.

'Hi,' the woman said, her tone friendly, her smile wide, showing even white teeth.

'Hello,' croaked Paula. She tore her eyes away from the woman's breasts, small and perky and so high that she was even tanned underneath them. Embarrassed, she crossed her arms over her own chest, even though she was wearing her bikini. 'I'm so sorry, I didn't realise anyone was in here.'

'S'all right,' the woman said. 'There's more than enough room for both of us in here.' She grinned at Paula, pushed herself upright and stuck out a hand. 'I'm Anna. Anna Masi. It's good to meet you.'

Chapter 7

They chatted for a while. Anna bit her lip to stop her amusement showing at just how uncomfortable Paula was.

'Are you looking forward to seeing the Northern Lights?' she asked, casually stretching out one leg and admiring her pedicured painted toenails.

'Oh yes, very much so,' Paula replied. 'But my husband said we might not see them, they're not always visible.'

Anna nodded. 'It's certainly down to luck.' She narrowed her eyes as she watched the other woman in the semi-dark of the room. 'But I've got a good feeling about this trip.'

Paula smiled – stiffly, Anna thought. Hiding her own smile, she stood up, raised her arms above her head and stretched. Paula put her head down, pretended to fiddle with the tie on her bikini.

'Right, enough for one day.' Anna picked up her towel and let it drape behind her as she made her way towards the door. She stopped, turned around to face Paula. 'Want me to put some more water on the coals for you before I leave?'

Paula, looking anywhere but at Anna's naked body, shook her head. 'No, that's fine. I should go find my husband soon anyway.'

Anna smothered a smile and slipped out of the door, sure she could hear Paula's sigh of relief as she closed it gently behind her.

Outside the sauna, she worked quickly, wrapping the towel around herself and picking up the poker in the box next to the door. She fed it through the door handle, careful not to let it clang as she released her grip. Then she padded soundlessly down the hallway, pausing at the lockers and grinning again as she spotted Paula's bag on top. Obviously, the woman hadn't bothered to stop in the spa reception and get a key.

She ducked into a changing room and pulled on her clothes. When she left, the spa area was still silent, still empty. She smiled to herself as she walked towards the exit, swiping Paula's bag off the top of the locker as she passed. Once outside the door, she flipped the sign over to read *Spa Closed*, then made her way down the corridor.

–

Paula stared at the door long after the strange woman had left. Who sat in a sauna totally naked? And her body! Regretfully, Paula pinched the spare flesh on her own stomach. The woman must work out every day to look like that.

She picked up her towel and rubbed at her face, realising just how hot she was. Suddenly a walk on the open-air deck seemed like the perfect way to finish off her afternoon of indulgence. If she could track Tommy down, maybe he'd come with her, explore outside before they got dressed for dinner. She looked at her watch and saw she'd been in the sauna for almost an hour. No wonder she was sweating so profusely. And that hour was plenty of time for Tommy to have cooled off.

She stood, grabbed her towel and pushed at the door. It didn't budge.

Frowning, she pushed it again, but it was stuck fast.

'No,' she whispered. Putting the whole side of her body against it, she shoved at it again and again. 'No!' She could hear the panic rising in her own voice.

Was it her imagination, or had the sauna suddenly got hotter? She let go of the handle, and lurched over to squint at the thermometer. It read 110 degrees – she knew it should be between 70 and 100 – and she had already been in there too long. What would happen if no one came to let her out? Would she pass out from heat exhaustion, or become dangerously dehydrated?

She slammed at the door again and banged on it with her fists. It was unlikely anybody else would come along soon; the rest of the passengers would be gearing up for the first night's dinner and celebrations of the maiden voyage.

'HELP!' she shouted, grabbing at the handle again.

It slipped out of her sweat-slick fingers, and with a howl she slid downwards, her fingernails breaking as they scrabbled at the wood. She threw out her left hand to steady herself, and her fingers connected with the wooden bowl that contained the water. It splashed onto the coals, hissing and spitting, the heat immediately rising as the water fizzed and bubbled.

'Oh, God,' Paula wept, the tears drying on her cheeks as soon as they leaked out of her eyes. 'Please, help me!'

–

After walking around on deck for a while, Anna was cold enough to return inside. As she headed along the glass-walled corridor that ran past the bar area, she pulled her short hair forward and peered through her fringe. Tommy was in there, not drinking morosely as she had half expected, but surrounded by a cluster of men. They were laughing and chatting, and Anna felt a stab of pleasure that he had not felt the need to go in search of his wife.

She speed-walked to the sixth deck, smiling with satisfaction at the sign on the spa door, which was just as she'd left it. She turned it over again and slipped inside, pausing in the doorway for just a moment before heading towards the sauna. The poker was still in place, and there was no sound from within.

Taking a deep breath, she slid the poker soundlessly out and set it down underneath a pile of towels. Then she gripped the handle and opened the door wide.

Paula was huddled in the corner, on the furthest bench from the door. In the dim light Anna saw her raise her head.

'Goodness! You're still in here?' Anna gave her a friendly smile. 'Did I leave my bracelet in— Oh, there it is!' She scooped up the silver chain, then stopped, the smile slipping from her face to be replaced with a look of concern. 'Hey, are you okay?'

Paula let out a deep, shuddering breath as she clambered off the bench.

'Don't let that door close!' she shrieked. She pushed past Anna and practically threw herself through the door. 'Oh my God!'

The tears came then, as Paula gulped great lungfuls of air. Spotting the water cooler, she staggered over to it. Anna went to stand beside her, taking the cup from the woman's shaking hands and filling it for her. Paula grabbed at it and drank greedily. When she had finished, she reached out her arms and pulled Anna into an embrace.

'I was stuck in there,' she cried. 'I thought I was going to die!'

Over Paula's shoulder, Anna rolled her eyes. 'What do you mean, stuck?' she asked.

'The door wouldn't open,' whispered Paula, her eyes darting fearfully to the sauna.

Anna moved back to the door, closing it and opening it again easily.

'It wouldn't open!' Paula cried. 'I swear, it was stuck fast.'

'Did you push it, or pull it?' Anna asked, swishing the door open and closed as if to prove her point.

'I-I don't know,' Paula said. 'I'm just so glad you came along.' Her eyes filled with tears again and she pulled out a chair and sat down.

Anna studied her. Never had she seen a person's cheeks so red. Paula's hair seemed to have swelled to three times its normal size, standing out in a frizzy halo around her head.

'I can't believe you've been down here all this time. Did your husband not come looking for you?'

Another tear tracked a path down Paula's face as she shook her head.

'Right, well it's nearly dinner time. Come on, you look a bit shaky. Let's get you back to your cabin.'

'My bag!' Paula stopped and wrenched her arm free of Anna. She stared at the row of lockers. 'My bag isn't here!'

Anna moved over to the lockers. 'Which one did you put it in?'

Paula shook her head. 'I didn't, I couldn't open them. I put it on top.'

Anna twisted the knob on one of the lockers and pulled it open. 'You didn't get a key from reception?'

'They wouldn't open when I tried them!' Paula's words caught on a sob and she scrubbed at her eyes. 'I can't believe all this is happening to me.'

Anna turned back to her. 'What was in your bag? Your purse, phone? Anything valuable?'

'No, just my make-up… a coin purse, I think.' Paula pulled at the lanyard round her neck. 'At least I have my cabin key.'

'We'll report the bag missing. Hey, maybe you didn't actually bring it in here. Might you have left it in your room?'

Paula's features swam with confusion. 'I don't know.' She looked at Anna doubtfully. 'Maybe.'

Anna patted her shoulder. 'Let's get you back to your cabin.'

–

As she allowed herself to be led by Anna through the stairwells and corridors, Paula began to relax. By the time they reached the Expedition Suite, she felt almost like her old self, as well as thoroughly embarrassed by the tears and panic she had shown in front of the other woman.

'Oh, we're practically neighbours,' said Anna when Paula stopped outside her door. 'I'm in the suite on the corner.'

Paula pulled at the towel wrapped around herself, which was wringing wet from her escapade in the sauna. 'I can't tell you how glad I am you left your bracelet in there,' she said. 'Anna, are you on this cruise alone?'

She nodded. 'I am. I'm treating myself before work gets crazy again in the new year.'

Paula wondered what sort of job this young woman did. On impulse, she took hold of Anna's hand. 'Please, will you join us for dinner tonight? I'd like to say thank you properly. It's our treat.'

'Oh, well, I think our meals are already paid for in the price of the tickets,' replied Anna. At Paula's mortified expression, she squeezed her hand. 'But I'd love to join you. Thank you.'

'Good.' Paula straightened her shoulders and slipped her key card in the slot. 'We'll meet you here in an hour?'

Inside the safety and relative expanse of her cabin, Paula sank onto the bed. Never in her whole life had she felt as frightened as she had in that sauna. She pulled off her bikini and inspected herself in the full-length mirror on the back of the bathroom door. Her skin was red and blotchy, her face was dry and her hair was like straw. She pulled at it, wincing as several strands came away in her fingers. What the hell had she done to herself in that awful sweat box? Tears filled her eyes again at the thought of the amount of money she spent to keep her hair and skin in tip-top condition. She didn't even have time to wash it, and actually wasn't sure if she dared, due to the amount that seemed to be shedding from her scalp.

She reached for her coconut oil, smoothing it along the shafts of her hair until she could get a comb through it. Slicking it against her head, she pinned it up and scowled at her reflection. This was not how she had intended to spend her first night on board.

And where was Tommy? As she reached for her phone on the side, she belatedly remembered her lost bag. She darted around the room, opening cupboard doors and bedside drawers, searching for the bag she was sure she'd taken to the sauna with her.

Feeling emotional again, she stabbed at Tommy's name, clicking her nails on the side of the sink as she waited for him to answer.

Her nails! In horror, she looked at her left hand, remembering now the nails that had chipped and split as she scraped them against the sauna door in her desperation to escape. They were jagged and broken, the expensive manicure that she'd had the day before a complete and utter waste of money.

'Hey, babe.' Tommy's voice came down the phone.

Paula dragged her gaze away from her ruined hand. 'Where are you?' she asked, hating the sound of the choked tears in her voice but unable to quell them.

'On the lower deck,' he replied, and down the line came the sound of male laughter.

Paula swallowed down the sobs that threatened to break free. In the mirror, her skin flushed an even deeper scarlet. 'It's nearly dinner time,' she said, hoarsely.

'I'm coming back now,' he replied, oblivious to her emotional state. 'I'll be in the cabin in five.'

Fifteen minutes later, she had done the quickest possible repair job on herself. She looked like shit, she thought, with the coconut oil clinging to her jet-black hair, making it appear greasy and unkempt. The aloe vera cream had done little to soothe her overheated skin, and the nails on her left hand were now a good few millimetres shorter than those on her right. She had chosen a floor-length maxi dress in baby blue, hoping that the subtle shade of the material might tone down her high colour. It didn't. She just looked like somebody wearing a summer dress in the middle of winter.

Right on cue, the door clicked and Tommy sauntered inside, throwing his key card on the bed and lowering himself into the bucket chair by the window.

'Did you have a nice afternoon?' he asked as she emerged from the bathroom. He sounded as though he was over his sulk.

Paula bit her lip. 'No, I had a really bad afternoon.'

'I met a group of fishermen in the bar,' he said, as if she hadn't spoken. 'They were really nice guys, had a good chat, they were telling me all about the Northern Lights—'

A sob emerged, tears rose, and she lowered her head.

'Babe?'

She dabbed at her eyes with her fingers. 'I had a really shitty afternoon. I got locked in the sauna.' She pointed to her head. 'Look at my hair, look at how red my skin is.' Miserably, she inspected her arms and hands. 'The woman next door rescued me, and I've invited her to join us for dinner tonight as a thank you. She's travelling alone,' she added as an afterthought.

''Kay,' said Tommy. 'Guess I'd better get ready then.'

He pushed himself out of the chair and walked somewhat unsteadily over to the wardrobe, flicking through the clothes that Paula had hung up earlier.

She knew her eyes were still watering. Mentally she pulled herself together. They had a guest with them for dinner. If Paula couldn't get her emotions under control, Tommy would refuse to eat with her. He would probably go off with his new buddies, and the woman next door – Anna – would think Paula was even more of a loser than she did already.

She bit her lip and sat down in the chair that Tommy had vacated.

She would have to get through dinner, but all she really wanted to do was crawl under the covers and forget this day had ever happened.

–

In the cabin on the corner Anna selected her most spectacular dress. A gold sequinned number, muted and matt, demure enough not to be sleazy, but cut high enough in the leg and low enough in the neck to give a hint of what lay beneath. As she carefully applied her make-up, she thought of Paula next door, and her awful blotchy, practically burned skin and terrible straw hair. She smiled as she dashed the bronzer along her cheekbones. Maybe she would suggest accompanying Paula to the salon tomorrow, get a deep-conditioning treatment put on her hair.

Taking one final look in the mirror, she scooped up her clutch bag and Paula's tote that she had swiped off the top of the locker earlier and strode the few feet down the hall to Paula and Tommy's cabin. Raising her hand, she rapped smartly on the door.

It opened immediately, and Anna's heart lurched a little as she surveyed the pleasing form of Tommy. He was dressed in a smart black suit and a crisp white shirt, with no tie. He managed to look casual but also as though he fitted right in.

She smiled, stuck out a hand and gripped his firmly. 'Hi, you must be Tommy. I'm Anna, your wife very kindly invited me to join you for dinner.'

He smiled back, showing white teeth, and ushered her inside. 'Come on in, we're just waiting for Paula. God knows what she does in there that takes so long,' he laughed. 'She comes out and I don't see much of a difference.'

Interesting. Anna raised her eyebrows. His first words were a put-down of his wife. Ordinarily, it would be a warning sign. This was, after all, the man Anna intended on leaving the cruise with in ten days' time. Most women with their eye on a guy would be put off by a man who spoke about his wife so dismissively. But Anna wasn't here for hearts and flowers. Language and attitudes didn't matter, not in the long run. She figured if she could live with old William the way she had, time spent with Tommy Ellis would be far more fruitful, despite his attitude to his current wife.

Tommy moved over to the semi-circular bar area and held up a bottle of gin. 'Drink?' he asked.

Anna was about to accept when the bathroom door clicked open and Paula emerged, her eyes almost as red as the skin on her face.

'Oh, Anna, hi,' she said. With a resigned shrug of her shoulders, she smiled. 'This is the best I could do.'

As Tommy sighed behind her, Anna scrutinised Paula's face: 'I have some powder in my bag, would you like to use some? I got extreme sunburn in the summer in Mexico, this worked wonders until the skin healed up properly.' She pulled it out and at the same time held Paula's tote bag aloft. 'Oh, and I went back to the sauna, found this on the reception desk. I think it belongs to you?'

'My bag!' Paula smiled and reached for it and upended it on the floor. 'Nothing's missing,' she said.

A sudden stillness came over the room and Paula looked up at Anna. 'How did you know it was mine?' she asked. 'There's nothing with any ID in here.'

Anna fought to control the flush that threatened to creep up her neck. Was Paula calling her out? Had she figured out who had both locked her in the sauna and stolen her bag? She felt her eyes glinting dangerously and consciously softened her expression.

'I never saw anyone else in the spa this afternoon apart from you. I figured it must be yours.'

Her tone was flat and hard; she heard it and wondered if Paula would challenge her. She darted a look at Tommy, still behind the bar, checking his watch.

'Are we going to dinner then?' he asked.

Paula stood up. 'Yes, let me just put this away.' She held it up, shook it at Tommy as she walked past him. 'Look, Anna found my bag that I lost in the spa.'

He raised his eyes. 'So, you got locked in the sauna and lost your stuff? Good going, even for you!'

Oh, how barbed and nasty their relationship was, thought Anna as she watched the exchange with interest. And yet Paula didn't react. Was she so used to her husband's scathing remarks that they just sailed over her head these days? Or did she wear a mask for him, only to cry in private? Perhaps the prize of the five-bedroom house and all the trimmings that came with it was enough to allow her to put up with the disrespect?

If it was, Anna could identify with that.

–

'That powder was great, thank you,' said Paula as the three of them left the cabin and walked down the corridor. The hallway was narrow, and the two women walked together, Tommy in the lead.

'It's a good one, I got it in New York and I always stock up when I'm there.' Anna smiled at her. 'You can keep that one.'

Paula blanched. 'Oh, I couldn't, it's obviously expensive.'

Anna put a hand on her arm. 'I insist.'

Paula darted a glance at the woman beside her. In just a few minutes she had already let them know that she'd been in Mexico in the summer, and was a frequent visitor to New York. Add in this cruise, not to mention the designer dress she was wearing and the expensive face powder she had given away so freely, and there was clearly no shortage of money.

'What do you do for a living, Anna?' she asked as they paused next to the lift that would take them to the restaurant.

'I oversee a nationwide firm,' replied Anna. 'My team are mostly freelancers, and I ensure they're all in work. It's a tough job – we're in the process of going international, so I need to be available all the time, literally day and night.' She smiled suddenly and swept her arms in a wide arc. 'A holiday like this is my reward!'

Paula blinked. This tiny woman with the body of a boy oversaw an entire company? And earned enough money to keep herself in luxury and allow her to go on holidays like this one several times a year?

'Wow,' she muttered. 'That's impressive.' She paused, eyes narrowed. 'What does your husband do?'

Anna laughed. 'No husband, just me. I never had the time nor the inclination for husbands or kids or all the mess that comes along with them.'

Tommy, previously uninterested in the women's conversation, swivelled his eyes to regard Anna, a move that Paula didn't miss.

'And what do you do, Paula?' asked Anna politely as they stepped into the lift.

A silence descended. Usually Paula answered that question with a hint of pride that she had a husband who earned enough that she didn't have to work herself. But somehow, next to the pocket rocket beside her, the answer she normally gave would just seem... sad.

'I keep house,' she managed, aware even as she spoke that it sounded lame.

'Oh, housekeeping?' said Anna. 'I was a part-time cleaner when I was working my way through college.'

Paula heard the disconnect, and swallowed as Tommy smirked in her direction. 'No, I meant I just look after our house.' She paused. 'I don't work,' she clarified.

The lift sped on down to the dining deck, opening with a little chime as they emerged, and Paula wondered if Anna had actually heard her. As the other woman walked ahead, Paula yanked on Tommy's sleeve. 'She thinks I'm a cleaner!' she hissed.

He pulled his arm free and straightened his cuff. 'For God's sake, relax,' he said, moving up to stand beside Anna as they waited to be seated.

Paula remained behind them, inexplicably hurt by both Anna's assumption and the fact that Tommy didn't seem to care. In front of her, Anna said something that made Tommy throw his head back with laughter. As a waiter appeared and led them through the restaurant, Tommy lifted a hand and rested it on the small of Anna's back.

Paula trailed behind.

'A garden salad,' Anna said as she passed her menu back to the waiter, confident that the meal she had selected would be enough to sustain her.

She glanced at Paula beside her, at how the straps of her dress cut into the flesh on her shoulders. Yes, the salad was a good idea.

She waited without remark as both Tommy and Paula ordered the steak fillet, with extra butter and fries.

Fries! And not even of the slightly healthier sweet potato variety.

Paula gave her menu back and looked a little abashed. 'I missed lunch because of all that sauna business,' she said.

Anna nodded. She had missed lunch and breakfast too. Inside, she glowed with pride.

Paula touched her arm and leaned in. 'Um, just to clarify, I'm not a cleaner, or a housekeeper. I don't actually work, you know?'

'Hey, guys!' A sudden shout from Tommy made Paula jump, and both women looked up. 'It's the boys from this afternoon,' he explained as he pushed his chair back. 'I'll be right back.'

Anna smothered a smile and turned to face Paula.

'So, what did you want to do? When you were young, I mean?'

Paula stared back blankly. 'What do you mean?'

'Well, nobody aspires to be a trophy wife, do they? I mean, when you were at school, when you were younger, what career did you want?'

'Oh.' A pained look crossed Paula's face and she froze in her seat.

'Paula?' Anna tilted her head, concerned.

Paula shook her head and uttered a dry little laugh. 'It's funny, my best friend said something along those lines to me just the other day. "Don't lose yourself," she said.' She smiled wryly. 'It pissed me off.'

Anna flinched. 'I'm so sorry, I didn't mean to be rude.'

But Paula's eyes were locked on something across the room. Anna followed her gaze to see Tommy immersed in his new group of buddies, back-slapping and handshakes all round as they congratulated themselves on how fantastic they all were.

'A trophy wife,' muttered Paula quietly.

Anna grabbed her hand. 'Listen, I only just met you, right, but I can tell you're so much more than a trophy wife.' She gestured to the table. 'Look at this. I would have been eating alone if you hadn't been kind enough to invite me to dinner with you tonight.'

She patted Paula's hand and laid it softly back on the table, pleased she had been able to find a compliment to pay the woman.

Paula smiled, but to Anna it seemed forced. 'Ignore me, I think it's the after-effects of this afternoon's horrific disaster.'

Anna sat back. She could feel the anger creaking through her very marrow, and she breathed deeply to contain herself. Being locked in a spa for an hour was *not* a horrific disaster. Being forced to lie with an old man so he continued to pay your salary was awful. Homelessness and sofa surfing was horrific. Joblessness and poverty was disastrous.

She bit her lip to stop it trembling. Inside her mouth the familiar metallic taste of blood brought her back to the present just as her salad was placed in front of her. She regarded it carefully, running her hand over her concave stomach. There were no curves now, hadn't been since she had been a teenager. At least that was one part of her life that she could control.

'I'm going to the salon tomorrow,' she said conversationally, looking away as Paula cut into her steak. 'Maybe you'd like to come along, get a deep-conditioning treatment on your hair?'

Tommy slid back into his chair, rubbing his hands together, and tucked into his steak with relish. 'The boys are doing a bit of deep-sea fishing tomorrow; they've invited me to join them,' he said with his mouth full. 'It should be fun.'

On the other side of her, Anna felt the look that Paula aimed at her husband.

'Really?' she asked. 'On our first full day?'

Anna glanced at Tommy, saw the eye roll. She nibbled at a piece of lettuce as the tension grew like a cloud of black smoke. She could practically smell the hurt coming off Paula in waves.

Eventually Paula addressed Anna. 'I'd love to come to the salon with you tomorrow, thank you.'

Anna smiled and pushed her plate away.

She was done.

'Good morning, this is your captain speaking. Today I would like to bring your attention to the Square of Pegasus. Pegasus can be seen in both the northern and southern hemispheres, but in the southern hemisphere it is upside down!

'Pegasus, our winged horse, consists of four stars of almost equal brightness. This two-thousand-year-old constellation can be tricky to see with the naked eye, but a simple pair of binoculars will show you all the stars within the square.

'According to Greek mythology, Pegasus had a hand in defeating Chimera, a fire-breathing monster, and was duly

rewarded by being presented with the seventh largest place in our skies.

'Pegasus is one hundred and ninety-six light years away from earth, which if you think about it makes you feel really rather small in our otherwise limitless galaxy...'

Chapter 8

Paula pulled the duvet tighter around herself as she listened to the captain's daily briefing over the tannoy. She liked his updates, the little titbits of information that he spoke about in authoritative but slightly camp tones. She wondered if Tommy enjoyed them as much as she did. She turned over to face him, but found a space in the bed, an indent on the pillow the only evidence he had been there at all.

She sighed, stretching as she ran her fingers through her hair. As she did so, she remembered that her appointment at the salon was at ten o'clock. She dragged herself out of bed, and without looking in the mirror pushed her hair back and wound it up with a band. She dressed quickly in skinny jeans and a plain black shirt.

'Tommy?' She called his name, but the room was empty. He must have left for the fishing expedition with his new mates.

She sighed deeply, remembering the days when he would kiss her awake just to tell her he was going to work. It seemed like a long time ago, and vaguely she wondered when it had stopped. It seemed that she'd spent most of this holiday so far on her own, and weren't they supposed to be having an adult discussion about starting a family? Since the night he had presented her with the cruise tickets, it hadn't been mentioned.

A horrible thought came to her mind. He hadn't 'presented' her with the tickets; he had distracted her with them. And now he'd vanished again, off on a deep-sea fishing day trip with his new mates instead of spending time with her, his wife. He'd never expressed an interest in fishing before. Or had he? After all, she hadn't known anything about his apparent passion for astronomy before this trip either.

She glanced at her phone on the bed. It was time to swallow her pride. She snatched it up, keyed in a number and closed her eyes as she waited. When the person on the other end answered, she swallowed audibly.

'Julie?' she said tentatively.

'Paula?'

There was a connection there, relief in both women's tone, and having known each other for so long, they both heard it.

'I'm so sorry!' bleated Paula.

At the same time Julie said, 'I'm so glad you called!'

There was no need for an apology, though both of them spoke the obligatory words. There was no need for explanations as to what had made them act the way they had. To Paula's relief, they simply picked up where they had left off.

'I saw your cruise news on Facebook. How's it going out there?' Julie asked, her voice muffled.

'What're you eating?' Paula suddenly realised that she wasn't going to have time for breakfast before they went to the salon. She glanced at her watch, saw it was a quarter to ten already. Breakfast was out today; she would have to have an early lunch instead.

'Muffins – went to Starbucks this morning.'

'Without me?' She laughed. 'I miss you, Jules.'

'Me too, but what's it like? Are you freezing yet?'

As Julie said the words, Paula realised she hadn't been up on deck and out in the open air since they set sail, just before her fateful trip to the sauna.

She shuddered. 'Jules, you won't believe this. I went to the sauna and got locked in. Locked in! I thought I was going to die.'

Expletives and murmurs of sympathy came down the line. Paula settled back against her pillows. She should have called Julie straight after it happened.

'How did you get out?'

'This woman came along, luckily. She was in there when I first went in. Oh my God, Jules, she was naked!' Paula's eyes widened at the memory. She was no prude, but it seemed so totally inappropriate.

'Eww,' said Julie.

'Yes, so she came back and luckily let me out. I invited her to dinner with us last night, she's here on her own.'

'Why'd she come back to the sauna?' said Julie.

'She left her bracelet in there or something. Lucky for me she did; nobody else was coming along. Oh, and then I lost my bloody bag. I thought it had been stolen from the sauna, but Anna – that's the woman who let me out – found it and returned it.'

There was silence at the other end of the phone.

'You still there?' Paula asked.

'Yeah. Just, it seems like this woman is your guardian angel or something,' said Julie, and Paula noted the careful tone she used.

She frowned as she looked at the phone. Was Julie *jealous* of her new friend?

'What're you on about?' she scoffed.

'Is she single?'

Paula nodded. 'Yes, and skinny as a rake. Seriously, Tommy and I had the most beautiful steak dinner last night, and she only ate half a plate of salad!'

'Careful, sweetie. There are women who make it their life's ambition to nab men like your Tommy. Just be on your guard,' said Julie.

Paula felt a flare of irritation, just as she had on the shopping trip. The woman was just one constant lecture. And what was with the continual digs at Tommy, the insinuations that he was going to go off with another woman? Just because it had happened to Julie...

She took a deep breath, not wanting to get into another fight with her best friend. 'She doesn't need to "nab" Tommy, she's very wealthy herself, got a good career, her own business.'

'So, she's skinny, independent, got her own money; she doesn't sound very desirable at all,' replied Julie drily.

'She barely even spoke to Tommy, she hung out with me,' said Paula defensively. 'Anyway, I have to go now because she's picking me up soon. We're going to the hair salon together.'

'It's your first full day on the cruise, where's Tommy?' asked Julie.

'On a fishing trip with some guys he met.' Paula closed her eyes and clutched the phone tight, suddenly unable to listen to the disapproving sound of Julie's silence. 'Gotta go, babe, I'll call you again!'

She hung up just as a knock sounded on the suite door. She hurried over, opened it and greeted Anna, noting as she did the spots of colour in the woman's high cheekbones and the thick winter coat she was wearing.

'Have you been out on deck?' she asked.

'Yes, just waving the boys off on their fishing trip,' Anna said. 'I thought you might be there.'

Paula frowned. She hadn't been invited to wave them off, she hadn't even known what time they were leaving. How had Anna known?

'I had a lie-in,' she answered lamely. 'Did Tommy tell you what time they were going?' And if so, when? she wondered. They'd not spoken much last night, and she was sure he hadn't mentioned the details of the fishing trip.

'No, I was just taking a walk up there before our appointment. We're already at Bruges, you know. It was great docking and watching the day-trippers speed away on the boats. We're docking again later in Ouddorp and picking them up there.'

Suddenly it seemed to Paula that Anna knew an awful lot more about her husband's trip than she did. She hadn't even realised the cruise ship would dock to let them off and collect them again later at a different place.

She thought of Julie's words of warning and felt something dislodge inside her. Why hadn't Tommy asked her if she'd see him off this morning? She smiled brightly at Anna, pushing her paranoia deep down inside. After all, if Anna was trying her luck with Tommy, she could have easily gone on the fishing expedition herself. 'I'll be sure to meet them when they get back,' she said as she glanced at her watch. 'But first, let's go to the salon and get my hair sorted out!'

Chapter 9

Before

My mother was both a prostitute and a drug addict.

Or so I was informed on my first day at secondary school.

At eleven years old I knew the basics of sex, but to me it was what people in their twenties did, not women like my mother. And drugs?

I thought of Kevin, our neighbour who sat in his back garden and puffed away on big white roll-ups, the unmistakable scent drifting over the fence, reaching my nostrils as I sat out there in all weathers, waiting patiently for my mother to finish up with her customers.

That was all I knew of drugs: funny-smelling fags that weren't such a big deal seeing as you could smell them practically everywhere you went on my little council estate.

The girl who told me what I hadn't known about my mother was called Suzanne. She was small and wiry and looked like a ferret. Like me, she was friendless, and looking back, I think now it would have made sense for us to reach out to each other. But in her desperation to be liked, she bullied me.

She made her announcement in front of my brand-new class, before the teacher came into the room. In shock, I said nothing. Instead, I thought about my home, the door to the bedroom that I mustn't enter if it were closed, the matches and ashtrays and that peculiar scent that I'd put down to Kevin next door but often smelled like it was coming from upstairs.

I wasn't sure which was worse: my mother the prostitute or my mother the drug addict.

The girls in the class, those well-adjusted, well-liked girls that Suzanne and I would never be, jumped on her proclamation. *Whore, druggy, slag, scag.* Words that started as a whisper were picked up and passed around, until the classroom was roaring.

'She's not!' I found my voice at last, and even though it trembled, I said what I was supposed to. I denied it.

'Settle down, come on now.' The teacher came in, bodies scattered into seats, laughter and pointed looks hung in the stale, sweaty air.

From beneath lowered lids I watched the girls who had called my mother those names.

'Where's your dad?' hissed Suzanne. 'Was he one of her punters?'

Punters.

My mother called the men in her room 'customers'. They used to be referred to as her 'friends', but that had changed since I'd got older. Two different words that meant the same thing.

The teacher stood in front of the class, coffee-stained shirt, bright eyes and unflattering glasses. As he settled in behind his battered desk, he promised us that the next few years would be among the best of our lives.

He lied.

-

79

For once, my mother's door was open when I got home, and she was in the kitchen, propped up against the worktop, still in her dressing gown.

I watched her for a while, trying to remember the last time I had seen her in clothes. My mind worked backwards until I recalled her taking me to town at the start of the summer holidays to buy my new school uniform. Six weeks ago.

'Mum,' I said as I closed the kitchen door behind me.

She tipped a fag out of the box and clutched it between her yellow fingers. I waited for her to ask me how my first day at school had gone, but she simply lit her cigarette and continued staring out of the window.

'What're you looking at?' I asked, coming up to stand beside her.

'Nothing,' she said.

I remained there for a little while, next to her, breathing in the cigarette smoke and trying to ignore her overpowering perfumed scent. It was warm in the little kitchen and I pushed up my sleeves, laying my arms on the cool of the worktop. I waited for her to comment on the scars that criss-crossed my arms and wrists, but she said nothing.

'Mum, can I ask you about my dad?' I held my breath; I'd never asked her anything like that before.

She uttered a laugh as she crushed out the cigarette in the sink. 'Nope,' she said as she pushed herself upright and stretched. 'Will you put some dinner on while I have a bath?'

Without waiting for a reply, she slouched away, her heavy tread on the stairs signalling the end of that particular conversation.

There was a girl at my new school who was living an even worse life than me. Her name was Rebecca Lavery, and she was dirty and smelly and thin as a rake. I wasn't any of those things because I'd learned how to use the washing machine when I was seven, and the iron and the shower, and I'd been cooking for myself and my mother since I was eight. I took comfort in the fact that Rebecca's sorry state of affairs was briefly more interesting to the other kids than the fact that my mother was a prostitute and a drug addict. I got a reprieve, for a short amount of time.

One day, I was sitting outside the nurse's office after having an accident with a scalpel in the art class. I'd given up cutting myself for sympathy, attention and physical comfort. Turns out when you're no longer tiny and cute, the teachers and nurses don't give a free hug with every incident that involves a bandage or a plaster. I still cut myself, though, because along with the blood came a feeling of release and relief. It was short-lived, and I tried not to do it often, but the sight of the sharp blade and the anticipation of that blessed emotion had been too tempting that day.

The nurse told me I looked pale as she deftly and efficiently patched me up, and I was to sit in the outer office until she was sure I wasn't going to pass out. I waited for her to comment on the faded scars that adorned my arms, but she said nothing.

As I perched on the chair, thinking of nothing and nobody, thin-as-a-rake Rebecca came in from the corridor.

'Mr Heston told me I was to come here,' she said, and it was a moment before I realised she was talking to me.

I shrugged. I hadn't summoned her; why was she telling me?

'Rebecca?'

It was the nurse, the same one who had bandaged me up. She hurried over to Rebecca and crouched down next to her, putting her arms around the thin girl's shoulders and pulling her close. From my corner, I watched in awe and envy.

'We're going to ask you some questions,' she said, her voice muffled as she spoke into Rebecca's hair. 'They might be difficult for you, but it is very important you tell us the truth.'

They moved as one into the nurse's room, and two official-looking suited women followed them in. Later, just as I was deemed fit to return to class, Rebecca came out with the two women. Her eyes were red, and both of them had their arms around her.

'It's okay, you won't ever have to go back to your home again,' murmured one. 'You'll be staying in a temporary home. The people are very kind, and they're very much looking forward to having you stay.'

The news was all over the school. Rebecca was being assaulted at home by a man she called 'uncle'. Many men came and went, apparently, and I couldn't help but think of my own house.

I never saw any of my mother's customers; they had no interest in me, or perhaps they didn't even know I existed. I wondered what they would do if they saw me when they had finished with my mother. Might they take an interest in me, an unhealthy interest like the 'uncle' had had with Rebecca? Would I then be summoned to the office and treated with tenderness and kindness and put in a home where people were nice to me? It was a thought that would stick with me.

There were tears, crocodile ones mostly, from the girls who had shamed Rebecca for the way she looked and the way she smelled. But all I felt was envy. She had been rescued and was moving to a home where only love and kindness and care were waiting for her.

Chapter 10

Paula leaned her head back against the sink and sighed with pleasure. Across the salon she could hear Anna's soft voice as she spoke to the stylist. She wondered what Anna was going to have done. Her hair was already short, shaved up the sides, longer on top. An out-there style that Paula would never have been able to carry off, but she had to admit that with Anna's petite and boyish frame, it looked very high-end. The woman had no roots to speak of either.

'We're going to leave the conditioner on for around thirty minutes,' said the stylist as she massaged Paula's head.

'Great idea, reverse some of the heat damage from that sauna,' murmured Anna.

She sounded very close, and Paula opened her eyes, closing them again as the conditioner flicked across her eyelids.

She felt Anna's hand then, on her shoulder, and she relaxed.

'What are you getting done, Anna?' she asked, wincing as the woman behind her tugged at her tangled hair.

'Hmm, just a trim. I was thinking of highlights, but you know, I think I like it how it is at the moment,' replied Anna.

The salon phone began to ring, and the stylist's hands stilled in Paula's hair. 'Are you all right if I just get that?' she asked.

Paula waved her away.

'I hate that,' she said in a low voice to Anna, 'when salon stylists have to double up as receptionists.' She paused and gave an awkward laugh. 'Do I sound like a snob?'

'No, it's a particular bugbear of mine too,' replied Anna. 'I mean, we pay enough money for them to hire someone to answer the phone, right?'

'Yes!' Paula smiled and settled back against the basin. 'Hey, do you want to get an early lunch when we're done here?'

'Ms Masi?' A second hairdresser came into the salon, and with a bright smile she summoned Anna over. 'I'm ready for you now.'

Thirty minutes later, Paula's stomach rumbled noisily as the stylist unwrapped the clingfilm from around her head. She looked over at Anna, realising the other woman hadn't answered her question about lunch. She opened her mouth to enquire again, but clamped it closed as she ran her eyes over Anna's impossibly skinny body. She had barely touched her salad last night, what if she had an eating disorder? Would it be horribly insensitive to keep on inviting her to meals?

'What are your plans for the rest of the day, Anna?' she asked.

Anna shrugged. 'I think we're stopping for a couple of hours when we dock to pick up the men. I might get off, have a look around.'

Paula nodded. Clearly, Anna was planning to be there when the men boarded. Was she intending on picking one of them up? Julie's warning rang in her mind again. Was she going to be there in the hope of bumping into Tommy in particular?

'*Merda!*'

Paula didn't understand the language, didn't even know what nationality her stylist was, but she got the tone.

'What?' she asked. She looked up and around at the other woman.

The stylist's face had drained of colour.

'What?' Paula asked again. She reached behind her, pulled her hair over her shoulder and peered down at it. 'Oh my God,' she muttered. Looking back up at the stylist, she held up the strands of hair. 'What *happened*?'

'What is it?' Anna's voice floated across the salon.

Paula couldn't speak. *It's hair, just hair. It's not your health, it's not a death. It's just hair,* she told herself.

But it wasn't, not really.

Anna's gown whispered as she crowded around with the two other stylists. Paula heard a gasp, long and drawn-out, and she felt the hairdressers' fear in their silence.

'Is this bleach?' asked Anna sharply, lifting a hand to pat at Paula's hair. The look in her eyes was of sympathy mixed with horror.

Despite the two hairdressers talking in crisp tones at each other, gesturing to the dish that had been used for the deep-conditioning treatment, Paula did not ask again what had happened. She did not demand that it be put right, that she receive a refund and further complimentary treatments, or insist that she speak to the manager of the salon. There was nothing that could fix this in the here and now.

'Just… dry it,' she said, her voice thick.

In the mirror she watched the three women behind her exchange worried glances. She heard her own breathing accelerate. Suddenly feeling very constricted, she pulled at the neck of the gown that covered her. The Velcro peeled away and she stood up, leaving the gown on her chair.

'Forget it,' she said in a strange, strangled voice, and as the others watched, she hurried to the door of the salon and pushed through it.

In the corridor, she paused, one hand on the wall, and was it her imagination or were the walls closing in on her? She heard the click of heels approaching from inside the salon, and she pushed off the wall and darted through a door, up the winding stairs, feeling dizzier and fainter as she went round and up and round.

Out of the corner of her eye she spotted a door, large and metal, and she pushed on it and burst through. The wind, howling and bitter, made her gasp, and belatedly she realised she was out in what must be minus temperatures in a thin top with no coat. She wrapped her arms around herself and, putting her head down against the wind, made her way to the railing.

Eyes stinging, she forced her head up and looked to the sky. It was a metallic grey with dark, swollen clouds. Fat raindrops cascaded around her, stinging her skin and soaking her already wet hair.

Her hair.

She caught a fistful of it and peered sideways. It was bleach, she knew instantly. Anna had been right. That wouldn't have been so bad had she been blonde, but the mixture had turned her glossy black hair a garish orange colour. And not all over, which might also have been a little bit better, but in splodges.

How had the bleach got in the dish? Had it been left over from a previous customer? It didn't matter anyway, she thought, as she tilted her head back and let the rain lash down to rinse the horrid mixture from her hair. There was no changing it.

She put a hand on the cold railing and stared out to sea, hoping to catch a glimpse of Tommy returning from his adventure. But there was no sign of life on the choppy ocean; it stretched dark and barren and empty all the way to the horizon.

–

Anna stood in the reception and tapped her nails on the counter. Behind the desk, the stylist who had worked on Paula's hair stared at her, a troubled expression on her face.

'She's your friend, no?' she asked in a low murmur.

Anna shrugged. 'Not really, I just met her yesterday.'

The stylist nodded and lowered her eyes. Anna let the silence stretch on.

'I don't understand how it happened,' the hairdresser said, her voice a thin, painful whisper now.

Anna said nothing, wondering what the woman expected in response. Platitudes? Sympathy?

Finally, the stylist stabbed at the computer till and pushed a receipt across the desk.

'It was very upsetting to witness,' said Anna without glancing at her bill.

A single moment, then the stylist flushed a deep red. She picked up the receipt and screwed it up, dropping it into the bin.

With a small smirk, Anna nodded to her and made her way out of the salon.

In the elevator, she pushed the button for the top deck and, holding her shoulder bag close, watched as the numbers ticked off.

The deck was deserted when she pushed through the heavy door. She didn't notice the sting of the wind and rain as she walked briskly to the rail. From her bag she pulled out the bottle of hydrogen peroxide and ammonia. She shook it, once, and the milky white dregs glowed bright against the gloom of the day. Then, pulling her arm back, she threw it as far as she could overboard. There was no splash. The bottle bobbed for a moment and sank in the white-plumed waves, to vanish forever in the trail of the fast-moving ship.

–

At lunchtime, Anna gave in to her body and ate a small bowl of soup. She spooned it mechanically, taking no pleasure from the flavour. Food meant little to her. It was a chore that she had to succumb to on occasion to keep her strength up. At times, as well as the light-headedness, she experienced other symptoms. Colours, vivid flashes of greens and blues affected her vision, along with a dense headache. She found the flashes diverting; she imagined the Northern Lights would look similar, if she were ever lucky enough to see them.

As she pushed her discarded bread roll to one side and sipped at her cup of water, she heard a commotion in the doorway. She looked up and sat a little straighter when she saw the fishing expedition boys come piling through the door, headed by Tommy Ellis. The dining area was empty but for her, and he hailed a hearty greeting as he made his way over to her.

Anna sat back and crossed her legs. 'You boys are back early,' she remarked.

'We had to turn around. Have you been on deck? It's wild out there,' said Tommy as he pulled out a chair uninvited and sat down.

'Drink, mate?' asked one of his fishing buddies.

'Pint, please,' said Tommy. He glanced at Anna's water. 'Anna?'

She pretended to mull it over. 'Gin and tonic, thanks,' she replied.

Tommy pulled off his jacket and slung it on an empty chair. 'How were your salon appointments?' he asked, and before she could answer he reached a hand towards her face.

For a second she thought he might touch her hair, and she held her breath, but his finger stopped just short of her. 'Looking good,' he said, and the roughness of his voice had gone, to be replaced by a softness she would never have thought he possessed.

'Good, thanks. Paula had a problem, though.'

His pint landed in front of him, and a heavy hand shoved gin and tonic towards her. She barely glanced at the man as she murmured her thanks.

Tommy took a long sip. 'What problem?' he asked.

She shrugged. 'Something wrong with the conditioner they used; it might have been a colour or something.' She shrugged again, allowing her oversized jumper to slip deliberately off one thin, tanned shoulder.

'How's that a problem?' he asked, his eyes travelling to the bare patch of skin. 'I'm sure it looked okay, didn't it?'

'I don't know.' Anna lowered her eyes. 'She stormed out and I haven't seen her since.'

Tommy's face fell, and she knew she had got across what she wanted. That Paula had had a tantrum; that she was hiding somewhere on the ship in a sulk.

'I'm sorry,' he said.

An apology. On behalf of his wife. Interesting. She smiled at him. 'It's not your fault, is it?'

He ran his large hand over his closely cropped hair. 'Nah, but she can be a bit...' He trailed off helplessly.

Anna debated whether to cover his hand with hers, offer sympathy. All the while the unspoken words that she would never behave that way would hover between them.

But no, she decided, it was too soon.

He pushed back his chair half-heartedly. 'I should track her down,' he said, though he remained seated.

Anna took a long swallow of her drink and crossed her legs. 'I think she wants to be alone... she'll probably want to sort out her hair.' She leaned forward, presenting him with an eyeful of her bra-less chest inside the deep neckline. 'Why don't you give her a few hours, then text her to come along for dinner? We can all eat together again, yes?'

For the first time she acknowledged the other men who had taken seats at their table. 'In the meantime, you can all regale me with your morning's adventures.'

—

The wind had picked up to what seemed like gale force when Paula finally peeled herself off the railing and walked slowly back inside. She was numb from her head to her toes, and the deep freeze had settled in the very marrow of her bones. In the elevator, she held her hands up in front of her face and clenched her fingers. Sharp pains shot through her knuckles and she gasped as she looked closer at the split skin.

With a barely concealed sob, she shoved her hands in her pockets.

The elevator door opened to a hive of activity and she looked around in confusion. She had ended up in the bar and dining area, and her stomach rumbled noisily, reminding her that she had missed both breakfast and the early lunch she had planned after the hair appointment.

But it was too close to dinner to eat something now, and catching sight of herself in the mirrored wall, she shuddered and retreated into the lift. She had never looked so awful. She turned away, but not before she had caught sight of her hair, still wet, tangled and with those awful pale bleach patterns.

She felt tears well up again at the sight of the people already congregating for dinner, laughing and drinking and—

She blinked.

Tommy and Anna. Sitting together, their faces close, Anna throwing her head back to laugh at something Tommy had said.

When had he got back? And why was he with *her*?

She slammed a hand on the panel to stop the doors closing, but they swished shut and with an efficient hiss the elevator swept upwards.

He had texted her, she saw as she closed the door of the suite behind her and picked up her phone.

> We're all in the restaurant, we're eating with the fishing boys tonight as the trip got cut short. Anna is already here. Come down as soon as you're ready.

She sank down on the bed, tapping her finger thoughtfully on the screen. It was more information than she usually got from him in a text, and it seemed to explain why he was already back. *And* he'd acknowledged that Anna was with him. Didn't try to hide it, not like some men would have.

She tapped out a reply.

Give me twenty minutes xxx

Pressing send, she threw the phone on the bed and hurried into the bathroom. Taking a deep breath, she studied her reflection. There was no salvaging her hair, except… In a flash of inspiration, she upended her make-up bag into the sink, scrabbling among the various items until she found what she was looking for.

Hair mascara.

A few months ago, she had found a single errant grey hair. In a state of panic she had plucked it out and immediately raced to the shops. She couldn't put a colour on; that was done by her very expensive stylist and she wasn't due an appointment for another four weeks. If grey hairs were going to start prematurely springing up, she needed something on hand for immediate use.

As luck would have it, no more grey hairs had appeared, and now she had a full tube of jet-black hair covering. It wouldn't do long term, she noted as she scraped the wand over the worst of the blotches; tomorrow she would go back to the salon as soon as they opened and demand that they fix the mess they had made of her hair.

And she would go alone.

She paused mid stroke, wondering why she had thought that. It was hardly Anna's fault that the hairdresser had messed up. She dashed the thought away and scrutinised her reflection. Perhaps the stylist could lighten her hair all over so that the orange bits blended in. She put the mascara wand down carefully on the edge of the sink and shook her hair out. She'd never been a blonde. And weren't they supposed to have more fun? She thought of Anna, her tousled sun-kissed hair flying around as she laughed with Tommy, and shivered.

When had Paula last laughed like that with him? They had certainly laughed a lot at the beginning of their relationship, when they were both students, when nothing seemed very important and life was all about fun. Then came jobs and responsibility, new houses and mortgages. And even though they were the most financially comfortable they had ever been, there didn't seem to be much to laugh about these days.

She missed the way they used to be. She realised that so far they had spent barely any time together on this holiday. They were supposed to be making a baby, and yet he hadn't even come near her. Once again she thought of him downstairs, with his fishing buddies and Anna.

After dinner they would come back to the suite, she vowed. They would spend the evening in bed, she would even open a bottle of champagne, and later they would sit in the big chairs in front of the French windows and watch the stars and, if they were really lucky, the Northern Lights.

-

There was something different about Paula as she made her way out of the elevator and raised her hand as she spotted them.

Anna tilted her head as she studied her. The hair...

It was Paula's normal glossy black hair. Had she returned to the salon? But no, there was no way they would have been able to repair the bleach damage in such a short space of time.

Tommy, previously attentive to Anna, saw his wife approaching, and Anna watched, increasingly disconcerted, as he smiled, wide and happy. He raised his hand, bellowed out for Paula to come over. When she arrived, he stood up and kissed her cheek.

'You look great,' he said. 'Where've you been? Anna said there was a problem at the salon.'

Anna reached out a hand and touched Paula's fingers, mustering up the enthusiasm to sound friendly. 'It looks great,' she said. 'Did they sort you out?'

Paula fixed a smile on her face. 'I'm going back at some point, but it's okay for now,' she replied. She turned to Tommy, her back to Anna now. 'How come you're here? What happened to your trip?'

With his arm around his wife's shoulders, he pulled her down to sit next to him. As he repeated his story of the wild seas and torrential wind and rain, Anna sat back in her own chair. It was all very civilised, and she was still at their table, but somehow it was as though she had lost. Husband and wife talked quietly together, their heads close, looking just like he and Anna had done all afternoon.

Resigned, she came to the conclusion that it was over for today.

But just for one day.

Tomorrow she would start again.

She murmured some excuse to the remaining few men who had been on Tommy's day trip with him and stood up, walking briskly away from the table towards the elevator. As she waited for it to arrive, she watched the couple carefully.

Maybe it was time to step things up a bit.

–

As Anna made her way up and out onto the top deck, she thought about Tommy Ellis. He was easy on the eye, fit and strong, and as long as he was talking about something that interested him, he was a good conversationalist. But all of those plus points were irrelevant. He was a man with a home and very good financial security. He had no children who would lay claim to his inheritance; he had no siblings, no dependants. Soon he would be a widower.

It was such a simple idea. It wasn't that much different from what she had planned with William, though that had ended sooner than she had banked on. *Because of his son.* If Jason hadn't suddenly appeared, Anna would have spent a good few more years squirrelling away William's money, siphoning transactions here and there. Laying a base plan for her own survival so that she never had to go back to the way her life had once been.

And that was why she had changed tack. Once Tommy was on his own, there would be nobody to stop her. No son or daughter swooping in to take care of their dad. There was only one snag: he needed to think less of his wife. She had seen it at the beginning, the tension that simmered between them, the discord, the niggles. She needed to widen that gap of dislike and distaste, and she'd thought she had been succeeding. Only tonight, when Paula had arrived for dinner, Tommy had looked at his wife with something that was almost a new love.

It wouldn't do.

It wouldn't do at all.

She walked to the side of the ship and rested her hand on the narrow gate set into the railing. Spotting a bolt at the bottom, she reached down and slid it back, then pushed on the gate. It opened easily, and she stood in the gap. Just one step forward and she would be below in the waves, no hope of survival.

She closed and bolted it again, then cast a glance around her to make sure nobody had witnessed what she had just done. Why on earth would the gate be there in the first place? She resolved to ask the captain when it was her turn to dine at his table.

Shivering now, she made her way back along the deck towards the inner corridor. At the door, she paused and looked up at the night sky. It was cloudy, the sky threatening rain again. There would be no chance of any sighting of the Northern Lights tonight.

Just then, the door swung open, and a crew member stumbled out, colliding with her.

'Miss, I'm so sorry,' he said, whipping his hand behind his back.

She caught the scent of hand-rolled tobacco, saw the smoke that spiralled up behind him. She smiled. 'I had exactly the same idea,' she said, 'but I left my smokes in my suite.'

He gave her a lopsided grin. 'Suite?' he asked. 'Not a cabin?'

'The Arctic Suite,' she confirmed. 'Pretty big for one person, I know, but hey.' She smiled, raised her eyebrows, hoped he'd got the message.

He leaned against the wall as he offered her a pre-made roll-up. She accepted it, bending forward as he cupped his hands around it to light it.

'What's your name?' she asked.

'Mark Taylor,' he replied, 'at your service.'

She nodded to herself. A man other than Tommy wasn't in her plan for this cruise, but men were generally stupid, led by their lower half, and this Mark might come in handy. She studied the insignia on his thick woollen coat. Three stripes meant he was at the higher end of the staffing scale. Her mind turned over; he would have access to cabins, the master key to all the suites. He could come in useful, very useful indeed.

'Mark, what is the gate for, in the middle of the railings down there?' she asked.

He dragged deeply on his own cigarette and looked to where she gestured. 'There are several of them. They're for the lifeboats. In the event of an emergency, we can just open the gates and crane them out. See where they're stored, behind those panels there, and the metal joints they're attached to.' He pointed with his cigarette and shrugged. 'It's a time-saver.'

She nodded and moved a little closer to him. 'Isn't it dangerous?' she asked. 'A kid could come along and open one and fall into the sea!'

He smiled; a patronising smile, she thought. Slightly irritating, but she waited patiently for his reply.

'Nah, they're padlocked,' he said. 'Only crew members can open them.'

One of them isn't, she thought. But she wasn't about to tell him that.

'It's my day off tomorrow,' he said. 'Maybe you'd like a tour of the ship?'

She smiled. He was hooked.

—

Within half an hour, Mark was in the Arctic Suite, naked, on top of Anna on the enormous bed, an almost-empty bottle of champagne clutched in one hand, a lit cigarette dangling from his full lips.

Anna counted silently inside her head. For her, sex, much like food, was something to be endured; an act that was sometimes necessary but from which she derived no pleasure. As Mark finished and let the champagne bottle drop from his hand to the floor, he muttered something into the pillow, words she didn't catch, then shifted position and closed his eyes.

She plucked the cigarette from between his lips and placed it in her own mouth. Within minutes, he was snoring loudly. She slipped from the bed, and as she walked to the bathroom, she picked up the keys from where he had carelessly tossed them as he divested himself of his clothes.

In the bathroom, she turned the shower on and laid the bunch of keys on the floor. She identified the padlock keys easily, the ones that would open the gates in the railings. She moved past them; the gate she had her eye on was already unlocked. No, it was the master keys she was after, the ones Mark had shown her earlier. Unlike the credit-card-type keys the passengers used, the masters were actual keys. Four of them in all, and as she located the one that locked and unlocked the suites, she slipped it off and put it in the pocket of her robe. As an afterthought, she pulled off the key for the public restrooms.

When she went back into the bedroom, she put the keys carefully back next to Mark's coat. On the bed, he slept on.

'Tonight, fellow passengers, may prove a lucky night, as the forecast is clearer than previous evenings. Not only do you have the chance to see the promised Northern Lights, but also shooting stars from the Leonids as well as the waxing gibbous moon, cloud cover permitting.

'So, midnight walkers, make sure you look up to the skies if you are taking a late-night stroll on the upper deck, and keep your eyes open for some unexpected surprises!'

Chapter 11

Paula groaned as Tommy shook her awake. She batted him away, pulling the quilt over her head.

'Wake up!' he hissed.

She lunged through the fog of sleep, arms windmilling as she struggled out of the covers.

'What's wrong?' she cried. Glancing at the glowing digits of the clock, she saw it was 2:30 a.m.

Tommy loomed over her, fully dressed, pulling his coat on. 'It's a clear sky!' he said excitedly. 'We're going up to the deck to see if we can see the Northern Lights.' He did a funny little dance on the spot, his excitement apparent as he thrust a glass at her. 'Drink this, it'll wake you up.'

Paula put a hand on her thumping heart and scrubbed at her face. 'It's the middle of the night.'

In the darkness of the cabin, his face glowed white in the moonlight. She saw something in his eyes, a disappointment, and her heart sank at causing him hurt. 'Give me a second, let me just get dressed,' she said.

She accepted what she thought was a glass of water from him and threw it back. 'This is vodka!' she gasped, coughing and spluttering.

He nodded eagerly and brandished the bottle, topping up her glass. 'It'll keep you warm, it's gonna be cold on deck.'

Still clutching the bottle, he moved away to the window, peering out anxiously.

As she pulled on her jeans, she caught a glimpse of the pillow, and the black stains that adorned it. The hair mascara. If it was on the pillow, it meant it was no longer on her hair. She would need a hat. She shivered. Tommy was right, it *was* cold. She swallowed back the vodka and held out her glass for him to refill it again.

He grinned at her, and suddenly, standing half dressed in the middle of the night, she was reminded of how they used to be, back when they were teenagers. It was a good feeling, and she giggled, already light-headed. Impulsively she planted a kiss on his lips.

'Go,' she said. 'I'll meet you on the upper deck.'

He grinned, shoving the bottle of vodka at her as he hurried from the room.

In his wardrobe she found his hat, big enough to stuff her hair inside. She put it on without looking in the mirror and vowed again that she would be outside the salon door when they opened in seven hours.

Out in the corridor, she pushed open the door to the spiral steps that led up and outside. All was quiet in the other suites, and she cast a glance back at Anna's door. What had Tommy meant by '*We're* going up to the deck'? Who was 'we' – his fishing buddies? Or Anna? She shivered, wondering when this had been arranged, or if someone had texted Tommy to tell him about the clear sky and the prospect of the Northern Lights.

Up and up she went, and as she pulled herself from stair to stair, she realised how utterly different the ship was in the midnight hours. From deep in the bowels of the boat she heard clangs and metal scraping. The low hum of the engine, which she couldn't remember hearing in the daytime, whirred beneath her. Everything else was deathly silent. She pushed herself to move faster.

For some reason, she had expected the top deck to be lit up. Instead, it was in total darkness. On the floor were tiny glowing circles, like emergency lighting strips in a hotel hallway. She pulled her coat tighter around her and wobbled as the vodka hit in the fresh air. She couldn't remember the last time she'd thrown back so many shots in the space of a minute.

She hesitated, staying perfectly still, cocking her head as she listened for sounds of chatter that would lead her to Tommy, all the while trying to get her eyes to focus through the alcohol haze. She called his name, once, but heard nothing in reply. She wished it was lighter out here. The deck couldn't be lit up, though; it would detract from the view of the Northern Lights. Still, it was a little intimidating, walking in the pitch-black.

With her arms outstretched in front of her, she made her way to the left side of the deck and clutched onto the railing. She peered over the edge, and found herself staring into nothingness. The sea was there, she could hear it, but the darkness was a hole, broken only by white foam as it shunted the side of the ship.

She looked up; what was that, at the far end of the ship? Dots of light floated in the air, tiny beams against the night sky. For an insane moment she thought of a UFO, and then wondered if this was the famous Northern Lights. But no, she'd seen photos of them, pictures on the internet. This wasn't them.

Tommy! He was there, and judging by the pinpricks of light, he was with others, the torches on their mobiles or perhaps camera flashes lighting her way. She smiled. It wasn't the Northern Lights, but never had she been so grateful to see light or people.

She opened her mouth to shout to him, to tell him to stay there, she was coming, but the wind had got up again, and it whipped her words from her mouth to carry them away over the dark sea. She held onto the railing, put her head down and moved forward. The wind was against her, but if she clutched onto the side, she would be fine.

The wind dropped, suddenly and swiftly, and she let go of the rail and stood up straight, amazed at the sudden calm. Tommy's hat, a little too big, slipped down, and she reached up with both hands to adjust it. Ahead of her, the lights seemed to have vanished, and she stepped up her pace.

She thought it was Tommy coming at her, the speed and suddenness just like him. She half turned, expecting him to grab her round her waist, pick her up effortlessly and swing her around to make her shriek and beat at his chest. She was already smiling, already relieved that someone bigger and stronger than her was there, so she could cling onto him as they made their way to the bow, rather than gripping the railing. She started to speak, words she wouldn't remember later, but as the person kept coming and didn't slow their pace, she knew that this wasn't Tommy, that it was the wrong shape.

'Hey!' she said, and there was a smile in her tone, because the way they were charging towards her meant they were probably drunk, and perhaps didn't know they were heading straight for her. 'Hey!' she said again, a little louder this time, and instinctively she raised her arms, crossing them in front of her.

The person slammed into her and she staggered backwards, feeling the railing behind her crush her breath out in a whoosh. She wheezed, bent double, and her assailant put their arms around her but said nothing.

That was the moment she realised she was in trouble, she thought later, the lack of speech. No apology, no shocked words, just a body against hers, and then the realisation that this person was still moving, still coming at her, and now they were both sliding along the railing, until the cold metal at Paula's back vanished and suddenly there was nothing any more.

She went down painfully on one knee, grabbing at anything she could: the decking beneath her with one hand, the unknown assailant with the other.

And still they pushed her, and there was nothing behind her, nothing apart from the deep, dark sea that churned far below.

It was over as soon as it had begun. Just as her right leg slipped off the ship altogether, she spotted the gap in the railing and threw her arm up. Clutching onto the rail to her right, she heaved herself upright.

'TOMMY!' she screamed, and she shouted his name again and again, her words trailing off to a single thin scream.

The pressure against her vanished as her assailant let go, but the knowledge that they were there, still close, frightened her almost as much as if they were still attacking her. Footsteps came now, hard and pounding, and she shifted position, crawling along the deck, slippery and cold, as she continued to shriek. Feet skidded to a stop beside her, three or more people there now, and finally, there was Tommy, on his knees in front of her, pulling her up to slump against him.

–

Tommy fed her a shot of whisky as she sat in the chair by the window. Her teeth knocked against the glass and he pulled the duvet tighter around her. She swallowed hard to stop herself gagging at the strong taste, and the sharp tang of bile rose in her throat.

'I'm not cold,' she protested, pushing the suffocating quilt away.

The late-night unscheduled announcement from the captain rang in her head. *Keep your eyes open for some unexpected surprises!* She shuddered, and a strangled cry emerged. When she had listened to his words over the sound system it had been magical, a hint of promise of something spectacular. Now, after the event, it seemed like a warning.

One she had not paid heed to.

'She's in shock,' said Dermot, one of Tommy's fishing friends. He pulled up a stool and sat down in front of her.

She looked up at him, noticing him almost for the first time, then pushed herself out of the chair and grabbed his sleeve. 'He wore a coat like this, waxy,' she said, her voice trembling as she rubbed it between her fingers. 'It was green, I think, just like this. A dark green waxed jacket.'

'Well, I was with Tommy when the accident happened,' said Dermot after a moment's uncomfortable silence.

She winced; she hadn't been accusing Dermot. An apology poured forth from her at the misunderstanding. 'I'm so sorry, I didn't mean that. I'm not saying it was you, just that this is exactly what he was wearing when he pushed me.'

'It's a common jacket,' replied Dermot. 'Lots of fishermen wear them.'

'Maybe someone had had too much to drink,' said Tommy.

'I thought that!' said Paula. 'I thought they'd just staggered into me, but they grabbed me, they didn't let go, they pushed me into that very specific gap where the railing had broken.' She heard her voice splinter with unshed tears and looked from Dermot to Tommy. 'I was pushed,' she finished quietly.

There was a moment of silence before Tommy spoke again. 'I meant you,' he said. 'That maybe *you'd* had a bit too much to drink.'

She gaped at him. 'No, I didn't!' But belatedly she remembered the vodkas she had knocked back less than half an hour before. 'I wasn't drunk,' she protested.

'Maybe the ship rocked, or a gust of wind...' The two men turned to each other as they mused upon the situation.

Paula sank back into her chair. 'I was pushed,' she said. But her words were so quiet the men didn't hear her. Or if they did, they didn't respond.

Fatigue overtook her and she breathed deeply. As traumatic as it was, she went back in her mind to the deck. Had she really been pushed? Or had the wind been so strong that it had buffeted her to the ground?

Her eyes wandered over to the bottle of vodka on the side. Nausea overcame her and she swallowed rapidly. Maybe she *had* been drunk. But if she had, she was stone-cold sober now.

'Hey, I thought I heard voices. Is everything all right?'

Anna was standing in the doorway. To Paula she looked as perfect as ever, not a hair out of place, her eyes not remotely sleepy as she tightened the belt of the thin robe she wore.

Paula looked down at her hands in her lap and prayed silently that Tommy wouldn't tell Anna what had happened to her. It was only the third day of their cruise, and already she had had more mishaps than most people usually had during a lifetime of holidays.

At the sight of Anna, Dermot sprang up and went over to her, and Paula watched as they talked quietly by the door, Anna nodding, gasping, casting worried glances Paula's way.

'I think I need to rest,' Paula said to Tommy.

He stood by the French windows, staring out at the black night. The clouds had dulled the moon; no chance of seeing the Northern Lights tonight. Besides, it was getting on for morning now. From the corner of her eye, Paula saw Anna drift over, ghost-like, a vision in white.

'I'm fine,' she said before Anna could speak. 'But severely sleep-deprived.' She attempted a smile, but failed miserably. 'I'll catch up with you tomorrow.'

Anna nodded and leaned forward, kissing Paula's cheek. Her lips were cold as ice.

'See you at breakfast, Tommy, Dermot,' she called, and slipped out of the room as silently as she had arrived.

Paula watched her go, realising that their romantic holiday had suddenly become a group outing.

'I'll walk you back,' said Dermot, skipping smartly out of the door. 'See you guys tomorrow. Paula, get some rest.'

The door closed behind them, and Paula looked over at Tommy, still motionless by the doors.

'How are you feeling?' he asked, coming to kneel beside her.

She allowed him to hold her, and leaned her head on his shoulder. 'I was sure someone pushed me, Tommy,' she whispered.

She felt him stiffen, before his arms circled her even tighter.

'It was a gate, not a gap in the railing,' he said. 'I'm going to speak to someone about it, make sure it's shut and locked.' He held her by the shoulders and looked into her eyes. 'I could have lost you.' His own eyes were shining, and she was moved by the emotion that she so rarely saw from him.

'I'm okay,' she replied, because that was what she was supposed to say.

But she didn't feel okay. Not at all.

–

Anna plucked a lemon from the basket on the table and placed the small vegetable knife next to it as she reached for the half-bottle of gin.

The sun was trying to push through, but hazy grey clouds almost smothered the weak orange rays that she could see on the horizon. She poured a healthy slug of gin and knocked it back. In the cabin next door, everything was quiet, and she wondered what the pair of them were doing in there.

As far as she could tell, no crime had been reported yet. And from what she'd managed to get out of Tommy's friend Dermot, it seemed that none of them had actually witnessed what had happened. A drunk man had crashed into Paula was what they were assuming, even though Paula herself was adamant she had been attacked.

Anna clutched the glass so hard it was in danger of cracking. As she huddled in the chair, she swore quietly. It had been her chance, the best chance she was going to get, and she had failed.

Anna didn't like failure. She was used to working hard to get what she wanted and she had become an expert at biding her time and not missing once-in-a-lifetime opportunities. Now Paula would be careful, on the lookout. She would cling to Tommy and his gaggle of mates as though they were bodyguards.

Anna drank again.

She had missed her chance.

A tap at the door, and she rose and walked across the room, tightening her robe. She hoped it wasn't Dermot; it had been obvious when he walked her back to her cabin that he was angling for an invitation to come inside. For a moment she had debated with herself, but she knew enough about him to confirm that he wasn't a suitable prospect for her plan. Too many relatives; an ex-wife, children too.

As she unlocked the door, hope flared briefly. Perhaps it was Paula, come to seek refuge with another woman, stifled by the men and their macho protectiveness.

She pulled the door open, a welcoming smile on her face.

'Oh,' she said. 'It's you.'

Mark, her bedfellow of the night before, leaned against the door frame and grinned at her. 'Sorry it's so early. Can I come in?' he asked.

Anna hesitated. Mark had served his purpose. But on the other hand, he was staff, and he might have information on whether anything had been reported by Paula and her clan.

She opened the door wide and stepped back. 'Come on in.'

She walked back to her chair and grabbed another glass from the shelf. 'Drink?' she asked, one hand subtly loosening the belt on her robe. She leaned over to pick up the gin.

He narrowed his eyes, his gaze flicking from her face to her chest. 'Go on, then,' he replied, lowering himself into a chair. 'Good view,' he said, gesturing to the horizon.

She murmured her agreement as she filled their glasses and picked up the knife and lemon.

'Not as good as the top deck, though,' he commented.

She kept slicing, but felt the ice as it ran through her veins. There was something in his tone, a caginess that had her hackles rising. She made no reply.

'Did I leave any keys here the other night?' he asked.

The knife stilled; she put the lemon down on the cutting board and turned to face him. 'I don't think so,' she said.

He crossed one leg over the other and smiled up at her. The smile didn't reach his eyes.

'You unlocked that gate on the deck. You had a fight with the woman from the Expedition Suite.'

She blinked slowly. The incident hadn't even been reported when she was in Anna's suite. How did Mark know about it? Was it possible he had seen her? She thought of Dermot, of the hushed excitement he seemed to exude when he told her about what had happened. She imagined him trailing through the rest of the ship, informing all and sundry about the night's adventures.

She said nothing. In Anna's experience, it was a sign of weakness or guilt to even attempt to take part in the conversation with an accuser. She slid the knife into the sleeve of her robe and fixed her gaze on him without saying a word.

He stared back.

Don't look away.

Mark blinked.

Anna allowed herself a small smile.

Wrong-footed, he bit his lip and tried another tack. 'Everyone's keys are being checked. Two of mine are missing.' He smiled strangely at her. 'You and I can come to an agreement. Compensation, say, for the fine I'll face.'

She wondered what sort of compensation he had in mind. Money, or her body? But she didn't ask him. She remained still, fighting the urge to do something – take a sip of gin or light a cigarette or even sit down or walk away. All would be signs that he had edged in front of her in this strange two-horse race.

'You're fucking mental.' His words were careful, considered, and held just a hint of unease.

She readied herself. His next move would be to mask his fear with a reaction, and he would use the only power he had over her: his physical strength.

He went to stand, planting his big hands on the armrests. Anna took two steps forward and raised her right hand. The knife slid out, an extension of her fingers. She didn't look at his eyes, or his hands, but kept her focus solely on the target area as she bent slightly and deftly flicked. The blade sliced cleanly through his carotid artery. The blood gush was instant.

One... two... three...

She put one hand on his shoulder as he bucked forward, angling herself so she stood clear of the jet. She watched its trajectory, up and over, hitting the glossy drinks cabinet, running down bright red against polished white wood.

Four... five... six...

She glanced down at Mark, his mouth flapping uselessly. Eight seconds for him to lose consciousness. She applied a little more pressure to his upper arm to keep him from moving to plug the flow.

Seven… eight…

It was done.

She moved back to survey the damage. The blood could have been worse; it hadn't touched the rug underneath the chairs, just the cabinet, which was dripping still, running in rivers to pool on the floor. She would tend to that first.

She slipped off her robe and worked naked, to avoid the danger of getting blood on her clothes. She hung the robe neatly in the wardrobe, pleased to see not a single drop of Mark's blood on it.

From her suitcase she pulled a large plastic sheet, which she tucked behind his shoulders, wrapping it around his front like a shawl. On her hands and knees, she mopped up the puddle and roughly cleaned the cabinet with cloths that had been packed alongside the sheet. When there was no risk of the blood getting on anything else, she opened the French doors and stepped out onto the balcony. The sun was fully up now, silvery white and yellow beams against a perfect blue sky. She walked over to the railing and squatted for a closer look at it. No gate here, unfortunately, unlike the top deck.

She looked back inside at Mark's inert body. He was a big guy. She'd put him at twelve stone at least, maybe more, almost double her own weight. The railing on the balcony came up to her chest, and though it was a clear drop down into the ocean, there was no way she could lift his corpse up and over.

She ran her hand over the railings again, feeling for the bolts. Just two in each, joining the white rails to the side supports. If she had a spanner, she would only need to remove one rail and she could slide Mark's body out.

She glanced around, grateful for the solid brick walls that divided her from the deck to the left, and Paula's Expedition Suite to the right. The white walls were floor-to-ceiling, offering total privacy from all angles, meaning she could work in peace; the only possibility of exposure was a passing ship or sailing too close to land on the starboard side.

There was only one sticking point: she needed to find a spanner.

Dusting off her hands, she pulled herself upright and walked back inside, closing the doors behind her.

–

'We're docking again today. D'you want to get off the ship for a while?' asked Tommy as they sat down to breakfast in the restaurant.

Paula looked over the menu half-heartedly. What she really wanted was to go home, to be safe in her own house, with the electric gates and the burglar alarms, and call her regular salon to make an appointment to sort out her damn hair.

She put the menu down and pulled some strands of hair around to inspect them. The covering mascara had all gone now, and the horrid orange bits were even worse than she remembered. Pulling a band out of her bag, she twisted her hair up and tied it in a bun.

'Babe?' prompted Tommy. 'Do you want to get off and have a look around?'

'Where are we docking?' she asked. 'And for how long?'

'Åndalsnes, in Norway,' replied Tommy as he stuffed a bread roll in his mouth. 'It's the last stop before Iceland, so if you want to stretch your legs, now's your chance.'

It was all 'you', she thought as she pretended to peruse the menu again. She remembered a time when Tommy had planned outings for the two of them, whether it be a picnic in the park when they were students, or a night at The Ritz when he first started earning a good wage. These days, he didn't seem too concerned if she didn't come along with him. If she didn't get off the ship in Åndalsnes, he would probably hook up with Dermot, or one of the other fishing boys, or even a complete stranger. They would wind up in a little bar, the beers would flow, Tommy would get boisterous and loud.

On the other hand, the *Ruby Spirit* was becoming claustrophobic, and if this was the last chance to step onto dry land before the three-day sail to Iceland, she thought she should take it. But there were things to be dealt with first.

'Did you report my attack?' she asked, lowering her voice so the neighbouring table couldn't hear her.

Tommy stared at her. 'I'm going to ask why the gate wasn't closed,' he said carefully.

Paula looked away, towards the floor-to-ceiling windows that offered a view of the sea. It wasn't an answer. Well, it was, but it was a placatory one. He had chosen his words deliberately. It was an answer that meant he didn't believe her version of events. She twisted her fingers together, staring down at them until her knuckles turned white.

He was probably right. She had drunk too much and it had been bitingly cold; her senses had been dulled. The accident was her own stupid fault. After all, who on this ship would want to hurt her?

But a niggling doubt pulsed in her head like the beginning of a migraine. Tears pricked behind her eyes and she blinked them away.

'What time do we dock?' she asked. 'I'd like to try and book an appointment at the salon before we get off the boat.'

'You're going back there? Even after…' He raised a hand and circled it around her head.

'I have to,' she said. 'It's the only hairdresser on board and I really don't want to spend the rest of my holiday like this.'

'There might be one in Åndalsnes. I could find a pub while you're—'

She shook her head. 'I'll go to the salon now. I'll find out what time we dock and I'll meet you at the gate.'

Pushing back her chair, she gave Tommy one last lingering glance. *Tell me that you believe me about what happened last night. Tell me that my hair's not too bad. Tell me we're going to have a nice day together.* But he had already turned away from her.

As she waited for the elevator to arrive, she moved back a few feet and watched him. He had his phone out now, stabbing at the screen with one hand while shoving a bacon roll in his mouth with the other.

At that moment, the lift doors opened, and Anna's unmistakable figure appeared. She looked every inch the centre spread in a glossy magazine, with her blonde hair styled under a pink beret, wearing a tailored black coat with a tiny pink dogtooth design. Paula kept dead still as she watched her. Anna scanned the room, her gaze alighting on her target, and she glided through the restaurant towards him, feigning surprise to see him there. Paula's insides churned as the two of them launched into an animated conversation.

She turned and stepped into the lift, not waiting to watch as Anna pulled out a chair and joined Tommy in a breakfast for two.

–

They fawned over her in the salon, three stylists working all at the same time, deliberating, explaining, choosing colours that would not only rectify their error but enhance her hair, make it better than it had been before the incident.

That was how they referred to it – 'the incident'. Paula thought of it as 'the fuck-up with the bleach', but she would never say that. The girl from the day before was young, younger than she'd seemed at the original appointment, and now her superiors didn't leave her side, commanding her to watch and learn and not to touch.

And the result was worth the hours spent in the chair. For the first time in her life, her hair wasn't dark and glossy. Now it was honey blonde, with highlights that made it look sun-kissed. To Paula's surprise, the stylists had been right: she was *enhanced*.

At the till, she pulled out her purse, but the senior stylist waved it away. 'No,' she said. 'I'm just glad we could fix it.'

Paula nodded and turned to the younger woman who had wrecked her hair. 'Thanks for sorting it out,' she said. 'And don't worry, everyone makes mistakes.'

The girl said nothing, simply offered a pinched smile before walking away.

Paula realised that the boat had stopped and that they must have docked. She wondered if Tommy would still be waiting for her, half hoping he wasn't; if she was with him, he would simply be interested in searching for a pub. She was looking forward to exploring the little town on her own.

She paused at the gate, wondering where that thought had come from. Once upon a time, she had hated doing anything by herself and had felt unconfident even in a town she knew. It was why she always called Julie to go shopping with her; she had a deep-seated need for other opinions, as though she didn't trust herself. She touched her new hair, which ran silky and soft through her fingers. Even this colour had been someone else's idea.

Why was she even thinking all of this? Where was it coming from?

She sighed, pulled her coat collar up and walked the last few feet to the gate.

'Paula!' Tommy grinned and adjusted his beanie hat. 'Looking lovely.'

She touched her hair self-consciously and smiled back. 'Thanks.'

Behind Tommy, melting into the crowd of passengers who seemed to be swarming off the ship, Paula saw a cap of blonde hair: Anna.

She turned to her husband. 'Did Anna say anything over breakfast this morning?' she asked.

'Like what?' asked Tommy as he took her hand. 'Come on, let's go.'

Paula averted her gaze, seeking Anna, but the woman had disappeared.

'*As we pause in the waters of the port of Åndalsnes, you might be interested in one of the fishing trips that takes place* in the famous Norwegian fjords. Popular catches are herring and mackerel, pollack and coal fish, among others. Of course, if you are feeling slightly more adventurous, why not try your hand at deep-sea fishing?

'Beware, though, as the waters here can be amongst the most dangerous in the world. Have you heard of Edgar Allan Poe's "A Descent into the Maelstrom"? The maelstrom is a tidal system of strong currents and eddies that has been responsible for many shipwrecks and lost lives throughout history. Even Jules Verne spoke about it in his famous novel, Twenty Thousand Leagues Under the Sea.

'Now the maelstrom, like all tides, is caused by the birth of a full moon. And it just so happens that the next full moon will be upon us... tomorrow...'

Chapter 12

Anna walked with purpose through the cobbled streets of Åndalsnes. The town was small, unremarkable, but it had what she needed and she headed straight there.

The bell tinkled as she pushed open the door of the hardware store. A sleepy-looking elderly man was perched on a high stool in the corner. He looked her up and down before returning his attention to the open magazine in front of him.

Anna turned into the first aisle, moving slowly, flicking her gaze left and right.

'You need help?'

She glanced towards the voice. The man had moved to the top of the aisle, standing bow-legged, scrutinising her.

'No, thank you,' she replied, turning back to commence her slow journey.

'Sometimes a man knows more about what they are looking for,' he said. 'We don't see many ladies in here.'

Anna stopped but didn't look at him. 'I don't need help,' she said.

After a few moments she turned back, but he had retreated to his magazine.

At the till, she waited in silence as he slipped her purchases into a paper bag. 'Doing some DIY?' he asked, his English holding only a trace of a Norwegian accent. 'Are you local?'

To the left of the till was a pot of screwdrivers, all different shapes and sizes. She thought how easy it would be to pull one out and stick it in his neck, in one quick, fluid motion. She let her eyes travel over the rest of the store. It was a dark and dingy place, and she was the only customer. It was old-fashioned and likely to contain no CCTV cameras. The windows that faced the street were filled with big boxed lawnmowers, bird boxes and stepladders.

How easy it would be.

She ran a finger over the handle of one of the screw-drivers.

'You want one of them too?' he asked.

His voice pulled her back to the present, to the reason she was here, which was to clean up a previous unplanned attack. That was her priority, not dealing with this weaselly, sexist little man.

She looked into his watery blue eyes and saw William. Her grip tightened for a second on the screwdriver before she forced herself to let it go. She laid her palm flat on the counter.

'Nothing else, thank you.'

The exchange of package, money and receipt took place without further conversation. The bell tinkled pret-tily as she left.

Åndalsnes was very green, thought Anna as she moved through the small, unremarkable town centre. Soon enough, she found herself at the bottom of a steep path that wound up, up, up. From where she was standing, it seemed to reach to the clouds. The pathway didn't seem particularly well-kept; tree roots blasted out of what seemed like hastily made concrete steps. But she had a while, and suddenly she found she wanted to be up there, looking down at the little people milling around, unaware of her watching them from above.

She slung her bag over her shoulder and started to climb.

After twenty minutes, she put a hand to her chest, felt her breath coming thin and uneven. The stone steps swam hazily in her view. She felt her head fall forward, recognised the feeling at once.

From her bag she pulled out a breakfast roll. She hadn't covered or wrapped it; the bread was hard and flaky. She broke off a tiny corner and shoved it in her mouth, chewing slowly as she resumed her journey.

As she went higher, she thought about Tommy, and their chat over breakfast. He was out here somewhere, with his wife. He planned to catch some game at a sports bar he had googled.

'What are Paula's plans?' she had asked.

He'd shrugged as he scraped the last of the egg from his plate. 'Shopping, I suppose,' he replied, his mouth full.

Oh, they were such a clichéd couple, she thought now, a small smile breaking through the grimace on her face at the toughness of the hill. She didn't much care; she wouldn't try to change Tommy when he was hers at the end of this holiday. She would keep him around for a while, see if there was anything that needed doing to the house, make sure he took out some decent life insurance, ensure his will was changed to name her. They might not have enough time to get married, but as long as all the paperwork was in order, that was all that mattered.

Her thoughts turned to Mark, back in her cabin. Mentally she ticked off the steps she had taken that morning. She had wrapped him in the plastic and moved him close to the patio door, behind the two-seater sofa.

The 'do not disturb' sign was on, and a chair had been pulled as close to the door as possible, in case House-keeping ignored the sign and tried to get into the room.

She nodded to herself; all was good back on the ship. There was no need to rush.

Finally, she reached the last set of steps, and staggered up them to find herself on a platform. Her breath caught in her throat as she turned to survey the view. Ahead of her was the Romsdalshornet mountain, breathtaking in its vastness. Rivers ran around it, sparkling emerald green in the sudden sunshine, the banks lush and covered with wild flowers. Beneath her was the port of Åndalsnes. She stared at the tiny figures moving around the town that she had climbed from.

'Excuse me!'

She jumped, yanked from her solitude and appreciation by a loud, American-accented voice directly behind her.

She turned, scowling, as she came face to face with a couple she hadn't even known were there. She looked them up and down, saw a middle-aged man and woman, red-faced and breathing heavily, the climb evidently harder for their heavier frames than it had been for her own starved body.

'Yes?' she asked.

The man held out a camera. 'We wondered if you would mind taking our photo?' he asked, as he and his wife gave her matching Hollywood smiles.

She nodded and took the camera carefully, studying it as they made their way to the edge of the platform, fussing with each other, checking over their shoulders to ensure the mountain was in the centre of their intended shot.

The camera was a Hasselblad; one of the most expensive pieces of equipment out there, Anna knew. She

123

weighed it in her hands and wrapped her fingers around it. Glancing up, she imagined the finished photo, suddenly sad that she would never see the quality of it. She took a few shots, then moved in for a close-up. The couple changed position, and she lowered the camera to wait for them.

How easy it would be to march up to them and swipe them off the platform with a simple back-handed blow. A smile twitched on her face as she looked over the edge at the rocky face that led to the river below. The camera sat heavy in her hands and she gripped it a little tighter. How wonderful it would be to leave this beautiful spot with a camera like this, a piece of equipment that even with William's money she couldn't afford.

She tapped her finger thoughtfully on the lens and considered any potential problems. This couple could be sailing on the *Ruby Spirit*, and she wasn't sure whether they did some sort of head count when the passengers returned from their day trips. She thought of Mark, back in the Arctic Suite. She couldn't send him out to sea until the *Ruby Spirit* was in the open ocean, and she wanted him gone as soon as possible. A delay wouldn't do.

Reluctantly, she handed the camera back.

'Thank you,' gushed the woman. 'Would you like us to take a picture of you?'

Anna turned away from them. 'No,' she said.

Before long, she was back at the *Ruby Spirit*. She hung around as the other passengers drifted back onto the boat. Nobody was checking who was boarding, and now she saw a sign that had been erected by the entrance: *This boat will not wait if you are late.*

She nodded to herself. No head count then. She stored away the knowledge to be used in a few days' time, at their next stop in Iceland.

–

Paula stared at the cobbled main street, disappointment evident on her face. The few shops that lined the road were of no interest to her.

Behind her, Tommy tapped her shoulder and nodded across the road. Paula's heart sank even further as she spotted the sports bar he was gesturing at.

'Pint?' he asked, hopefully.

She sighed and looked back the way they had come. Behind her, the street opened up to a large expanse of green water, a slow-moving river that twinkled as it caught the light of the glaring sunshine.

'Maybe we could take a walk,' she said. 'Down the river, maybe find somewhere to have lunch.'

Tommy nodded and checked his watch. 'Tell you what, you have a look around, I'll catch the first half of the rugby, then we'll go and have some lunch.'

Paula lifted a hand, a half-hearted gesture that he took as permission. He swooped in to land a kiss on her cheek and darted across the cobbles, vanishing into the gloom of the bar.

Paula turned around and walked back down towards the river. Across the water, the *Ruby Spirit* loomed large, and she sat down on a bench to admire it. She still couldn't get over the size of it, and she wished very much that Tommy was there with her.

But he wasn't.

He never was.

Suddenly Paula felt very lonely, hit by the realisation that she was in a perpetual state of solitude. This wasn't a new thing; the feeling was constant, always there, even when Tommy was beside her. To make up for it, she bought stuff, things that were pretty and expensive, but items that she would give up in a heartbeat for a man who wanted to be with her more than he wanted to hang out with the lads or watch the rugby.

'I'm lonely.'

She said the words out loud, her voice breaking as she admitted to herself for the first time that something wasn't working the way it should. She bit her lip and wondered how she could make it right. The image of a baby – that phantom miracle-working child she'd thought about so often over the years – popped into her mind. It was a cliché, she knew. It would be a Band-Aid baby, a patch to cover the open wound of boredom. But underneath, the scars would remain.

'Shit,' she whispered as tears stung at her eyes.

Finally, the truth hit her: a baby was the furthest thing from Tommy's mind. It was a joke. They hadn't even made love yet on this holiday. And despite the fact that she had told Julie he had agreed to have a child, she knew now that that wasn't the case. He had placated her with this cruise, just as he had appeased her last year when she had brought up the subject by buying her a new car. The year before that he had mollified her with the house.

She had been so stupid. She had believed that the car (a family one) and the house (also a family one) were signs that he was preparing for their little unit to grow.

She swiped at her cheeks as tears dripped down them, cold rivers on her face. Where did that leave her? She was thirty-five, the years were rolling on. Soon she would be forty, with nothing to show for it. It was too late to start again, and even the thought of it was enough to make her feel sick. How would she cope on her own, with no skills apart from the ability to keep a beautiful home?

Anna popped into her head. Beautiful, independent Anna who needed no man, who oversaw a whole company and took holidays on her own. A woman who sat naked in saunas, showing off her body with absolute confidence; who moved easily into conversations and friendships with strangers.

A jagged gasp escaped, and she put her gloved hand to her mouth, very aware that it could easily turn into a scream. How could she be like Anna when she had gone from her childhood house to shared student accommodation to a home with Tommy? She had never been on her own, wasn't cut out for it. She didn't have a job or a career or an ambition. She felt swamped, drowning in realisation of facts she had never before let herself acknowledge.

She pushed herself up from the bench and turned in the direction of the bar. Her head was swimming with things she didn't want to feel, but she shoved the thoughts and fears away and went to find her husband.

There was nothing for it; she had to make it work.

There was nothing else.

–

Tommy had a prime seat in the bar, underneath the large flat-screen TV. Around him sat a dozen other men, pints in hand, eyes fixed on the game.

Paula looked around, saw no other women, wondered where the spouses of all these men were. Not shopping, not in this hick town, that was for sure. Or maybe they didn't even have wives or girlfriends; maybe they were locals, bachelors, living the kind of life that would have suited Tommy just fine.

She put her head down and moved through the crowd to his table, where she slipped onto an uncomfortable bar stool and offered him a tight smile.

'Babe, that was quick,' he said, his eyes flicking back to the screen as a roar went up from the crowd.

She said nothing; instead, picked up the wine menu and pretended to read it. The bar was dark, the small, narrow windows near the ceiling the only source of natural light. The tiny strips of bright blue sky hurt her eyes and her heart. She shouldn't be sitting in a bar; neither of them should be. They were in Norway! They should be outside in the bracing cold, exploring a foreign city together.

Swallowing hard, she slipped from the stool.

'Get us another one, will you, babe?' Tommy asked without even looking at her.

She walked the length of the long mahogany bar. It was brighter here, and there was a blast of cold air as someone entered. She didn't hesitate. Didn't stop to think. Throwing the wine menu on the bar top, she carried on walking, to the door, through it, and down the cobbled street back towards the *Ruby Spirit*.

–

Anna watched from the first deck as Paula traipsed back onto the ship. There was no sign of Tommy, and from up here, Paula seemed sad and dejected. But her hair! Anna narrowed her eyes. It looked... well, it looked great. Even better than before the bleaching incident.

She waited to see where Paula was headed, and when it became clear she was walking in the direction of the stairwell that would take her to her cabin, she nipped smartly into the corridor to wait for her. As the sound of footsteps started up, she began to walk down the hallway, reaching the door of the Expedition Suite just as Paula turned the corner.

'Hey!' she said, giving her best smile. 'I was just about to knock for you, see if you wanted to grab a coffee.'

Paula offered a weak smile. Automatically her hand went to her head.

Still self-conscious, thought Anna with an internal sneer.

'It's looking... fine,' she said hesitantly, fully aware that her tone was cautious, as though the hair was only a slight improvement on the mess it had previously been.

Paula's face fell and she shrugged.

'So, coffee?' prompted Anna.

Paula hesitated, then nodded. 'I'll make us one, though, in my cabin. Is that okay?' she asked.

Anna smiled. It was more than okay.

Inside, she took a seat by the doors that looked out over the port. This suite was almost the same as her own, a mirror image. Minus the corpse that sat behind the very spot where she was currently sitting. At least Mark was undisturbed; she'd checked on him before deciding she didn't want to stay in the room with him.

Anxiously, she checked her watch. Less than half an hour before they set sail. When she returned to her cabin, she would try out the tools she had purchased on the bolts on the balcony railing. Later tonight, when they were travelling at top speed and the rest of the passengers were sleeping, she would get to work on unscrewing the rail. Then it would be goodbye, Mark, and by the time anyone realised he was missing from duty, it would be too late to find his body.

'Is decaf okay?' Paula held up a coffee pod.

Anna nodded as she pulled her pink beret off her head. 'Decaf's good. Where's Tommy?' she asked. 'Still in the bar?'

She saw the look of suspicion that Paula shot her, and smiled. 'Isn't that where they all go when they get day release?' she laughed.

Paula laughed with her, but to Anna it sounded forced. She put the mugs underneath the fancy coffee maker in turn. When they were filled, and the aroma filtered through the room, she gestured to them before heading to the bathroom. 'Back in a sec,' she said, closing the door gently behind her.

Anna sprang into action. From her pocket she withdrew a small vial of crushed zolpidem and divided it between the two mugs, giving them a shake to mix the dark powder with the granules. Then she moved to Paula's bag on the counter and peered into it, careful not to disturb the objects inside. Spotting what she was seeking, she pulled out Paula's iPhone and pressed the home button. A text from Tommy flashed up on the screen, a short message asking where Paula had gone, telling her he had bumped into the lads and was having a drink in the restaurant. She should come straight down to dinner when she was ready and meet him at their normal table.

She let the screen fade to black before returning to her chair and slipping the phone into her own bag just as Paula emerged from the toilet.

'How are you feeling now, after your nasty fall on deck?' she asked.

The kettle clicked off, and Paula silently filled the mugs.

'Milk?' she asked. 'Sugar?'

'No, thanks,' replied Anna, accepting the cup Paula passed her.

Paula sat down heavily in the other chair. 'You called it a fall,' she said bluntly.

Anna creased her brow in faux concern. 'Yes, I saw Tommy this morning at breakfast and asked how you were. He said you'd had a nasty fall, were really shaken up.' She paused. 'I was here last night. You were very upset. Did you hurt yourself?'

Paula's face drained of colour. 'Tommy said I fell?' she asked, her voice suddenly hoarse.

Anna frowned. 'Yes, Dermot said the same.' She leaned forward, looked Paula in the eye. 'Why do you ask?'

Paula's face crumpled, and just for a second her emotions were there, plain as day. Then they were gone, and she sat up straight and gulped at her coffee.

'I don't know what happened,' she said, her voice clear now, a bitter sound to it, ringing out into the room. 'It was just a shock, is all.'

Anna nodded and set her cup, still full, down on the table between them.

Paula didn't trust her.

It was an interesting development, and a potentially devastating one. She needed the woman to have faith in her, to confide in her, not to be suspicious or sceptical. If that wasn't possible, she would just have to move her plan along at a quicker pace. She stood up.

'Best get back, I've got some emails that I really must reply to.' She smiled. 'See you at dinner?'

Paula nodded and raised a hand. 'See you later.'

—

When the door closed behind Anna, Paula reached over and picked up the other woman's coffee. She'd hardly touched it. As she drank it, she noticed her hands were shaking slightly.

Tommy was telling everyone that she'd fallen.

She thought back to it again, that certainty that she hadn't tripped, hadn't lost her footing on what might have been a slippery deck. She had been assaulted, attacked, and yet nobody believed her.

She closed her eyes, reliving the night before. The surprise as she had been barged into, the shock in the sudden realisation that it wasn't an accident, that her perpetrator wasn't about to haul her to her feet and apologise. Then those terrible seconds as she was dragged to the gap that would take her into the crashing waves below.

The bottle of vodka still sat on the table, mocking her, it seemed.

You were drunk.

A noise sounded in the room, like a sheep bleating, and belatedly she realised it came from her.

She stood up, smoothing down her shirt, and reached for her bag.

Even if someone on this ship hadn't tried to hurt her, a flaw in the ship's design had almost killed her.

And if Tommy wasn't going to report it, then she would.

They'll ask if you'd been drinking.

The voice of caution whispered to her. Ignoring it, she slipped her feet back into her boots and stamped over to the door, yanking at the handle.

The door didn't move.

She ran her hands over the tiny gap between the door and the frame, seeking locks, seeing nothing. She turned the handle once more, knowing even as she pulled at it that it wouldn't open.

She was locked in a room again. Just like in the sauna on that first day.

Breathing heavily now, she moved away from the door and reached into her bag, her fingers searching for her phone to call Tommy to come and let her out.

It wasn't in there.

–

In the suite next door, Anna stepped around Mark's inert body and let herself out onto the balcony. The wind rushed at her, sent her staggering into the railing, and she gripped it tightly, cursing as she almost dropped the bag she was carrying.

Down on her knees she went, head lowered against the biting gale as she pulled the spanner from the bag and angled it against the railing. It was a battle to get the first turn, and it took every ounce of strength she had, but finally the bolt moved a little.

Breathing deeply, a burning sensation in her chest, she pushed herself up and moved back inside.

Hopefully when they moved out to sea the wind would change and it wouldn't be so hard to remove the bolts.

She placed the spanner on the side table next to her handbag and pulled out Paula's phone. Opening the wardrobe, she slipped the phone into the pocket of the waxed jacket she had stolen yesterday.

Chapter 13

Before

When I was fourteen, I met one of my mother's friends. His name was Carl. It was a Friday afternoon, and when I let myself into the house, he was there in the hallway.

'Well, well,' he said, 'who's this, then?'

He was a small man; his smile was grey and yellow and brown. His hair was pulled back into a straggly ponytail and he wore a checked shirt and saggy, baggy jeans. I stared at the sleeve of his shirt, rolled up. I could see the faded colours of a tattoo peeking out. He caught me staring.

'Wanna see it?' he grinned.

I shuddered. No, I didn't want to see it. I didn't want to see his tattoo or any part of him.

He laughed, and my mother drifted lazily down the stairs. 'S'my girl,' she slurred.

'Pretty,' he said.

With that one remark, I knew that I had to get out. I was a teenager now, and I had grown in places that this man, and all the other ones, liked to stare at. I looked at my mother now, her gown hanging open, the skin between her breasts like crêpe paper.

She moved past Carl towards the kitchen, and another thought occurred to me. My mother would not protect me from these men who hung around her house like flies buzzing around dirty plates in summer.

Throwing my bag down in the hall, I hurried upstairs to my room.

I listened for a while, but the front door didn't open and close, and I knew he was still here. He had been on his way out when I came in, but he hadn't left.

I pulled the chair from my dressing table and propped it under the door handle. From the bedside table I took my favourite knife. I slipped off my trousers and slid the blade along my knicker line. As the blood trickled out, my fear flowed along with it. Soon I was breathing easier. I slapped a wodge of tissue against the cut and snapped my underwear elastic back into place.

I no longer cut my arms, nor anywhere that showed. My panty line was a recently discovered perfect secret place. Nobody saw it, and the fine dark hairs that were another recent addition hid the scars.

As I leaned against the headboard, lost in a world that nobody else visited, I heard a creak on the stairs. I sat upright, every part of me on alert now. Sure enough, after a moment, the doorknob twisted round. The chair moved half an inch; there was a grunt, a laugh and then the door was pulled shut.

'See you again, pretty lady,' said Carl.

I didn't answer, and soon I heard his footsteps descending the stairs, and the front door banging behind him.

It was safe, finally, so I opened my door and padded quietly down the stairs. In the kitchen, a cigarette was burning down to the filter in the ashtray. I stubbed it out and went in search of my mother.

I found her in the living room, curled in a ball on the sofa. The room was in darkness, and the curtains – unused to being opened – released a flurry of dust as I pulled them to the sides. I watched the motes spinning in the air, and made a mental note to take the drapes down and wash them tomorrow.

I turned my attention to my mother.

In the sunshine I could see her clearly, her eyes tiny milky slits as she regarded me. Around her left arm was a soft cotton belt. My belt, I realised. Though why my mother would tie a belt around her arm was beyond me. On the floor was a needle, like the kind I'd recently seen when I'd had my inoculations at school. Inside it, a murky brown liquid bubbled. Beside the needle was one of our tablespoons. I bent down to look at it, and touched the brown stain then sniffed at it. I didn't know what it all meant, but somehow I knew it wasn't good.

I undid the buckle and slipped the belt from my mum's arm. A little blood had stained the neon pink, and I sighed. I didn't have any money to buy another belt. I rubbed at the blood, wondering if I could use a stain remover to get rid of it.

Then there was more blood, trickling out of my mother's arm. I reached for a tissue and wiped at it, then pressed it against her arm until the blood stopped. In the messy drawer in the cabinet I found a plaster, and I stuck it to where it looked like the blood had come from.

I collected up the belt, the spoon and the needle and carried them all through to the kitchen, placing them beside her packet of cigarettes. Then I returned to the living room, where I draped a blanket over her inert form and got to tidying up the rest of the room.

All the while, she slept on.

It was an awful existence, no way for a teenage girl to live. But up until then it had been bearable. I kept the house clean, along with myself, and washed our clothes and ironed them and changed my mother's bed sheets. I didn't mind doing any of that.

My mother didn't trouble me, didn't bug me to do homework or lecture me about the dangers a young girl might face. She never kept track of my movements, and because of all this, I never rebelled like so many of my classmates. A threat had never been there until now.

Until Carl.

He gave my mother heroin. That was the brown stuff and why she needed the needle and the spoon and the belt, and from the snippets of conversation I heard between them, it was really, really expensive. Carl took 'payment in kind', and because he could name his price, sometimes he took more than the use of her body. Money that we kept in a jar for electricity vanished, as did pieces of my mother's jewellery. She had never done heroin until he came into her life. He had introduced her to it, and I knew it was dangerous. And I soon learned that she couldn't live without it.

'Don't let him in,' I pleaded with her after he'd taken all the cash in the house.

She stared at me. 'Where else am I going to get it from?' she asked. 'This is the best deal, he doesn't always take money.'

It was unspoken, but that was what I was afraid of. I knew Carl would accept the use of me as payment for Mum's habit, and I couldn't – *wouldn't* – live like that.

'Do you have any cash hidden anywhere?' I asked her.

She shrugged, unable to remember, unable to care.

Later, when she slept, I turned the whole house upside down and came up with forty quid. When she woke, I held it up to her.

'If he comes, don't let him in.' I moved the four ten-pound notes in front of her face. She followed them with her eyes. 'I'll get your stuff, just don't let him in.'

She needed it, I knew that much. At lunchtime I'd gone to the library and read up on addiction. There was no point trying to make her stop; the brown stuff was too big for both of us.

I considered asking Kevin, our weed-smoking neighbour, if he knew where I could get some from. But by then I knew that heroin and marijuana were very different drugs, used by two very different types of people. Although I'd learned that the weed Kevin smoked was something called a 'gateway drug', and one day he might move on to my mother's drug of choice too. So that night, when it was nearing midnight, I went out on the streets and headed to the rougher part of town, the Billingham Road. I wondered if I looked out of place in my winter tweed coat, my hair hidden under a black woollen hat and my mother's scarf concealing the bottom of my face. To my relief, as I moved among the emaciated, toothless users, nobody gave me a second glance. Horror crept in as I realised that I must have looked like I belonged there.

I moved past the teenage youths, knowing they would be dealing weed or pills, and edged my way into a cluster of men. 'Got any brown?' I asked.

Three men melted away into the night, leaving one who looked me up and down. 'For you?' he asked.

I tried to detect a hint of surprise in his question, but realised he was just being careful, making sure I wasn't a decoy.

'For me,' I confirmed.

'What you got?' he asked.

I took thirty pounds from my pocket. He looked bored, and I pulled the last tenner out. He snatched it, rubbed the notes between his fingers; then, to my astonishment, he handed me four packages wrapped in tin foil. Then, as suddenly as the other men who had been with him, he was gone.

I put the foil envelopes in my pocket. I couldn't believe I had got four. Heroin, it seemed, wasn't a very expensive habit after all, in spite of what Carl had told my mother.

I left Billingham Road and all the horrors it held, winding my way home. Across the road was a little cluster of people, dolled up, fancy. I pulled my hood up and watched them. A couple, an older man and woman, walked either side of a young girl. I looked at the girl with envy. She wore a pretty dress with a full skirt, and a hip-length white fur coat. Her hair was long and luscious, her face carefully made up. Her heels clicked on the pavement and I drew in a sharp breath.

It was Rebecca Lavery. The girl from my school who had been removed from her home and sent to a loving family. Were these her foster parents?

I chewed on my nails as I watched them, vaguely wondering why they were out so late. Wherever they had been must have been somewhere nice. I leaned against the wall, imagining a dinner with three courses, white tablecloths and crystal wine glasses.

They stopped to cross the road and Rebecca turned in my direction. Her glance swept over me with no hint or sign of recognition, but I couldn't pull my gaze away from her. She was beautiful, yet that lovely clear-skinned face, those eyes, they still held the same look that she'd worn at school.

Sad, worried, filled with pain.

I raised a hand in greeting, a tentative half-wave. Rebecca blinked. Her lips parted. Just as quickly, she turned and was gone.

I pulled my coat tighter around me and started home. Maybe she just looked like that because it took time to get over what she'd been through. I told myself that I was happy for her, but my clenched jaw and fingers that curled into fists revealed the lie.

–

At home, my mother was in her usual place, on the sofa, wrapped in her dressing gown with a blanket over her knees. She was shivering violently.

'You took my money,' she hissed when I came into the room. 'Carl came round and I couldn't get my stuff off him because you took my money.'

I took a seat opposite her. 'I told you not to let him in, don't you remember?' She stared at me blankly, her teeth chattering, her tongue slipping in and out of her mouth. 'I said I was going to get it for you, so you don't need to let Carl in any more.'

As I spoke, I drew out one of the foil envelopes and she lunged for it. I went to pull it away – I wanted to talk to her first, to ask her if she could try and get better – but I was too slow and she snatched it out of my grasp.

Into the kitchen she moved at speed, rifling in the drawers, getting her spoon, the needle, digging in the pocket of her gown for my belt.

'Mum, I need to talk to you,' I pleaded. 'I really want to try and help you to get better. I don't want to have to live with you like this.'

Impatiently she brushed me aside and headed back to the living room. 'I know, I'll stop soon,' she said as she set about heating the spoon with her lighter.

I watched the spoon as it turned brown and acrid. She didn't even keep her paraphernalia separate. I would eat from that spoon, once I'd washed it up. A slow burn began inside of me, and I felt something close to hatred as the liquid began to bubble.

I left the room before she put the needle in her arm.

—

I withheld the remaining three packets of brown. With a butter knife I removed the lock from the toilet door and fitted it to the outside of my mother's bedroom door.

Later, I helped her up the stairs and put her to bed. As carefully as I could, I removed my belt from around her arm, rubbing her withered skin to get the blood flowing. Irritated, she pulled away from me, and burrowed under the bedclothes like a child.

I placed three large bottles of water and a bucket on the floor by her bed. On the windowsill I put two pots of yoghurt, a banana that was already on the turn and a packet of biscuits. I stared at the snacks, knowing she wouldn't eat them, but it felt like a nurturing thing to do. It was the kind of thing a mother would do if she had a sick child.

My mother snored and whistled, and I backed out of the room and quietly closed the door. I took a deep breath and slid the lock into place. Then I sat down with my back to the door and waited.

Chapter 14

Paula upended all her bags, checked the pockets of her jeans, her coat, the carrier bags by the bed that contained the few souvenirs she had purchased. She opened the wardrobe, rifled through the clothes in there, even checking the pockets of Tommy's body warmer and dinner jacket.

With her hands on her hips she stood in the centre of the suite and turned in a full circle. Had she even had her phone when she went out today? She thought back, tried to remember the last time she had used it. She hadn't pulled it out to take any photos when she was in Åndalsnes today. She hadn't been in the mood.

Abandoning her search, she went to the sliding doors and slipped outside. The howling wind pummelled her face and she gasped and hurried back in, pulling the doors closed behind her. The ship's horn blasted, signalling that they were about to leave port. Through the glass she stared across the narrow strip of water to the area lined with benches where she had sat earlier, and as the ship rocked gently, she groaned at the thought that her phone might be left behind on land.

Turning her back on the dockside, she ran across the room to the door and pulled at the handle again, holding her breath. When it didn't move, she exhaled, tears spiking at her eyes. The captain's cautionary tale over the loud-speaker came back to her: the maelstrom, the deadly whirlpool that sucked ships and passengers to their death. They were sailing near it; what if there was an accident? What if they were pulled into it? She would be left here, in the cabin, unable to get out and make it to the lifeboats.

Her breath came quicker. Beaten, she rubbed at her face. Her eyelids were heavy, as though she'd been awake for days, and she moved over to a chair and sank into it. She noticed she hadn't closed the sliding doors fully, and the curtain flapped in the breeze, the chill coming into the room making her shiver.

Should close the door, she thought, but suddenly it was too much effort to lean forward and slide it completely shut. With the wind howling outside, she leaned her head back and closed her eyes. Confusion overcame her, just moments before sleep.

–

For dinner, Anna dressed in a simple black jumpsuit, a thin gold chain around her neck and her make-up natural. She grabbed her black clutch, put on her tallest stilettos and let herself quietly out of the suite.

The corridor was empty and silent, and the ship's engine hummed a gentle tune beneath her feet. She smiled; they were on the move, and tonight, after the meal, they would be far enough out in the open ocean that she could dispose of Mark. But first, she had other plans to attend to.

Outside Tommy and Paula's suite she stopped and pulled Mark's master key from her purse. He had been more than happy to tell her all about the workings of the ship, and the most surprising one had been the keys. In the event of an emergency – striking another boat, or terrorism, or something else that threatened life – the passengers were to return to their suites or cabins. At the captain's discretion, all the doors would be locked from the outside. Controversial, Mark had said, but sometimes necessary. Also, not something that the shipping line advertised.

And it had worked, Anna saw now. Just one turn of the key when she had left the Expedition Suite earlier and the red light was still glowing on the door handle button. She inserted the master key now, and with the softest of clicks the door opened. With a palm flat on the door, she pushed it open far enough to slip inside. The room was in darkness now, but the outside balcony lamp cast a strip of light that cut through the centre of the room. In the chair nearest the door sat Paula, her head back, her breathing deep, heavy and even.

Anna smiled to herself and backed out into the hallway, pulling the door to but not closing it fully.

–

The restaurant was heaving, the passengers seemingly revived and in high spirits from their day on land. Anna made her way to the far side, near the floor-to-ceiling windows and Tommy's usual table.

He saw her approach and stood up, waving to her with a yell. 'Anna!' he called. 'Over here.'

He really was rather animalistic, she noted with distaste as she smiled her hellos to the table and sat down in the empty seat next to him. It was clearly being saved for Paula, and she waited with interest to see if he would mention his wife.

'Did you have a good day?' he asked, and without waiting for a reply he went on, 'Found a cute little sports bar, didn't I?'

She watched him eat, realising he was already on his main course. She frowned, and asked, 'Where's Paula?'

He glanced up, something flickering across his face. 'Didn't she come down with you?' he asked.

She shook her head. 'I was late getting ready, so I assumed she would already be here.'

He stood up, and Anna was surprised that he would be so chivalrous as to go and look for her. Instead, he picked up his empty plate. 'Back in a sec,' he said, and wove his way through the tables towards the buffet.

After a moment, she got up and followed him. She gave in to her body's demands and selected a small lamb chop with a rocket side salad. She had heavy physical work to do later on tonight and the last thing she needed was to become light-headed and topple through the railings, following Mark to his watery grave.

She picked at the meat, trying not to let her disgust show as a white strip of fat glistened on the bone. She pushed it to one side, eating only the darker, well-cooked meat. She forced the rocket salad into her mouth and washed it down with copious amounts of water. After a few minutes she was entirely full.

One by one the other occupants of the table fell away, until it was just Tommy and Anna. Without a word being spoken, they moved to the plush couch by the glass wall and looked out at the black night. It was impossible to tell where the sky ended and the sea began. Grey-black clouds drifted across the moon.

'No Northern Lights tonight,' said Tommy gloomily as he put his beer bottle down on the table.

Anna stared at it, then glanced at the five other empty bottles on their dinner table. He would have had several in the sports bar too. She sipped at her own lime and soda before abandoning it – the carbonated water only served to make her feel uncomfortably bloated.

'I might turn in,' she said with a smile. 'Shall we walk back together?' She leaned forward, her normal trick of allowing him a good view down her low-cut top, though only for a second, as she reached for her clutch bag.

He nodded dumbly, and together they made their way through the almost empty restaurant.

In silence the elevator sped upwards, and Anna angled herself so that she was almost touching Tommy's side. As the lift came to a stop, he jerked as if stung, and looked down at her. Anna smiled at him and together they exited.

'Thank you for being my dinner date,' she said huskily as they walked along the hallway.

He stopped outside his own suite, and she saw the frown on his face as he clocked that the door was slightly ajar.

'See ya,' she said, pretending not to notice, and threw him a small wave over her shoulder. She made no mention of Paula, and as she slipped inside her room, she was aware of him still watching her until she closed the door silently behind her.

–

In her medicated sleep, Paula dreamed of the Northern Lights. She lifted her head and watched the green glow as it filled the sky, then wrapped her arms around herself, feeling troubled. She had thought the lights would be beautiful. Instead, they were sinister, shrouding her, wrapping her up too tight. So tight that she couldn't breathe.

Beneath her feet, the ground swirled and rippled. It was the maelstrom that she had heard about. It pulled her into its magnetic grip until she was spinning and spinning, down, down, down. All the while Tommy stood nearby, impervious to her distress, his eyes on the sky, his face filled with wonder.

There was a loud noise, a repetitive clanging and banging, and a pressure on her shoulders. Through the fog of sleep, Paula pushed against it, forcing her eyes open. Her eyeballs stung and she winced at the harsh white light. The green was gone, and she was back in her chair in the Expedition Suite. Everything crashed back at her: she was locked in the suite, and her phone was missing, and Tommy... she didn't even know if he had made it back onto the ship. And now somebody was in her room, standing over her, looming and pushing at her.

She yelped, thrashed at the heavy shape with her arms, swinging and hitting, remembering being on the deck, the mass there that had shoved at her and tried to kill her.

She screamed. A hand, rough and big, clamped down on her mouth and a voice hissed in her ear.

'Jesus, Paula, it's me!'

She wriggled away. 'Tommy?'

He moved away to sit in the chair opposite her. 'You were dead to the world.'

She shuddered at his words and struggled to sit up. 'Did you see the Northern Lights?' she asked.

He shook his head. 'Nah, too much cloud tonight. Couldn't even see the moon. What happened to you at dinner?'

It had been a dream, she realised, those horrible, terrible green lights, the maelstrom. And... dinner?

She pushed herself up and out of the chair, staggered as her body kept moving even when she stopped walking. Tommy put a hand out towards her.

'Whoa,' he said, 'steady.'

She looked to the door, tightly closed, and strode over to it. Pulling the handle, she yanked it open and stared in disbelief.

'How did you get in here?' she asked.

'The door was open – you shouldn't leave it open if you're sleeping. You were out cold, anyone could have walked in here and taken anything.' As if to prove his point, he got up and walked to his nightstand, checking the pile of money that he kept in the drawer.

'It wasn't open,' she said. She pushed the door closed, more firmly than was necessary, and turned to face Tommy. 'It wasn't open. I was locked in, I couldn't get out.' Suddenly she recalled her mobile. 'Do you have my phone? I can't find it.'

He stopped counting the euro notes in his hand and looked at her. 'The door was *open*, it wasn't closed. You weren't locked in.' He shook his head. 'Wait, you've lost your phone?'

It struck her then, a realisation, a certainty, and despite knowing what Tommy's response would be, she voiced her concern.

'I'm being targeted,' she said, and her voice trembled with emotion. 'Someone's after me.'

She watched him carefully. He held her gaze for a moment, then averted his eyes. He scratched at his head.

'I don't know what you want me to say,' he replied, and his tone was weary, as though he'd heard it all before.

'Too much has happened, Tommy.' She moved over to him at speed, sat beside him on the bed. She hated the plea in her voice, but he had to know, had to understand that this wasn't in her mind. 'It's the second time in days I've been locked in; look what happened to my hair, the attack on deck…' She trailed off as something else occurred to her. 'That sleep, just now.' She stood up, wrapped her arms around herself. 'That wasn't normal. Oh my God!' She dragged her fingers down her cheeks. 'I was *drugged*.'

Tommy laughed. 'You're obviously not getting to grips with the locks,' he said. 'It's all right, it's a new place, locks and key cards and all sorts of security.' Noticing her expression, he pushed on hurriedly. 'I just think you're anxious; it's your first cruise and I admit the thought of being out in the middle of the ocean can be daunting.' Awkwardly, he put one arm around her. 'You just need to get a good rest and start over again tomorrow.'

At first she thought she was seething, shaking with anger. It took her a moment to realise that it wasn't anger, but fear. Was someone after her? Or – and the second thought was almost worse – was this all in her mind? From the corner of her eye she watched her husband as he gave her one last squeeze and went to the bathroom, leaving the door open. She walked back to the chair she had been sleeping in. Was it even possible that it was Tommy doing this to her? It was a frightening thought, one that she would never have even considered before this trip. He was capable of a lot; she wouldn't put it past him to have an affair, if she were totally honest with herself. She certainly wouldn't be shocked if he eyed up other women.

But this… She was being gaslighted. And in a million years she wouldn't have thought Tommy would have the capacity to do that. And why would he?

He was a narcissist, though, for sure. His response just now proved that.

'Something's happening,' she said. 'I don't know if it's you or me, but something's changing.'

She heard the toilet flush and the tap running in the bathroom. Tommy didn't hear her, or if he did, he didn't reply.

—

The wind had settled a little, and Anna pulled on the stolen waxed jacket and picked up a towel and a cushion and went out onto the balcony.

She laid the towel on the deck, put the pillow on top of it and knelt down. She stayed still and silent, listening for evidence that either of her neighbours might be outside on their own veranda. Next door, in the Expedition Suite, she thought she heard Paula's voice, shrill and high, panicked and frightened, though she couldn't discern the words. There was nothing to be heard from Tommy.

Satisfied that she was alone, she went to work on the bolts. Soon her fingers were red with blisters. It was so cold they didn't sting, and Anna very rarely felt pain anyway, but the look didn't really go with the stylish businesswoman persona she was trying to put out there.

In spite of the little piece of meat and the salad she had eaten earlier, the work was even harder than she had anticipated, and she rested as frequently as she dared, which wasn't that much because this needed to be done before first light. Today was Mark's day off; he had told her that, back on the night they had slept together. He had said it with a suggestive leer, not even a question, as though she would leap at the chance to spend the day with him.

But he would be expected to report for duty tomorrow, and when he didn't turn up, questions would be asked.

People might already be asking questions. She knew how workmates were; they generally hung around with each other even when they weren't on duty, a fact that was even more likely on a cruise ship.

She glanced over her shoulder at his body. Yes, he had to go tonight; she couldn't risk keeping him in her suite for one more night. She bent her head to her task and spun the bolts harder and faster. The spanner slipped in her bloodied fingers, but she kept going. Finally, the last bolt came free. She picked it up and put it on the threshold, just inside the door.

In the living room area, she stood beside Mark's body and removed all her clothes. She slipped on the shower cap that came free with the suite, and a pair of rubber gloves.

Now came the really hard work.

It took an age to roll him to the door, and over the threshold. Sweat poured freely down her thin body, and the heat of the chore was a strange contrast to the biting cold outside.

For the final few feet, she put her gloved hands on his thick, cold skin and wedged the corner of the plastic covering under her knees. Carefully she unfurled him, gripping the plastic and rolling it up. Finally, he was on the precipice, the gap just large enough for his bulky frame to be pushed through.

She clung onto his meaty arms as she scanned the horizon. All was quiet, the sea stretching for miles in every direction, black under a cloudy sky; not even a hint of the moon or any stars.

Still keeping hold of Mark, she leaned across him to look down at the balconies below. She clenched her teeth against the chill and with her free arm swiped her eyes clear of the tears that had sprung up in the biting wind.

He would fall straight down, she told herself. *He had to.* If a gust came and knocked him onto someone else's balcony, the resulting investigation would be catastrophic. There was nowhere to run to on a cruise ship in the middle of the ocean, unlike at William's house, where she'd been able to pack her things and walk away to another life.

She pushed herself back, gripping Mark with both hands now, and settled into a crouch. The wind was as still as it was ever going to be, and with a primal grunt she shoved at him as hard as she could. His limbs opened up as he fell, arms and legs spread, and for a moment he was flying. It was almost beautiful, she thought. There was no sound as he hit the water; the waves already crashing against the side of the ship disguised any splash.

She pulled her jacket around her and stayed in a crouch for a while, listening keenly for any shouts or sounds of a Good Samaritan raising the alarm. There was nothing, and eventually she stood up and made her way back inside.

–

'I don't know what you want me to say.'

Propped up against the pillows in the bed, Paula put her head in her hands.

His words had turned into a mantra. *I don't know what you want me to say.* Over and over and over again. Had he always been like this? So… dismissive.

Yes, thought Paula. And she wondered about the other women she knew, whose husbands were possessive and willing to raise their voices and fists in support of their wives, sometimes against their wives. Tommy was too laid-back for that. This was a different sort of control.

The sun had risen now, after a night of no sleep for either of them. Paula had been too frightened to drop off, and Tommy was... well, Tommy was simply mystified at her behaviour.

'I want to get off this ship,' she said now. 'I don't know what I've done for someone to target me so intensely. I just need to leave.' She waited a beat and then said pitifully, '*Please.*'

He had been pacing for a while, up and down, back and forth, pausing every so often to look out across the patio. Paula followed his gaze. The sea looked calm, blue and glacial, an almost perfect colour match to the winter sky.

'We don't stop now until Iceland.' He came over to the bed and sat down next to her. The mattress dipped with his weight as he leaned across and took her hand in his own. 'We get off for a whole day before we set sail for home.' He squeezed her fingers. 'You've just got cabin fever.'

She was sure that wasn't it. What even was cabin fever – a form of claustrophobia? If so, that wasn't her problem at all. She would have been quite happy spending more time in the sauna, or even in her plush suite, but she had been forcibly locked in.

'What did you do last night, when I was in here?' she asked suddenly.

He shrugged. 'Had dinner, some drinks with the boys.'

'Anna was here,' she said. She narrowed her eyes. 'Actually, she was the last one who went out of the door. As soon as she did, I couldn't open it.' She raised her hands, palms up, an unspoken question, and stared hard at him.

'She was in the restaurant, she had dinner with us,' he said.

'Oh. So, it wasn't just dinner and drinks with the boys after all?' Even as she spoke the words, she wanted to take them back. They were too combative, she shouldn't confront him like that.

He sighed and let go of her hand.

'Honey, when I came back, this door was open. It wasn't even just unlocked, it was *open*.'

Paula bit her lip. He'd told her that as soon as he'd woken her up. All along he'd been adamant the door had been ajar. And that heavy, heavy sleep she'd had... Turning away, she wrapped her arms around herself. Was it possible she'd dreamed the whole being-locked-in thing?

She shivered, despite the warmth of the room.

Was it her mind that was playing tricks on her, and not some stranger with a grudge?

The deck attack, the push, the missing railing... that hadn't been a dream. But she had been drinking the night she was pushed. Those three shots of vodka, one after the other. The way she had staggered and wobbled when she'd first come out on deck in the freezing night air.

As if sensing her hesitation, Tommy put his hands on her shoulders. 'Look, it's going to be a bright day. Why don't we have breakfast and then wrap up warm and go out on the deck?'

She looked into his face, into his eyes that she knew so well. Sometimes she thought she knew the contours of his face and body better than she knew her own. Was that what all this was about? The fact that they'd been together coming up for two decades? Things shifted and changed, and maybe everything that had happened to her on this trip, and the way he'd reacted to her recent misfortunes...

155

She felt her mouth turn down. She couldn't blame him; if she were him, she would be irritated with herself too.

She nodded reluctantly, her mind made up. 'Let's go and have some breakfast.'

He smiled and was up and off in an instant, pulling his shoes on, picking out his thickest coat and hat. She moved more slowly, disconcerted at how easily appeased he was. At how quickly he seemed to forget her troubles.

Chapter 15

Anna slept like the dead. The physical work of disposing of Mark's body had left her exhausted. Afterwards, she had been unable to shake the feeling that someone would spot him moving around in the waves, and so she had wrapped herself in her duvet and camped just inside the door of the balcony until the dawn light had started to spread its grey fingers across the ocean.

She had listened keenly through the shrieking wind. Nobody had raised the alarm. She hadn't heard the sound of anybody else's doors opening. No low conversation or startled screams. She had got away with it. Smiling, she had finally gone to bed.

When she awoke, it was almost nine o'clock and the sun was streaming through the doors. Another couple of days and they would be in Iceland. She remembered how she had locked Paula in last night. When she had slipped into the Expedition Suite, Paula had been dead to the world in her drugged sleep. She would be feeling terrible this morning; groggy, almost like a hangover. Which meant she had probably declined breakfast.

Which meant Tommy would be in the restaurant by himself. Or if not alone, with his pals.

She slid out from between the sheets and dressed hurriedly, pulling on skinny jeans and a thick knitted jumper. The jeans gaped at the waistband and she smiled.

It was going to be a good day.

–

Anna swept out of the elevator and into the restaurant, wrinkling her nose at the smell of the hot buffet. As if in reaction, her stomach growled noisily, and she frowned, holding her breath as she walked past. She poured herself half a cup of black coffee and took a single slice of melon before looking around the busy room.

There was Tommy in his normal spot, a full English in front of him, along with a newspaper. He was shovelling bacon into his mouth while turning the pages of the paper.

She hesitated, thinking that maybe she should wait until he'd finished eating like he was in some sort of competition. But she steeled herself and walked over to his table. Putting her coffee and melon slice down, she smiled at him.

'Good morning,' she said. 'Is this seat taken?'

His mouth was full and he chewed frantically, though her question hadn't been a request for permission. She started to pull the chair out.

'It *is* taken, I'm afraid.'

The voice came from behind her, and spinning around, she came face to face with Paula.

'Oh, er, hello, good morning,' Anna said, stumbling over her words. 'How *are* you?'

She'd got it wrong. She cursed herself, hearing the concern in her own voice, feeling the frown that knitted her brow. As though she already knew that Paula had had a shitty night locked in her suite. She waited, hoping neither of them had picked up on her tone.

'Good, thanks, looks like it's going to be a lovely day.' Paula nudged her way in front of Anna and pulled out the chair. 'Excuse me.'

It was awful, uncomfortable, and Anna froze, her mind unable to catch up with the faux pas. The tension dragged on until Tommy pushed Anna's coffee cup and plate to the left of him. 'This seat's free,' he said, over-cheerful, compensating for his wife's frostiness.

Anna pulled out the chair and sat down. She picked up her coffee cup and cradled it in her hands.

'Anything exciting going on?' she asked, gesturing to his newspaper.

He shrugged. 'There's a storm coming. Going to hit Europe, Iceland too.' He angled the paper so she could see.

'That's a shame. I really want to get off the ship when we dock, take a look around Reykjavík.'

Tommy guffawed. 'If you're anything like Paula, the weather won't matter. They've got a big shopping mall, all under cover.'

Anna caught the pained look that shot across Paula's face and leapt on it. 'Not a fan of the outdoors, Paula?' she asked innocently.

'I am, as a matter of fact. And I've been reading about the frozen lakes. I'll be taking a look at them, whatever the weather.' Paula's reply was even, but Anna detected the undertone. Cool towards herself, belligerent against her husband. But then her face flushed and she dropped her gaze to the tabletop. Anna nodded to herself; neither emotion came naturally to meek, mousy Paula.

Tommy glanced at his wife. 'You didn't say. I've been looking at trips to the natural springs, I wanted to go and see them.'

An uncomfortable silence fell, broken eventually by Paula. 'You can, I'll be fine.'

Anna cleared her throat and shifted in her chair to stare outside. Why didn't Paula just give up and return to her suite? Probably because she was scared she was going to be locked in again. She smothered a smile.

'Hey, look, this is near us!' exclaimed Tommy suddenly.

Anna turned back to him, but he had pushed the newspaper over towards Paula.

'Look, this poor old guy was found dead in a house in Ilford. That's not far from us.'

The smile slid from Anna's face.

Could it be…?

'Says they assumed he'd had a heart attack, but the police found evidence of foul play,' read Paula. 'Oh, God, they're looking for his *carer* in relation to the attack!'

Sweat prickled at Anna's hairline. Her heart pounded at double time. Discreetly, she smoothed her wrist along her forehead.

'There's a photo of her.' Paula showed the paper to Tommy, seemingly forgetting that Anna was even there.

A *photo*? Of her?

'Can I see?' she asked, as casually as she could manage.

Tommy passed the paper across to her and Anna peered at the article. Two pictures, one of William in his younger days, before she even knew him. And a second photo… and it was of her.

She was wearing the beret she favoured, walking across the road towards William's house, a shopping bag in one hand, her keys hanging loosely from the other. The photo was black and white, grainy on the page; her face was angled off to one side, her attention caught by something down the street.

Her mouth was suddenly dry, and her chest felt painfully tight.

How was there a photograph of her?

She read the article quickly.

> The body of William Hatcher, 82, was discovered at the bottom of the stairs in his terraced house in Ilford, Essex. It appeared that Mr Hatcher may have suffered a coronary episode, but Mr Hatcher's son, Jason, 45, subsequently reported that a large sum of cash was missing from the property.
>
> Jason Hatcher has been living abroad, and therefore was not aware that his father had a live-in carer. Mr Hatcher's next-door neighbour, Cameron Henderson, (75) told our reporter:
>
> 'Her name is Gemma, she's very young, in her twenties, I'd say. Gemma wasn't particularly friendly and I put that down to her just being shy. But I haven't seen her since William's death, and now this money is missing too.'
>
> Mr Henderson added that the whole neighbourhood is in shock.
>
> Anyone who has information regarding Gemma's whereabouts is asked to contact Central Essex Police on…

'It didn't say how much money was missing, did it?' Tommy asked.

Anna shook her head. She couldn't look at him, at either of them. If they studied the photo closely… And yet she felt a bloom of pleasure that old Mr Henderson had thought she was only in her twenties.

She blinked the feeling away and studied the paper again. How were they even looking for her? She had covered her tracks with the goodbye card she had left. She had been so careful not to mark his face when she had killed him. She went back in time to that dim, gloomy hallway where she had sat atop his body and closed off his airways. He had been struggling, she'd been forceful. His skin was old and paper-thin. Had she left imprints of her fingers on his face?

Another horrible thought caught at her: that she had worn the very same beret pictured in the newspaper when the boat had docked in Åndalsnes, and when she had gone to Paula's suite last night for a coffee. It was a deep, dark pink, unmistakable. Thankfully the newspaper was in black and white, but online, in the article that would be all over social media, the photo would be in colour. She had to ditch the beret and just hope against hope that Paula wouldn't see the same article online and remember that she owned an identical hat.

But she had Paula's phone, she remembered, so she wouldn't be scrolling through the news on that device. And the article had referred to her as Gemma, which was also good.

'Can't believe how close to us this is.' Tommy shook the paper in his hand.

Paula sat back in her chair. 'It's not that close,' she said. 'We don't live in Ilford.'

Anna narrowed her eyes. Was that snobbery in Paula's tone? Or was she trying to hide the fact that she was horrified that a crime had taken place in their vicinity?

'Where are you from, Anna?' asked Tommy.

'The city,' she replied without missing a beat.

'What, central London?' Tommy whistled. 'That's expensive.'

She met his eye. 'Yes,' she replied. 'I suppose it is.'

He was looking at her the way he had the first time they had met. Impressed, again, with her apparent wealth. Her eyes drifted over to Paula. The woman looked unhappy now, her husband's awe needling at her. Tommy folded up the newspaper and drained his coffee. Anna put her hand on the paper.

'Do you mind?'

He shook his head. 'Feel free.'

He looked at her again, really looked, and Anna maintained eye contact. Was he looking at her suspiciously, comparing her to the woman in the newspaper? Or was it lust? His eyes darkened, and she smiled.

Lust.

Paula cleared her throat.

'Shall we get on, then?' she asked, standing up.

Reluctantly, Tommy dragged his gaze away from Anna.

'See you later,' he said.

Anna smiled and raised her hand in a wave. Paula left the table without a word.

–

'You're pissed off,' said Tommy as they climbed the winding stairs to the deck. 'What's wrong now?'

Paula stopped short, glancing at the mirrored wall that ran alongside them. For a moment she studied her own face. No, definitely not pissed off. She looked *hurt*. She looked how she felt. How could Tommy be so blind, both to her and her true emotion? Couldn't he see that Anna

163

was blatantly flirting with him? Did he think Paula had missed those little looks that passed between them? How could he be so disrespectful as to behave like a simpering teenager, not even having the courtesy to do it behind her back?

They emerged from the stairs onto the top deck, a blast of icy air hitting her head-on. She gasped and pulled her hood up.

'I'm fine,' she said through teeth that chattered. 'I'm just cold.'

She pushed on, moving to the side to clutch at the railing as the wind buffeted her. In an instant she was back there, in the same place she had stood a few nights ago. Carefully she walked the length of the deck, not waiting for Tommy, not looking back to see if he was behind her. Where the railing curved to the bow, she stopped. There were no unbroken railings, and it all looked so different in the daylight. She turned again, started to walk back the way she had come. Tommy was standing still, staring out over the sea. As she reached him, she came to a stop.

'This is the gate that was open,' he said, and he tapped it with his ungloved hand. His wedding ring clanged against it, making a small, tinny sound. 'It's padlocked now,' he added, and he brought up a booted foot and kicked at the lock as if to prove his point.

Paula said nothing, just turned so she was facing the open ocean. The sea was choppy; frothy white waves slammed against the side of the *Ruby Spirit*, throwing up a fine spray of salty seawater. Suddenly she felt very small indeed. The expanse of the ocean, the size of the ship and everything that had happened to her on it made her shrink inside the oversized coat she wore.

'It wasn't locked that night. It was open,' she said.

He nodded. 'I know. We reported it, Dermot and me. They apologised but couldn't understand how it wasn't locked in the first place.'

'Doesn't matter now,' she said.

That wasn't true. An open gate on the side of a cruise ship was bad; it *did* matter, because anyone – little kids or older people – could have wandered through it and been seriously injured or died, just like what had almost happened to Paula. But it was what was behind the incident that mattered most of all.

She inhaled deeply, steeling herself to say the words he didn't believe. 'Tommy, I'm certain there was someone else there that night.'

'There were lots of people there that night. We were all there, looking for the Northern Lights. And we'd all been drinking.' His tone was gentle now, placatory, protesting against her argument that she had been pushed, even though she hadn't said the words here today.

And that was how the conversation would always go, she realised. She would protest that she'd been attacked, and he would say she or the person who had walked into her was drunk. Round and round in circles, just like their annual autumn conversation about babies and their lives moving forward together.

She swiped at her eyes, suddenly tired.

'Let's go back inside,' she said quietly.

–

Using Mark's master key, Anna let herself into Tommy and Paula's suite. She had watched them go up to the top deck, Paula looking miserable, Tommy looking strained.

It was freezing cold today, she knew, having followed them up there at a distance and melted into the little pockets of people milling around. They might not stay outside for very long, Paula especially.

She sneered as she thought of the woman's need for creature comforts and tried to imagine Paula having to deal with Mark's body the way she herself had done last night. There would be no chance that she could steel herself to do anything like that. She didn't have the back-bone, living the easy, privileged life she'd led.

Anna had done it before, even before William; she had been in a corner and fought her way out each and every time, learning from a young age that you couldn't rely on anyone apart from yourself. The only way to get out of a rut was money, and plenty of it, and not having to share it with anyone else.

William's money would soon be gone, and Anna needed more. It was as bad as an addiction, the primal need she had for security. And time was running out. Although the newspaper and old Mr Henderson had put her in her early twenties, she was actually halfway through her thirties. She looked good because she didn't eat, and she took care of her skin and worked out and kept herself looking young and elfin. But the terror age was looming, and she wasn't anywhere near where she needed to be when she reached forty.

This was her one big chance. The chance to have Paula's life.

She didn't know what she was looking for, not really. Just anything that could extend the rip that was already there in the couple's marriage. In the bathroom she opened the cabinet and looked inside. His and hers wash bags, Tommy's plain black, Paula's designer. She pulled Tommy's off the shelf, poked around among the razors, hair gel, aftershave and moisturiser. She rummaged around in her own bag and pulled out a box of condoms. Taking two out, she slipped one into Tommy's toiletry bag, which she put back on the shelf, then placed the other one so it was just visible.

She moved out into the main living area, opening drawers, the wardrobe, the suitcases that sat behind the couch. There was nothing of interest, she thought, feeling disappointed as she came to the end of her search. At random, she pulled a couple of Paula's tops and trousers out of the wardrobe and shoved them in her own bag. The woman had brought what looked like her entire wardrobe; Anna wondered if she would even realise there were items missing.

She hoped so.

She did another turn around the suite, verifying that Tommy hadn't left his phone in the room. She'd wanted that, wanted to prevent him from looking further at the article about William and the damning photo of herself. She sighed. Oh well, couldn't win them all.

And then, the last place, the bedside table. A pile of euros, not neatly stacked but haphazard piles and crumpled notes. She slipped some into her purse.

–

'Has anyone handed in an iPhone?' Paula asked at the information desk. 'I lost it a couple of days ago.'

The girl stared at her with narrowed eyes and shook her head. 'Nope,' she replied.

Startled by the woman's seemingly uncaring demeanour, Paula wandered back to Tommy. 'She was rude,' she said.

Tommy glanced back to the reception desk. 'Was she?' he asked through a yawn.

She sighed. She would have to accept that her phone was gone, probably back on the bench in Åndalsnes. It was the end of the Instagram posts she'd planned for this trip, not that she'd been in the mood to put anything on social media so far.

'What shall we do now?' she asked.

Tommy shrugged and offered nothing further. Tears stung Paula's eyes. She remembered the days when there was no question of how they would spend any precious free time. In bed, or driving out to a forest and making love on the bonnet of his car under a starry sky.

At that moment, Dermot and another pal, Angus, wandered past. Tommy grinned and there was much back-slapping and clasping of hands. Paula smiled weakly, hovering on the fringes of the group.

'Hey, we're going to try out the casino. Wanna come?' Angus said.

Paula brightened. The casino was one place they hadn't spent any time, and though they didn't have money to burn, they could certainly afford to enjoy an hour or so of indulgence.

Tommy said, 'Yes! Good plan, buddy.' He turned to Paula, put a hand on her arm. 'You don't mind, do you, love?'

'No, sounds great,' she said.

'Cool.' He dipped his head, landed an awkward kiss on her cheek. 'I'll see you later.'

And with that, he was gone.

Paula watched their departing figures with disbelief. From behind her came a snort of laughter, and she turned to see the woman on the information desk raise her hand to cover her mouth. All at once she recognised her as the stylist who had wrecked her hair in the ship's salon, and her rudeness suddenly made sense. The girl had been demoted. Banished from the salon to work on the inform-ation desk.

Paula's face reddened. She ducked her head and walked quickly away.

In her suite, she closed the door behind her. Leaning against it, exhaustion overcame her. More than anything she wanted to call Julie, and she reached for her bag, belatedly remembering that her phone was gone. She thought of Tommy, of asking if she could use his phone, and remembered he was with his pals in the casino, enjoying the lunchtime fun that she wasn't invited to.

How had this happened? she wondered as she pulled off her coat and slung it on the bed. How had a once-in-a-lifetime cruise turned into something so awful, and on top of that, how had it managed to highlight every single rotten piece of her marriage?

Tears came, in earnest this time, and she let them flow as she stumbled into the bathroom and pulled off some toilet roll to wipe her eyes. When her crying jag was done, she rinsed her face with cold water and towelled it vigor-ously. Looking in the mirror, she started, not recognising the woman who glared back at her with red-rimmed eyes and a pale, drawn face. She opened the cabinet, pulled out her make-up bag and rummaged for the powder that Anna had given her on that first day.

Shoving the bag back, she froze, icy fingers of dread creeping along her skin, making the hairs on her arms stand up. Her heart lurched so far up in her chest that she thought she might be sick. With hands that shook, she reached up to the other shelf and pulled Tommy's toiletry bag into the sink. As she stared down at the contents, the tears came again.

Anna sat herself down at the roulette table and picked up a pile of chips. Across the room, Tommy, Dermot and their mate Angus were standing at the slot machines. In perfect synchronisation they fed their coins into the machines, pulling the handles, their eyes low-lidded and glassy. Small-time players, she thought as she fingered the five-hundred-euro chips in her hand. She started low, putting in fifty euros, getting the feel of the atmosphere, playing small like the boys. At least until they noticed her.

And they would see her. She'd fed some highlighter into her hair last night, so that it was blonder than ever, and she'd tanned in the spa too. She was wearing skin-tight black pants, a thin, black off-the-shoulder jumper. She glanced around, at the fat, florid couples still wearing their duffle coats and wellington boots, in spite of the heat in the casino. Even the boys, all three of them normally very good-looking, appeared windswept and frozen and somehow out of place.

Anna smiled to herself as she placed a fifty on black ten. She barely watched as it spun, not caring about the loss; after all, this was just a warm-up. When the boys came over, that was when she would commence serious play.

In her peripheral vision she saw Tommy straighten up, his gaze sweeping the casino, his eyes alighting on her. He slapped Dermot on the back, gestured with his head. Moments later, she spotted their figures approaching, weaving in and out of the tables. She sat up straight, and placed her hand on her pile of chips.

'Two thousand five hundred covering the orphans,' she instructed the dealer, her voice loud and clear. She slid the chips along, placing them on 6, 34 and 17.

The wheel spun and she offered a smile to the newcomers to the table, her gaze lingering on Tommy. He caught her eye, and held it as the wheel came to a stop on number 6.

'We are approaching the peak date for the Leonid meteor shower. The show can be hugely impressive in a dark night sky. However, we have just left the full moon, narrowly escaping — if you remember — the perils of the maelstrom! For this reason, we are now in the phase known as a waning gibbous moon. It is neither full nor a three-quarter, so it sheds a lot of light throughout our atmosphere.

'The best chance you have to see the meteors is in the pre-dawn hours, so for you early risers, get out on deck and keep watching the skies!'

Chapter 16

Before

I didn't go to school the day after I locked my mother in her room. That night, she slept soundly, and knowing that in the morning things would be very different, I took the chance to sleep too. I had done my research, and I knew the next day or two wouldn't be easy on either of us.

But I had no idea just how bad it would get.

She started at five a.m. Dawn had arrived, the light was grey and pale yellow, and for a moment I ignored the banging and watched the world outside my window from my bed. Eventually she started to shout, and I dragged myself up and went to her door. The lock had held fast, and for that I was grateful.

'You have to stay in there, Mum,' I said. 'It won't be easy, but we need to get you off the drugs. You've got everything you need.' I paused, and when she didn't reply, I added, 'It's just for a couple of days.'

Silence fell on the other side of the door. I put my face close to it. I could hear her breathing, deep, heavy, dragging breaths.

'Are you fucking kidding me?' Her voice was quiet, and there was humour in it, as though it was a joke that she didn't quite get yet.

I shook my head, even though she couldn't see me. 'I'm serious,' I said. 'If you carry on taking that stuff, you'll die.'

I wondered why I'd said those words. Because if I was honest, I didn't fear or dread her death. In fact, if it happened, I would probably be better off. I would be moved to a foster home or a care facility, and people would look after me. They would cook my meals. They would wash my clothes. I wouldn't have to look over my shoulder for my mother's men wanting me to pay her debts in kind.

But still, she was my mother. I had to try to help her get clean.

My mind wandered then, and I allowed myself to think about the possibility of having a real mum. One who took me to town on Saturdays, who watched movies with me and helped me with my homework. It was unimaginable. I couldn't picture it in a thousand years.

A thump on the other side of the door made me jump. I scooted backwards.

'You've got water in there, plenty of bottles, and some food,' I said bravely.

Silence descended once more, and after a while I retreated to my room and burrowed back under the covers.

'I'm going out the window!'

The bellow was so deep and raw that for a moment I thought Carl was in the house. But it wasn't a man's voice, it was my mother's, and the change in her tone frightened me.

I went down the stairs and slipped out the front, staring up at her window. She was there, spread-eagled against the glass, one of the two fanlights open, her left hand outside, waving, her cheek pressed to the pane, her mouth stretched wide in that primal man's shout.

Satisfied that she couldn't get out of the window, I went back inside. As I closed the door, I saw Kevin in his front garden in the process of taking out the rubbish. One hand held the bin lid open and he stared up at my mother, his mouth a wide 'O' of shock.

I closed the door and trudged back upstairs.

'Are you drinking your water?' I asked through the closed door.

'My girl, my baby, please don't hurt Mummy like this.' Her voice had returned to normal, high-pitched and squeaky. 'Mummy loves you so much. Just get her some of her stuff and we'll never talk about this, I promise,' she wheedled.

I sat with my back to the door. That was the problem. We never talked about it. And after years of low-class drugs, she had slipped so easily into this. A smell, sweet and sickly, settled around me on the landing and I pulled my T-shirt up to cover my mouth and nose.

'Use the bucket,' I said.

'YOU BITCH!' she roared, the male voice back in full force. 'You bloody cu—' She broke off as she retched and vomited.

Later, much later, she spoke again. 'My bones are breaking,' she whispered. 'Please help me, someone… anyone…'

—

Late that night, when it was fully dark and the street was in blackness, Carl came to the house. He had one hand on his fly, already unzipping it as I opened the door.

I stepped back to let him in, and jerked my head towards the stairs. For a second his eyes widened, hope and excitement reflected back at me as he misunderstood my meaning.

As if on cue, she started again, thin screams now, her throat sounding raw. If he'd cared, he would have leapt up the stairs, taking them two at a time. Instead, he turned to face me, a question mark in his eyes. From behind my back I pulled out the knife I was clutching and held it loosely in my fist. My hands were not shaking, and for that I was grateful.

He bit his lip. Wondering if he could take me, perhaps. But quickly he seemed to come to the conclusion that he wanted no part of this. Why would he? There was nothing special about my mother apart from the fact that she was an easy target. He could get his kicks and sell his wares elsewhere; this town wasn't short of desperate, disadvantaged women.

I followed him to the door. 'Don't come back, Carl,' I said, and this time *my* voice sounded low and deep and filled with the promise of violence.

He moved down the path, his head low, his shoulders hunched. I watched him until he had vanished into the black night.

I didn't go to school the next day, and nobody called or came round to see where I was.

Nobody cared.

I'd thought that someone might report the disturbance that she made, on and off, night and day. I watched from the window, saw a few people from the estate walking past and angling their heads upwards at the screams and curses. I held my breath when I heard sirens, or when official-looking cars drove past. But nobody came.

Nobody cared.

It never occurred to me that I could call the social services, or the police. What did I know about safe-guarding at that age?

On the third night, somebody finally came. It was almost midnight, and I hadn't slept for two nights. When the knock sounded, my legs collapsed beneath me. I felt wetness on my face and I swiped at the tears as I pulled myself up and staggered to the door.

Two men huddled in the porch, dressed in black, their faces, thick and plump and red, creased in frowns. Word-lessly, I looked at them, but the gratitude I wanted to convey wouldn't come, so I stepped back and let them in.

'She's up there,' I said, pointing to the stairs.

In silence, they thudded up to the landing, giving me long, lingering looks on the way. I sat on the bottom step, wondered where I would go, and suddenly I was so, so tired that I could have slept right there. Would they let me stay in my own home just for tonight? I wondered. I thought of Rebecca and how she had been given to a family who loved and cared for her. My breath caught at the excitement of potential change.

Upstairs, sounds were magnified. The bolt slid across; an intake of breath; short, sharp words from one of the men. My heart spun in my chest: was she dead? I turned and crawled up the stairs, holding onto the wall for support as I turned the corner. One of the men lurched past me, shoving me out of the way as he put his arm over his mouth.

'I–I had to do this,' I said to nobody.

I peered into the room. By the bed, the bucket had been overturned, and liquid waste pooled on the carpet.

The bedclothes were pushed to one side, the sheets yellow and damp. My mother was slumped on the floor with her back against the bed. She was naked, angry red scratches criss-crossing up and down her arms. The remaining man leaned over her, his body blocking my view of what he was doing.

'I'll get you a dressing gown, Mum,' I said, and hurrying to my room, I snatched my own off the back of the door. I sidled back into her room, trying to hold my breath as I edged towards her.

I put the gown over her thin shoulders. The curve of her back was punctuated by bumps, and I could count every part of her spine. As I touched her, her skin rose in goosebumps and her eyes slid sideways to look at me. Here was a woman who was broken beyond repair, and yet a stone sat in my chest where my heart should have been.

The man had a strap around her upper arm: blood pressure check, I thought at first, and then I smelled a familiar scent, tart, like burning vinegar. It was the second man, coming back upstairs, carrying a tin, a tea towel wrapped around it.

Ignoring me, he set the tin down on the bedside table. From his pocket he withdrew a needle; swiftly he placed it in the tin and sucked up the fluid, passing the syringe to the man next to my mother.

I heard the sharp intake of breath, belatedly realised it came from me. The veins on my mother's arms stood to attention, erect and eager to receive, and I found my voice, found myself. Darting over to the man, I knocked the needle from his hands.

It fell to the floor, landing in the puddle of shit. He grimaced, and with thumb and forefinger, picked it up.

As he slid it into her arm, into the very vein that was shrieking for it, I put my hands over my face and sank to my knees.

'Carl?' I said. 'Carl sent you?'

They didn't answer me, and my mother smiled and hissed out unintelligible words as she laid her head back against the bed.

They removed the lock from the door. I watched as the paint flaked and drifted down to the floor. The first man slipped the lock into his pocket and moved past me.

He paused, and leaned his face very close to mine.

'Leave her alone,' he said, the only words he had spoken to me.

Leave her alone.

As though she were the victim here, and this was how I should be expected to live. I slumped down into a crouch and put my head in my hands.

I had to get out. I had to forge a life for myself that was as far away from here as possible. Because there was no fixing this; the situation wouldn't get better, no matter what I did. Two more years, then I would be sixteen and I could legally leave. I could leave right now, I realised, but I wasn't stupid. With no money and nobody to run to, I would end up on the streets. Eventually I would become the woman on the floor in front of me.

Two more years...

It was the early hours of the morning now, and I had to go to school today. I had to pick up my grades, work really, really hard so I had a chance of getting into a university. Uni life cost money, but scholarships didn't. And if anyone needed a scholarship, it was me. If anyone *deserved* a scholarship, it was me.

I washed my school uniform and draped it over a radiator. I checked the gas meter: it had fifty pence in it, which should be just enough to dry my clothes. In the meantime, I filled a bowl with bleach and water and returned to my mother's bedroom.

I scrubbed at the carpet, the pungent stench of faeces mixed with bleach making my eyes water. The chemicals turned the carpet white, but I didn't care. I liked it: a single clean spot in an otherwise rotten environment.

The work became soothing, mechanical, and in my mind I dreamed of Cambridge, of Durham, Leeds or Oxford. I didn't know what they looked like, or what subject I would study there, I just knew I needed to get to one of those places.

She slumbered on, happy in her heroin dreams while I cleaned her shit from the carpet.

I scoured and scrubbed, focused now, no longer trying to save her, no longer wasting my time trying to change her. I just needed to escape.

It was all about me now, and the future I deserved.

Chapter 17

In the Expedition Suite, Paula paced back and forth, clutching the two condoms in her sweaty palms.

He was intending to use them. *They* didn't use them, she was on the pill. Well, she wasn't, she remembered, a pang of guilt pulsing through her. She had flushed them down the toilet, hadn't she? Determined to get a head start on the baby that he continuously stalled on.

But as far as he knew, she *was* on the pill, which was laughable anyway, considering they hadn't so much as had a cuddle on this goddam holiday.

She needed to confront him, but she was terrified. What if he said it was over?

On the table, the bottle of vodka caught her eye. Unmoved and untouched since that night. She reached for it now, spinning off the cap, putting the bottle to her lips and swallowing down mouthful after mouthful until her throat burned and her eyes stung.

She slammed the bottle down, gasping and shivering despite the warmth of the room.

'Can you be on your own?' she asked her reflection in the mirror.

The woman who stared back shook her head.

No, you're not cut out for it. You worked too damn hard for this life that you now lead. You can't do without it.

'Maybe I can,' she whispered, with all the defiance she could muster.

The woman in the mirror laughed at her, long and hard. Paula turned blindly to reach for the bottle.

–

The drink was flowing in the casino, cocktails on tap, the waiter summoned by Anna as soon as Tommy's glass was empty. One by one his friends dropped out and wandered off in drunken, penniless stupors until only he remained.

Anna was winning as much as she was losing, she noted, which was good because she had used a massive chunk of William's money for today's task, and the pile was rapidly diminishing. She flung two more five-hundred-euro chips on the table, covering black with one, red with the other. Tommy was too drunk to notice the futility of this. All he saw was the masses of money that she was literally throwing away.

'Wish me luck,' she said softly, lowering her eyes as she leaned into him.

He lurched off his stool to stand behind her. Suddenly, without warning, he pressed his body against her, the whole length of him pushing into her so hard she felt her pubic bones jut painfully against the roulette table. She experienced a strange mixture of disgust and pride. And then something else, a sensation that she very rarely – if *ever* – felt with a man. The slow, unfamiliar dawning of desire.

His arms came around her sides to lean on the table. Subtly, she moved back against him. He breathed satisfyingly heavily in her ear. Maybe, she thought, just maybe, once she had his home and Paula's life and everything in it, she might keep him around for a while.

He murmured something unintelligible, and she turned her head slightly.

'Are you sending me lucky vibes?' she asked huskily.

He responded by grinding against her harder. She didn't watch where the ball landed – black, red, it was all the same to her. But across the room she saw movement, a woman standing by the slot machines, in almost exactly the same place that Tommy had been when Anna had first started playing.

She wore an oversized coat, a man's coat, Anna saw, as though she had picked up the nearest garment and thrown it on without looking. Her face was red, blotchy, streaked with tears that even now were falling down her cheeks as she watched the scene unfold before her.

Her jaw was slack, her eyes bleak. She looked like she had lost everything.

Anna smiled and bit her bottom lip.

'Tommy,' she said quietly, without taking her eyes off Paula. 'Your wife is watching you.'

–

Paula watched in disbelief as Tommy pressed himself up against the woman in front of him. Her breath came in jerky gasps, and in her pocket she fingered the sharp edges of the condom packets. She wanted to stalk over there, spinning her arms around and punching out at the pair of them, all the while screaming expletives. In her mind, she said them, the worst words she could dredge from her vocabulary. Words that nice, classy married women didn't use.

Words that Paula herself never said.

She wanted to do all this, but her legs were leaden.

''Scuse me, I'm on this machine.' The voice was that of an elderly lady, nudging her way in, scared that Paula was going to take all the money out of the machine she'd spent so many hours feeding.

Fuck you, Paula wanted to shout at the innocent woman, and in her pockets her hands curled into fists. Instead, she allowed herself to be carefully prodded aside. Her legs started to move of their own accord, taking her towards *them*, her traitorous husband and the vicious slag in front of him. And all of a sudden, the words came in a torrent, and the intonation was pure, bitter fury.

'You fucking bastard,' she said as she reached them, and she was glad her voice didn't betray her; it was low and guttural and rather quiet. Only the croupier caught her words, and he looked at her side-on, just a single quick warning glance.

They would throw her out of the casino if she made a scene. And Paula wasn't the sort to make a show of herself. Years of preening and priming herself into the woman she was had ingrained that in her.

'Uh…' Tommy said as he swallowed and pulled away from Anna, stumbling into the table. 'Just having some fun. Anna's winning.' He smiled lopsidedly, more drunk than she had ever known him. He didn't even look ashamed, or embarrassed to have been caught in the act.

Paula switched her attention to Anna. The scarlet woman met her glare head-on, unflinching, uncaring.

'You…' She leaned in, really close to the pair of them now, not wanting to shout the word that she never, ever uttered but that right now was the only word that would do. 'You pair of… of *cunts*.'

It seemed to sober Tommy, and his hand snapped out, grabbed her wrist. 'Hey,' he said sharply.

183

She pulled her arm free, a gasp emerging from her, incredulous that she had actually said the word. She was too far gone now, there was no turning back. She dug in the pocket of the coat of his that she was wearing and flung the condoms onto the roulette table. The croupier glanced at them, nestled on the green felt, before performing a sleight of hand and scooping them up before any other onlookers saw.

'Leave, please,' he said in a quiet but firm tone.

Paula nodded at him, her jaw set, clenching down on it, because she didn't want to cry in front of him, in front of any of them. Not in front of *her*, especially.

'Cunt,' she said, louder this time, directed at Anna, because there was nothing left to lose and she quite liked the feel of the word on her tongue. She turned on her heel and staggered back through the casino the way she had come.

—

'Nothing was happening, nothing happened or was going to happen.' Tommy's voice was a whine, long and scratchy, like a mosquito buzzing, or a broken record. Loud too, now they were alone in their suite.

She turned to the doors and put her sleeve in her mouth, biting down on the material to stop the word coming out of her. That awful word that she had never spoken, in all these years, and now she just wanted to spit it at him again and again.

'And what was with the condoms, for God's sake?' he hissed, self-righteous now, a true narcissist, putting it all on her because she was the one who had called him a bastard and a cunt in public, and shown him up by throwing the condoms on the table in the packed casino.

The croupier had asked her to leave.

Paula closed her eyes in shame.

'Where did you even get them from,' he shouted, 'and more to the point, why?'

She turned to face him. 'They're *yours*!' she exclaimed.

'What the hell do I want condoms for?' He threw his hands up in a gesture of disbelief.

'To screw her,' Paula shouted back. Had she ever even raised her voice to him before? If she had, she couldn't remember. 'You need them to fuck that awful wretched woman.' An unplanned sob escaped and she tried to swallow it down. 'I should be grateful you thought of that; who knows what you might have caught?'

'Fucking hell, Paula,' he said. 'I don't know what you're talking about.'

'Well, they're not for us, are they?' she cried, tears flowing now, a river of hurt. 'We don't use condoms, do we? I'm on the pill.'

A grin broke out on his face, so out of keeping with the current conversation that she blinked in confusion. He clapped his hands together slowly, and carried on smiling as he walked towards her.

'But you're not, are you, darling?' he said. His voice was vicious, cruel. 'You threw them away, didn't you?'

Paula swallowed. *How did he know?*

'What... how... h-how...?'

He came up close to her, and she backed away slightly. 'How do I know?' he hissed. 'Because you usually take the damn things every night, make a big bloody show of it, trying to make me feel bad. You've done it since we got married.' His finger came up to touch her chin. It felt like a red-hot poker on her skin. 'Not recently, though.

Right?' He looked triumphant, lips pinched, eyebrows raised in a question that he already knew the answer to.

He flicked his finger, the rough skin around his nail scraping her face. It was a gesture so spiteful that she flushed red. 'I-I don't...' She trailed off, not knowing where she was going, what she could say. Embarrassment mingled with guilt at lying to him. 'I'm sorry.' Finally, she pushed the words out.

He nodded and turned on his heel, stalking from the room. The door closed slowly, and she watched as he turned right and moved down the corridor.

Towards Anna's suite.

–

Anna remained in the casino. The small crowd of people playing the tables had gone back to their games after the few moments of excitement. The men looked her up and down. The women glared at her. Anna smiled and kept spinning the wheel.

She wondered when Tommy would come for her. That he would, she had no doubt; he had been furious that Paula had made a show of him. He had chased her back to the Expedition Suite, fire in his eyes, fury evident in the taut way he held himself. He would return to Anna. She would comfort him. She understood him. She would fix his masculinity, which Paula had temporarily broken.

Soon, she tired of the roulette wheel. Slipping off the stool, she moved across to the blackjack table, an onlooker now, whiling the time away until her man came back.

A tug at her sleeve. She looked to her left, into the face of a young steward she didn't know.

'Yes?' she said.

He wore fingerless gloves, and his nails were grubby. She moved out of reach of his touch.

'Sorry to bother you, madam,' he said. 'Can you... step over here for a moment?'

She looked him up and down, this youthful, feminine-looking man. Was he going to issue a warning over the fracas at the roulette wheel earlier? Who was he to do so? And anyway, it had nothing to do with her; *she* wasn't the one who had thrown foul words and condoms around.

She moved over to the wall with him and waited for him to speak.

His eyes lowered and he leaned closer to her. 'Forgive me, madam. I need to talk frankly to you. One of our staff members hasn't shown up for his shift, and we have reason to believe you may know him.'

Mark.

She arranged her face into a frown. 'Who on earth are you talking about?'

The man, who was no more than a boy really, flushed scarlet. 'Mark Taylor,' he said, and his voice was pitched high when he spoke the dead man's name. 'We understand he was... spending some time with you.'

She nodded sagely. 'I haven't seen Mark since we stopped in Norway. He had a load of his stuff with him, backpack and all that. I assumed his stint had finished and he was disembarking there.'

'Oh.' The young man scratched at his head, clearly perplexed.

Anna smiled and put a hand on his arm. The wool of his jacket was soft under her fingers. 'Why don't you call him? I'm sure he'll be able to explain the mix-up.'

'Yes,' he said, and his eyes darted everywhere except at her. 'Yes. Thank you.'

She watched as he scurried away.

When he had vanished from sight, the smile slipped from her face. Mark had told the crew about her; they all knew, and as far as they were concerned, she was the last link to him.

She rubbed at her face, thought about the newspaper with the photo of her, wanted in connection with William's death. The net was closing in, and there was still another day until they docked in Iceland. Then, of course, there was the journey home.

When they couldn't get hold of Mark, would they check the CCTV on board the *Ruby Spirit*? What areas did the cameras cover? Not inside the suites, she knew. There was no chance of the killing being captured on film. But what about the hallways? What if the last sighting they had of him was at her door?

Her stomach flipped at the thought. Walking fast, she moved towards the casino's exit and back to her suite.

–

After fixing her face, and putting on her own coat, Paula opened the door a crack and peeped out. There was no sign of Tommy. She bit her lip, wondered if he was in Anna's suite, in her bed; perhaps they were drinking champagne and feeding each other from the complimentary fruit basket.

She pulled the door closed behind her and hurried down the hall towards the lift. Was it too late to make this right? If she apologised for lying about taking the pill, perhaps he in turn would be contrite about his behaviour with that witch in the casino. He was drunk, after all, and they hadn't actually done anything.

More than anything she wanted to talk to Julie, and she wondered if there was an internet café or a bank of computers on board that she could use to communicate with her friend. She would ask at the information desk, she thought, and she hoped it wouldn't be the disgraced stylist on duty again.

She thumped impatiently at the button on the elevator, at a loss what to do first. She really needed Julie's advice before tracking down her husband. Julie would know what to do; she always did.

The lift pinged, and Paula froze as the doors swished open to reveal Anna. There was a terrible moment of nothingness, both women standing stock still. Then the doors began to close, and Anna put an arm out to stop them. At the sudden movement, Paula flinched. Anna stepped out of the lift, and as Paula slipped inside, the other woman turned around and smiled at her. As the doors closed, the last thing Paula saw was Anna's face, shining and happy and satisfied.

By the time the elevator opened on to the restaurant, Paula had abandoned the idea of locating an internet café and of finding her husband. The encounter with Anna had been chilling, awful – and, if she was honest, frightening. What sort of woman laughed when she came face to face with the wife of the man she was screwing?

Not screwing, not yet, Paula mentally corrected herself. *Just flirting, for now anyway*.

Semantics; the details were neither here nor there. The intention was the problem, and Tommy's acceptance.

She stepped out of the elevator, turning towards the heavy door that led to the winding staircase. She pulled at the neck of her coat, feeling as though it was strangling her as the sweat pricked her underarms and beaded her forehead. There had been women before, names mentioned at home a little too frequently, lustful glances at Christmas parties, lingering hands on arms. All easily dealt with when they recurred a little too incessantly. A horror story that she'd heard and passed on to Tommy about a man who had messed around with a colleague and whose standing in both his firm and society had suffered. He'd half listened, but knowing him so well and for so long, she'd been aware that it had sunk in. The message that risking everything for a bit of skirt wasn't worth it. The texts had stopped, and the meaningful glances, and the names had been casually dropped from conversation before anything happened.

And Paula had accepted this, because wasn't that just how men worked? All men, but especially those who had a lot to offer in the way of money, status and career. But something else was happening here, something that she had never encountered before. Anna wasn't a silly, wide-eyed young thing. She was something else.

Something frightening.

When Paula had been afraid before, she had gone to Tommy. He had talked her down, protected her, like that time she had thought someone was watching their house and he'd had all those fancy alarms fitted. He was practical in his fixing of things. Only this time, the problem was *him*.

Outside, on the deck, the sky was grey. Rolling clouds loomed on the horizon, and snow flurries drifted down to melt on impact with the wooden boards. The wind was back, howling, punctuated by screeches that sounded like a child screaming.

Paula staggered across the empty deck and gripped the handrail. The cold felt like a burn on her palms, and she wished she had brought her gloves with her. The wind buffeted her along the deck and she forced her head up to stare directly into the weather that spat and pummelled at her.

What would she say to Julie, if she had the means to reach out to her? *I'm frightened of this woman who wants Tommy. I'm scared because I think he wants her too. I'm anxious about a woman who is thinner than a supermodel, a woman who if she was out here right now would probably be swept overboard by this wind.*

She spoke some of the words out loud, spitting them into the wind only for them to be thrown back in her face. A great gust of wind swept across the deck, and she skidded back a couple of steps. Something inside her battled against the elements, an internal reminder that she, Paula, could fight too.

She walked backwards to the door and yanked it open, spilling inside, breathless at the sudden change in environment. Yes, she could fight. But she was so weary of constantly being on her guard to pull Tommy back from an affair they wouldn't recover from. And surely it wasn't her place to do that?

But it is, if you want to carry on living the life you've become accustomed to, a little voice whispered inside her.

Was that really all that mattered? What sort of woman thought like that?

A realisation hit, sudden and real and devastating. Paula clapped her hands over her mouth and allowed herself to think the words she had buried for so long.

If I met myself right now, I wouldn't like me at all.

–

Inside the Arctic Suite, Anna stripped off her clothes and walked naked to the glass doors. She pulled them open, holding onto the handles as the wind smashed into her. It was invigorating, and she screwed her eyes closed.

As she stood there, she thought back to seeing Paula at the elevator. The woman's face, her stance, her whole demeanour was like that of a frightened little mouse. And the look on her face when Anna had laughed at her! Paula had folded into herself even more, looking like she wished she could disappear. The last thing Anna had seen was the tears filling the other woman's eyes as the doors closed.

Reactions were funny things, she thought now as she came back into the room and moved over to the kettle, flicking it on. That moment in the casino was the closest she bet Paula had come to losing her shit in many, many years. It hadn't been a big thing: a few cusses and looks that could kill aimed at Anna and Tommy. Nothing physical, even though Paula was probably double Anna's own weight.

Violence didn't occur to Tommy's wife, and for Anna, that was important. What was even more important was that she had seen no evidence of any CCTV in the corridor that led from the elevator to the Arctic Suite. That was good news; it meant that Mark couldn't be tracked to her room. If he could have been, they would have watched the tape until they realised that he had never emerged again.

Of course he *had* exited, just from a different doorway.

Anna smirked.

But what of the CCTV along the external rails of the cruise ship? Was there such a thing? She grabbed her phone, put some searches into Google and spent the next few minutes watching irrelevant videos that came up. She bit her lip and placed the phone back on the table. She would have to take a walk around the decks of the ship to make sure. And if she did see any cameras on the starboard side where Mark's body had tumbled off her balcony, well... she would deal with that when the time came.

She put a coffee pod in the machine and picked up the fancy little sugar bowl. She took the lid off and stared greedily inside. Saliva filled her mouth. How long ago was it when she'd last allowed herself sugar? She couldn't remember.

As the kettle boiled, she made a decision. She scooped up a quarter of a teaspoon of sugar and added it to the mug. A few grains remained on the spoon, and after a moment's hesitation, she brought it to her mouth and touched her tongue to it.

Her taste buds roared with delight. Light-headed, she dipped the spoon in the sugar bowl again, filling it this time. Before she could change her mind, she thrust it into her mouth. The sweetness rippled through her, fizzing and bubbling all the way down her gullet. As it settled in her stomach, she sank to the floor, eyes closed, caught between pain and ecstasy. Too soon, though, the nausea came, and the pleasure was over almost before it had begun.

Later, she tipped out the now-cold coffee from the mug and poured in still-hot water from the kettle. Wrapped in the thin sheet from the bed, she sipped at the plain water. A lemon from the fruit basket caught her eye and she let her gaze linger on it longingly. But there was no chance now; the loss of control over the stupid sugar had ruined any chance of a tiny treat.

She drank the bland water that tasted of nothing and accepted it for the punishment it was.

Chapter 18

Paula finally found Tommy in the basement bar. It was a place they hadn't visited except to pass through, simply because it literally was just a basement, with no windows or views out to sea.

She stood in the doorway and looked around. It was gloomy, dimly lit, and could be any underground bar one might find in the city. Depressing, she realised now, and a glance at her husband told her that he was drowning his sorrows.

Hope pierced her. He wasn't with that woman; wasn't in her bed making love and drinking champagne from her welcome hamper. And he hadn't sought solace with his mates; there was no sign of Dermot or Angus or any of the other men who had suddenly become his bosom buddies.

Apart from him, the room was empty, and feeling brave due to the lack of audience, she walked over to the bar. He heard her approach, his head snapping up and round. Was it just her imagination, or did he look disappointed when he realised she wasn't Anna? She shook her head a little to banish the thought and slipped onto the bar stool next to him.

There was a long silence, and he turned back to nurse his whisky.

'Do you want a drink?' he asked, grudgingly it seemed to her, but at least he'd spoken.

'Yes, please,' she said softly.

He gestured to the bartender, ordered a vodka and soda without asking her. The bartender slid it over to her, his eyes lingering on the pair of them before he retired to wipe glasses in the shadow at the far end of the counter.

Paula sipped at her drink, biting the straw to stop herself apologising first. Tommy said nothing. Behind the bar, the second hand on an oversized clock ticked around and around.

'I'm sorry,' she said eventually.

Stony-eyed, he looked straight ahead.

She put a hand on his wrist. 'I *am* sorry,' she repeated, and as she said the words for the second time, she hated herself a little.

He shrugged and sighed. 'Okay,' he muttered.

She withdrew her hand and put it primly in her lap, unsure of what his response meant. Now was the moment when he was supposed to turn to her and tell her that he was sorry as well; that he had been drunk, not that it was an excuse, and he wouldn't do anything as crass as grind up against another woman again.

'Did you take any of my money from the bedside drawer?' he asked.

She blinked and frowned at the sudden change of direction.

'Um, no,' she said. 'Why?'

He shrugged again, and she felt a bleat of fury at the gesture, which was his answer to so many of her questions these days.

'I'm missing some,' he said. 'A couple of hundred euros.'

She was confused. His money had always been her money – *their* money. When they went away, they didn't have their own spending cash, it was all in. More to the point, she hadn't been anywhere to use any money.

A thought struck at her as she stirred her drink with the straw. 'Anna was in our suite,' she said. 'I went to the bathroom, that night when I was locked in, and she was alone in there for a while.'

He hissed out a breath. 'For God's *sake*.' He drained his drink and turned to face her for the first time.

She shrank back but forced herself to speak anyway. 'Why are you defending her?' It came out as a whine, and she clenched her fists in frustration.

He shook his head, held his hands up and stumbled backwards off his stool. 'I can't do this again, I can't go through your craziness again.'

Again. What was that supposed to mean? That she was always behaving crazy? Before she could ask him, he turned and made to walk away. She reached for him, snagging the sleeve of his coat, jerking him backwards, and he stumbled into the bronze handrail on the bar, banging his side.

He clutched at his ribs and glared at her. His eyes were filled with something she'd seen more times on this cruise ship than in all their years together.

She let her hand fall to her side. 'I'm sorry,' she whispered.

He simmered for a second before glancing at his watch. 'It's nearly time for dinner. Are we going to eat tonight?'

An olive branch, a peace offering. His face was creased with a scowl, but his words were a lifeline that she grabbed onto. She pushed herself off the stool, abandoned her drink and followed him as he left the bar without waiting to see if she was behind him.

–

At Tommy's suggestion they dined in the smaller Japanese restaurant on the other side of the ship. It was the first time they hadn't eaten in the main restaurant. It was quiet, and even better, nobody they knew was in there.

Paula sank into a chair and picked up the menu, pretending to read it while instead she scrutinised Tommy and tried to figure out what was going on in his head. His face was a blank; the scowl of earlier was gone, but his ready cheery smile had not put in an appearance.

She was on the brink, she thought as she watched him. Or rather, they were. On a precipice that could lead to her plummeting down into a lonely dark cave of singledom. She thought of Julie, how she sat in the house that she'd got free and clear of a mortgage in the divorce from her cheating husband. She had her home, she had a lifestyle allowance that he still paid monthly, and yet Paula knew she would give it all up to have her man back.

She bit her lip. For the first time, she knew how her friend felt. She didn't want to be sitting in a house that Tommy's pot of money had given her without him in it. But was it love, she wondered, or just fear? Either way, she couldn't think of how to make things right again.

'Not long until we dock in Iceland,' he said.

He had begun speaking to her again back in the suite while they were getting ready. She had walked around in her nicest lingerie, reaching back to the days when they were young and had made up the old-fashioned way after a fight. Today, as she moved around him in her underwear, deliberately and slowly, he'd kept his eyes on his phone, scrolling with his thumb, waiting patiently for her to get dressed.

'How long do we spend there?' she asked now, playing the game nicely in the way he wanted.

'All day, enough time to see the scenery.'

She nodded and rolled her shoulders, tried to dissipate the tension that had built and built over the last few days. 'Maybe see the Northern Lights,' she said, hopeful that his current favourite topic would perk him up.

'Maybe,' he conceded.

She watched as he pulled his phone out and started scrolling again.

She sat up straight. 'Can I borrow that?' she asked. 'I've not spoken to Julie in days; she'll have been sending me messages and she'll be worried that I've not answered her.'

He raised his eyes, and she shivered at the sudden intensity of his stare.

'Yeah,' he answered finally. 'Let me just finish this.'

She wondered what was he thinking about her request. Did he think she had asked to use his phone so she could skip through his apps, through his texts and calls and email to see if there was anything on there from Anna?

Back and forth went his thumb, scrolling, flicking, jabbing at the screen.

Deleting?

Miserable, she slumped in her chair. When he was finally finished and passed the phone across the table to her, she shook her head.

'Doesn't matter,' she said, smiling bravely.

With an eye roll, he put the phone back in his pocket, then the waiter arrived and Paula had to feign enthusiasm for a cuisine she didn't particularly enjoy.

It was a risk wearing the stolen waxed jacket, but it was the only weatherproof outerwear Anna had, and besides, it wasn't like she was going to go out in public wearing it. She stood on her balcony, leaning far over while adrenaline pumped around her body, bringing a fresh wave of dizziness that she harnessed and held close.

Below her, the waves smashed the starboard side of the *Ruby Spirit* and reached up towards her, six-, seven-, eight-feet-tall sheets of ice-cold sea. Curling tentacles grappled and fought each other to get to her, and she watched, mesmerised by the danger, until she remembered why she was out there.

She hauled herself even further over the same rail that she had removed and pushed Mark through. Turning her head to the right, she gasped, a strangled choking sound, as the wind punched at her face. Tiny flakes of snow mingled with needle-sharp rain, rendering her blind.

She withdrew, clambering off the railing and reversing back inside the suite. She shrugged off the coat, leaving it on the floor, and peeled off her clothes, then pulled a fluffy robe around her shivering body. Picking up her phone, she huddled on the chair by the window, watching the sleet pelt down outside. She thought about giving up on the CCTV surveillance. Surely if they had coverage they would have been here questioning her already?

A knock at the door had her snapping upright in the chair, as though they had sensed her thoughts, as though they had caught up with her. She shrugged inside the robe until it hung loosely around her, then tiptoed to the door and squinted through the peephole at the man who stood outside.

He was older, this one, wearing the same uniform as Mark had: three stripes on his arm with an insignia of an albatross on the sleeve.

She pulled the door open.

He nodded to her and gave a strange half-salute. 'Madam, I'm sorry to bother you. I'm First Officer Patrick Duane, and I wonder if I can have a moment of your time?'

She looked him up and down, compared him to the effeminate man who had spoken to her in the casino. This one was a whole different ball game, that much she could tell straight off. Power and authority spoke volumes.

She pulled the door open. 'Come in,' she invited.

He stepped through and removed his cap. Underneath, his hair was short, military style, greying round the edges. His face was tanned, with deep-set lines, and she could tell that underneath his clothes he was muscled. He clearly took care of himself. She noticed that his eyes did not travel to the plunging neckline of her robe. She would have to be careful.

'Is this about Mark?' she blurted.

His face betrayed no expression as he nodded. 'I understand you last saw him in Åndalsnes, when we docked?'

'That's right,' she said cautiously. 'His shift had finished, he got off the boat.'

He nodded, his granite eyes not leaving her face as he circled her and sat down uninvited in a chair by the window. 'Only his shift hadn't finished,' he said. He offered no further explanation.

'Oh.' Clutching her robe tightly, she followed him and sat down opposite.

'This is unlike Mark.'

She nodded in agreement.

'Did he tell you of his plans?'

She looked down and to the side. Outside the window the sky was white with the promise of further snow.

'Madam?' he prompted.

'He was meeting a woman, I think.' She spoke haltingly, her tone loaded with hesitation.

He nodded. 'Go on.'

Anna took a deep breath and exhaled. 'I've known Mark for a while, before this cruise. Our relationship wasn't what you think.' She picked up the belt of her robe and let it run through her fingers before glancing at Patrick. 'We were friends.'

Patrick tilted his head. 'So, he left his job to be with this… woman?'

Anna nodded. 'He asked me not to tell, but I can see you're all worried about him.' Even as she spoke, she berated herself. This was a risky lie, too risky. He would have told his crewmates that he'd slept with her. Locker room talk, boys together; Anna was a catch, of course he'd bragged about her. 'I'm sure he'll be fine,' she said. Her tone was one of finality, signalling the end of the conversation.

Patrick nodded gravely. Planting his hands on the arms of the chair, he pushed himself to a standing position.

'Did he come to the Arctic Suite often?' he asked.

Anna concealed a sigh. He was pressing her. 'A couple of times. We were friends, like I said.'

Patrick's mouth twisted in an odd smile. 'Were you also friends with his wife?'

It was as though the snow outside had entered the suite. A sudden chill, the realisation like a violent blow to her chest. He didn't believe her. And she hadn't known Mark was married.

She raised her chin. 'Yes, of course.'

He nodded again. 'Jasmin, isn't it? Mark's wife's name, I mean?'

She hesitated, just for a moment. 'That's right.'

He turned sharply, moved towards the door. As he passed the coat hook, he stopped and stared. She followed his eyeline to the pink beret, only partially hidden behind her tailored black coat. He glanced back at her, his gaze moving swiftly past to settle on the floor behind her.

She didn't turn around to see what he was looking at. She knew it was there, the stolen waxed coat. She remained defiantly still and silent.

Finally, he spoke. 'Thank you for your help.'

She released the breath she had been holding. 'If I can be of any further—'

'His wife's name is Belle,' Patrick interrupted her.

Caught in a lie.

When cornered, do nothing, say nothing, she reminded herself.

'I'll be in touch.' He smiled, but it was cold and distrustful.

After a moment, he put his cap back on and left the suite. As she listened to his footsteps out in the corridor, she stared at the door, which he had left open.

Caught in a lie.

With a strangled sound that she tried to push down, she ran to the door and kicked it closed.

–

'I'm going down to the bar.'

Paula sat on the bed and watched Tommy through the open bathroom door as he smoothed back his hair. She didn't push for an invitation; there was really very little point. It stung, though, and she sat up straighter and called through to him.

'I'll try and stay awake. Keep an eye out for the lights!' Her voice was falsely jovial, a tone she hated. She was only just beginning to realise how much she used it when she spoke to him.

'Sure,' he replied.

She didn't know if it was an agreement or a question. Either way, he had responded, and that was a good thing.

He was humming to himself now in the bathroom, and she felt her muscles relax at the sound. He was simmering down, their earlier argument drifting away. In the back of her mind she knew it was a bad thing that they hadn't actually discussed anything, either his inappropriate behaviour with Anna in the casino or her own deception about the pill. There had been no resolution, just bitter acrimony on his part that came off him in waves. She had backed off, apologised, fallen to her knees and accepted the blame for everything.

As usual.

A sour taste filled her mouth, the familiar taste of disappointment. More at herself than him. And now she was expected to stay alone here in the suite until he decided to come to bed.

There was a sudden flutter in her chest, an unprecedented urge to defy him, though she knew even as she felt it that if she did, it would swing his mood back to a black one once more. She closed her eyes and saw them again, plain as day. Anna looking like a goddess at the roulette table, her head tilted back slightly, her lips parted. And Tommy behind her, thrusting against her, his mouth slack and foolish.

She sat up and pushed her feet into her boots, reached for her hooded jumper and pulled it on.

'Where are you going?' he asked, emerging from the bathroom.

A little thrill ran through her at his question.

He does *care*.

She pulled at the cord around the neck of her hoodie. 'To see if there's an internet café, or a computer I can use. I want to message Julie.'

He kept his eyes on her for a moment before apparently deciding this was okay by him. With a 'see ya later', he picked up his key card and dodged out of the door.

–

She avoided the elevator; instead she took the stairs, circling down, down, down until the familiar mechanical hum told her she was nearing the engine room. There was a space down here, almost like a snug, that she recalled seeing one time. She rounded the corner and smiled as the bank of six computers came into view.

The lounge area was deserted – unsurprisingly, she acknowledged, seeing as most the passengers were probably up on deck searching fruitlessly for the Northern Lights, or eating a late dinner, or whale-watching or something.

She slid onto a chair, wiggled the mouse and the screen popped to life. It was free to use, not rented by the hour like some internet cafés. As it should be, she supposed, with the amount the cruise cost overall.

She logged onto Facebook, crushed a little by the fact that she had posted nothing at all on this holiday so far. She thought of the sights she had seen: the lush green mountain at Åndalsnes, the sheer majesty of the Expedition Suite and the views from the ship as the *Ruby Spirit* cut through the choppy winter waters. So many missed opportunities. So many breathtaking moments that she had experienced alone. Mostly because that woman had been hanging around, trying to snare Tommy, trying to lure him away.

She abandoned thoughts of Julie and instead typed Anna's name into the search engine, overcome by curiosity about the cuckoo trying to take over the nest that she had spent so long building.

There was a stream of results: Instagram profiles, adverts for lawyers, obituaries, influencers. A succession of clicks confirmed that none of them was the Anna Masi who was currently haunting Paula.

Puzzled, she sat back in her chair. Surely someone who oversaw a nationwide company, one that was soon to be international, should have a profile somewhere?

Eventually she clicked off the screen. The home page was a news site, and as she sat there chewing the skin around her thumbnail, deep in thought about the mysterious Anna Masi, she idly scanned the articles. The Essex thing popped up, the old man who had died, the one where the carer had vanished with his money.

The photo was there again, in colour this time. The carer's face was obscured as she glanced off to one side. The only thing that was really visible was her coat, black and tailored, and the pop of colour from the vivid pink beret that sat atop her head.

She doesn't look like the hired help, thought Paula as she scrolled down the page. She looked expensive and fierce and confident. She looked like everything Paula herself tried to portray but was never sure she actually carried off.

She was about to click out of the page, already thinking about returning to her suite, having a cup of tea and breaking open the box of chocolates from the welcome hamper that she had so far managed to resist. The mouse was hovering over the cross in the top right corner when her finger stalled.

She leaned closer to the screen and scrutinised the photo of the woman, and suddenly her heart began to beat in double time.

Slamming doors and sudden footsteps startled her. There was a flurry of activity in the previously deserted lounge. Paula sank down in her chair as bodies came from seemingly nowhere, not even casting a glance her way as they chattered excitedly about notifications they had received about the last of the Leonid showers, which were apparently happening right now. They moved in a herd, stampeding towards the elevators. Finally, there was the promise of the lights, the very reason for this cruise.

She watched as the last trickle of passengers squeezed into the lift. She should join them really, should look for Tommy and make sure he'd heard the announcement. Instead, she remained at the computer terminal, bound to her chair by a force as invisible as the lights had been thus far.

Soon, silence descended. She was alone again.

–

Anna paced in her suite. In the corner of the room was a pile of incriminating items. The waxed jacket. The pink beret. Paula's mobile phone. Mark's keys and phone. The plastic sheeting and the spanner.

She surveyed them all, the pieces that could be used as evidence against her, then she moved to the door, slid it open and stepped out onto the balcony. This time she ignored the snowflakes that the wind spat at her. Leaning over the side, she glanced down, saw the merriment of some sort of party on the balcony below. A handful of people, music from an iPhone speaker. They huddled in their coats, arms and voices raised, glasses clinking as they stared upwards, waiting for the last of the light show.

No chance of throwing the stuff overboard. She looked back inside. She would dispose of it in Iceland. She would pack everything in her rucksack and take it off the ship. If First Officer Patrick Duane should come back, she would be ready for him and her suite would be clean.

She pushed her hair back and shuffled inside. Perhaps she should get off in Iceland, melt into the Reykjavík crowds and start anew in a different country. But then this trip would have been a total and utter waste of time and money, and she would lose the biggest prize of all.

Tommy and everything he owned.

With her foot she slid the door closed, and sank to the floor with her back to the glass.

Cornered.

The net was closing in on her, and she was trapped.

Chapter 19

Before

The days went on, though not like before.

Carl became an almost permanent fixture in the horrid little house that was my home.

I had thought I was protecting myself, my mother and my territory when I brandished that knife at him. I had thought I was taking back control when I locked my mother in her room and forced the withdrawal on her.

Instead, I'd simply managed to lose the battle.

Winter had arrived, and with it the first real snowstorm that I could remember since I was a child. Roads were cut off, just like our heating, and I started to arrive at school earlier each day just to get some warmth into my bones.

I was a week off my fifteenth birthday when I was called out of science class and summoned to the head-master's office. Inside was Miss Hayle, my English teacher, and the head, Mr Clayton.

'Sit down,' said Miss Hayle, and I did as she asked.

I thought back to the medical room that day when they had taken Rebecca Lavery from her home and given her a wonderful new life. She had never come back to our school, and I'd thought about her often since seeing her that night I'd gone out to buy my mother's heroin.

Wherever she was, it was not in the same place as me. I hated her and envied her in equal measure.

But now I felt a tremor of anticipation. Had my teachers realised what was happening in my home? Was it my turn to be saved?

Miss Hayle was talking now, but it was clear from her smile and the enthusiastic nodding along of Mr Clayton that they were not there to save me like they'd saved Rebecca.

I barely listened; focused instead on the old-fashioned radiator that kicked out more heat in this one room than I had in my entire house.

'So,' Miss Hayle prompted me, 'what do you think?'

I stared dumbly at them.

It was a trick of mine, a way to save my soul at home. To block out the noises that came from my mother's room when Carl was in there with her. I'd never done it at school before. School was my saving grace. Learning was my escape.

'I'm sorry?' I asked, stalling for time.

Miss Hayle giggled. A girlish sound, in keeping with her whole demeanour. I hated her happiness.

She clapped her hands together childishly. 'We want to put your name forward for the Kerry Grant. It's a scholarship, and the prize is entrance and full payment to study two subjects of your choice at Edinburgh University.'

My throat closed up. I held my bag in my lap and moved my fingers underneath it, my nails prodding at the scars on my inner thigh through my tights.

It hurt. The sting told me this was not a dream.

How did they know?

'How did you know?' I blurted.

Miss Hayle's smile faltered for a second. 'How did we know what?' she asked.

'That this is what I've dreamed of?'

Miss Hayle tittered; Mr Clayton's lined face creased in a smile. I lowered my head. My words were stupid. I had shown them what I was feeling, and that wasn't how life worked, and now they were laughing at me.

I raised my chin and set my shoulders back. 'I deserve this,' I said.

Miss Hayle looked at me, uncertainty on her face. 'Yes, we know. That's why we'd like to put your name forward, if that's okay?'

It wasn't a mistake or a trick. It was *real*.

'How do I do it?' I demanded.

They produced papers, leaflets and pamphlets and spread them out over the desk. They talked over each other then, and I looked from her to him and back again, and down at the literature on the desk.

Edinburgh.

It was as far away as I could ever get.

My face ached, and I wondered if I was crying. I swiped at my cheeks to brush away the tears, but they were dry, and belatedly I realised that the strange sensation I was feeling was a smile. I never smiled.

'Take this away, talk to your parents. We're happy to meet with them, discuss any concerns or questions—'

'That's okay, you don't need to do that,' I said quickly, the smile slipping away, my face back to its usual stern and serious expression.

'Well, we'll need to talk to them anyway. Part of the scholarship requirements are access to bank statements, combined income, et cetera, et cetera,' replied Miss Hayle as she shuffled the papers together.

Miss Hayle and Mr Clayton at my house. That couldn't – wouldn't – happen. If they saw where I was from, they would realise they had made a mistake; they would take this away from me.

I looked at her, this happy, smiling teacher in her lovely clean dress and spotless shoes. I imagined her walking through my house, picking her way carefully, making sure not to stand on a stray needle or knock over one of the overflowing ashtrays.

I shuddered and glanced at the top leaflet on the pile she pushed towards me across the desk.

A glossy photograph of the university. The grey brick-work, the tall windows, the proud turret in the back-ground standing sentry over the students who passed through this coveted place. If these people saw where I came from, the scholarship would be taken away before I even won it.

Clipped to the brochure was another piece of paper. I glanced at it and my blood ran cold as I saw two names hand-written there. One of them was mine. The other was Rebecca Lavery.

'How many people get a scholarship?' I asked, my voice rushed. 'How many places are there?'

Miss Hayle's smile slipped just a little as she saw what I was looking at. Deftly she reached across the desk and snatched up the list that had broken my heart.

'Just one,' she said, the brightness back in her tone, but it was falsely jovial. 'So you need to continue working extra hard, up your game.'

'But she doesn't need it, she has so much money now. She doesn't even go to school here any more!' I blurted.

Her smile settled into one of understanding and sympathy. Neither emotion was of any help. I thought fast, and spoke before I lost my nerve.

'I have to go along Billingham Road to get home. I see her there.' I paused, and then added for effect, 'I see her there *all the time*.'

Miss Hayle, for all her niceness, knew what went on in Billingham Road. And she knew what I was telling her.

The smile slipped, properly this time, and she paled beneath her make-up.

'Right,' she said. 'I see.'

–

It was a lie, but not an awful one, I told myself as I went home. I *had* seen Rebecca. Not in the way I had insinuated, not buying or selling on Billingham Road, but I had seen her near there. That dress she had worn, the expensive restaurant I was sure she had been in… My fists curled. She didn't need this scholarship. *I did.*

But even if my lie had been enough to remove her name from the list, my battle wasn't over.

–

'Mum, I need to talk to you,' I said.

She was in the kitchen; a good sign. She wasn't dressed, but then I hadn't seen her wearing proper clothes in months, years even.

I studied her from the doorway, allowed my eyes to take in the home from a stranger's perspective. It was kind of clean, I made sure of that. I'd seen from where Rebecca came from that if you didn't clean your house, the aromas of filth transferred to your clothes and became common knowledge.

No, that wasn't the problem. Even though it was old-fashioned and tatty in decor, and freezing cold, the house itself wasn't an issue.

It was *her*. I narrowed my eyes, knowing that if these people were to come calling, the odds on catching her like this, a relatively good day, were not in my favour. And it was Carl who was to blame for that.

'Where's Carl?' I asked.

She turned around and I flinched at her face. Her skin was grey, her hair greasy and lank. Her chest, visible through the open neck of her house coat, was mottled with tiny scars. I knew those scars. When she took the brown stuff, she complained more and more of things in her skin, and she scratched and tore at her chest until it turned raw and bled.

She would need to wear a button-up shirt, or a polo neck, I realised.

'He's gone to get me some stuff,' she said.

Stuff, I knew, meant brown, and fags and booze.

'He'll be back soon,' she said.

I backed out of the kitchen and retreated to my bedroom to think.

–

Later, I moved around their still bodies as I searched the cabinets and piles of papers for bank statements and giro cheques. Our income was to be scrutinised, and it was non-existent. The money that came in was from the dole, and the money for the rent went out to the council.

I found a pile of statements, most of them unopened, and I took them out of the envelopes and smoothed the

213

creases away. She was overdrawn, I noticed. I looked at the benefits that went in and the rent that was deducted, and frowned. The rent was a bit less than the amount she got from the government. There was enough of a difference to allow for other essential items like food and heating.

I looked across the room at her, deep in slumber. The brown cost money, I knew that, but I also knew she hadn't been anywhere in a long time to withdraw money to buy it. I had assumed Carl was giving it to her for free, or in return for what she used to do with other men to earn some cash.

Those men never came here any longer.

A red-hot poker of anger stabbed at me. Carl was taking her money. The money that should be buying us stuff to eat, and gas and electricity. As if to prove a point, the single light in the lounge dimmed and went out.

I went to the cupboard underneath the stairs and pressed the button on the electricity meter. It blinked at me – zero. They no longer gave our home emergency credit; we'd used up that favour a long time ago.

Back in the living room, I picked up Carl's wallet from the coffee table. I looked at him as he lolled on the sofa, one arm thrown behind his head. A bubble of spit floated on his lips as he slept.

I took his wallet to the kitchen, and by the light of a torch I emptied it of its contents.

Business cards, credit cards, scrawled paper with phone numbers, a list of names with figures beside them. People who owed him money, I reckoned, and with a snarl – emotion that I rarely showed – I ripped it up and pushed the bits of paper down the plughole in the sink. A single bank card remained. I pulled it out, saw my mother's initials and surname embossed at the bottom.

I shoved the card in my pocket and was about to put everything back when I saw there was something else in the wallet. Behind a clear flap, there was a photo. I brought it closer to the torch and inspected it, realising with a jolt that it was my mother. It was years old; she was young and fresh-faced and happy, a dimple in her left cheek as she smiled for the camera. A dimple I never even knew she had.

Behind it was another photo, this one folded, and I plucked it out and opened it up. I heard a whoosh of noise, a thin breath — more of an exhalation really — and spun around to see who it was, dropping the photo so it landed face down on the floor. I clapped my hand over my mouth. The noise had come from me. In the living room, the two of them slept soundly on.

I knelt down, picked up the picture between my thumb and forefinger. It was a photo of me. It was also old; in it, I must have been around seven or eight. I recognised my bed, the pink flowery duvet cover that I still had now. I recognised the nightie that I used to wear, white with a yellow lace trim. I was sleeping, just as deeply as they were now next door. My nightie was pulled up to my neck, exposing parts of me that were never meant to be photographed at that age.

I had no knowledge, no memory of that picture being taken.

On the kitchen floor, I wept. Hot tears coursed down my face as sadness swirled inside for the little girl in the photo. I turned the torch off and went to bed, pushing my chair under the door handle so it couldn't be opened from the outside.

—

'You got something of mine, missy?'

It was days later, and the appointment for my teacher to call on us was imminent. I was surveying the kitchen with an exacting scrutiny. Every plate had been cleared away, every cup and spoon had been cleaned and scrubbed free of stains. It had been hard work; cold water didn't wash as well as hot, but we had none of that, so good old-fashioned elbow grease had done the job.

Carl was hovering, his eyes beady and black in his face.

'Like what?' I asked.

'My wallet,' he said.

He was holding it and I gestured to it. '*That's* your wallet.'

He slapped it down on the counter. 'Things are missing from it.'

I said nothing, though I wanted to scream at him that the things that were missing were not his. He came close to me. I backed up until I hit the wall. No way out, nowhere to go. I was trapped.

'I'm watching you,' he said.

It was nothing new; he was always watching me. I looked through to the dining room at my mother. She sat at the table, her back curved as she slumped in the chair. Her finger had found a hole in the tablecloth and she poked at it, stretching it and pulling at it until there was a gaping rip in the fabric.

At the supermarket there had been a cash machine. I'd inserted the card and typed in the PIN. I got it right first time: my mother's birthday. Not mine, because she never remembered it.

I tried to withdraw fifty pounds, then twenty, and finally ten when it was declined. The card was spat out and no money followed.

I'd put the card away. I would have to wait until the benefits went in, and slowly the account would crawl out of the red. In the meantime, I would have to fill up on free school dinners. As for heating, I would simply wear more layers at home.

In my pocket, I felt the edges of the photograph of myself and wondered what I could do about Carl. It was clear, that morning in the kitchen, that I could do nothing. He was a permanent fixture. If I tried to get rid of him, those two men might come round again. Them, or different ones. There were many of them, I was sure. If I told the authorities, it wouldn't matter. Carl was a charmer, able to talk his way out of any situation.

Edinburgh.

It had become my mantra. It was my escape, my salvation, my future.

I just had to hold on a little bit longer.

—

I didn't listen to what Miss Hayle said to my mother. Instead, I kept my eyes on Mum. She looked okay, I thought. I'd washed her and helped her to dress in a high-necked blouse and an old pair of black trousers. I pinned her hair up and patted powder on her face with a little bit of blusher.

She didn't look great, but she looked like some of the other mothers I'd seen at the school gates.

'Don't open your mouth too wide when Miss Hayle is here,' I said as I caught a glimpse of her brown teeth, whittled down far more than they should have been by her incessant jaw-clenching.

'Okay, baby,' she'd said, obediently.

I looked into her eyes as I rearranged her fringe. Deep pools of baby blue. She had beautiful eyes, I realised, if you ignored the redness in the whites of them.

I will never become you.

I brushed off her gratitude and thought of where I would be when I was her age. I would have a beautiful home, with a kind husband; there would be money for heating and lovely clothes, and hot water would come out of the tap, and I wouldn't have to read books by torchlight.

She was forty, my mother. It was too late for her, but not for me.

Miss Hayle talked on, showing Mum the same leaflets she had shown me. Every so often she looked up and around the room, and I wondered what it was like to see my home through a stranger's eyes.

Everything bad was hidden. The burn mark on the windowsill from one of their cigarettes had been covered up with Tippex that I'd stolen from school. The hole in the tablecloth was concealed by a lamp I'd placed strategic- ally over it. The lamp didn't work because the electricity meter was empty, but it did the trick.

How easy it was to hide the rot, I marvelled, my mother especially. She looked decent, clean, *normal*. If you scratched at the surface, though, it was all so different. The scars on her chest, the sense of absence in her eyes when you looked a little too closely.

'You can keep those,' I said as Miss Hayle picked up the bank statements and benefits letters that I'd found.

She looked at them briefly, the only sign that she was shocked a slight widening of her eyes as she glanced at me. I kept my gaze locked on hers. *Yes, see, miss, I need this scholarship.*

She left soon after, and I sagged with relief as I showed her to the door. She said goodbye, and I sucked in a big breath and put my hand on her arm.

'Miss,' I said, 'is... is anyone else on the scholarship list?'

Her lips pressed together in a straight line. That everready smile slipped again, and she put her hand on mine and patted my fingers.

'No, dear. There's nobody else applying for the scholarship.'

I tried to hide the joy in my sharp inhalation. Miss Hayle had kicked Rebecca off the list! Something fluttered inside me. Guilt? Or a sense of accomplishment? I couldn't decide, and I flicked the emotion away.

I deserved this. I *needed* this.

I dropped my guard; I was smiling as I let Miss Hayle out. Then Carl's dirty old van pulled up.

'I'll see you later, Miss Hayle,' I said hurriedly, practically pushing her down the path.

Too late, too slow. Carl was there, grinning, showing his gaping black hole of a heroin-ruined mouth.

'She's a good girl, isn't she?' he leered, putting his arm around my shoulder. I fought against the urge to squirm away, felt my face hot and red, out of keeping with the winter air.

'This is my mother's friend,' I rasped, my voice disintegrating at Carl's touch. 'He doesn't live here, though.'

It was a lie – he was here more than he wasn't – but I knew we'd had to provide household income for the scholarship. I glanced at him as I shrugged him off me. Not that it mattered; his bank statements were probably in worse shape than my mother's.

'Can't believe you're taking her away from us.' Carl shook his head sadly. 'Don't know what her mother and me will do without her.'

'Miss Hayle was just leaving,' I said desperately.

'Ok-aaay.' She nodded, put her hand out to shake Carl's.

I inserted myself between them and led her to her car.

'Thank you,' I said. My voice shook, was still hoarse.

She smiled over my shoulder. 'You've got a nice family,' she said as she got into her car.

I watched as she drove away and thought about her words. *You've got a nice family*.

It really was easy to hide the rot.

Chapter 20

Alone at the bank of computers, Paula read the article again, slowly this time. It didn't help; phrases and words jumped out at her – *bruises on his face... fingerprint marks... airways blocked* – and with every paragraph, she found her eyes wandering back to the photo.

She zoomed in, but it only served to make the image blurrier. She zoomed out again, looked at it in its normal composition. The woman the police were hunting was Anna, she was sure of it. That beret, the tailored coat, the stance of the figure in the picture. Caution pricked at her: these were not unusual items, the clothing was not enough to pin it on her.

The hat might have hidden her hair, but it was likely to be short, just like Anna's was. If the woman in the picture had long hair, surely there would be some strands hanging down, unless she'd pushed her full head of hair underneath the beret?

There was something else, something confusing. A kind of recognition or knowledge of this woman. Not that it was Anna, but someone else, someone or something that tugged at Paula's memories.

Her mind went blank and she frowned as she clicked off the website. She checked her watch and saw that it was late. The lounge had been deserted since the sudden flurry of people racing for the deck. She shivered at the knowledge that she was totally alone down there.

Grabbing her key card, she hurried back towards the stairs.

-

It was after midnight, and Anna hauled herself to her feet and dressed. She felt like a sitting duck here, a criminal just waiting for the officer to come and arrest her.

In a few hours they would dock in Reykjavík. Was that what they were waiting for: for the passengers to disembark so there wouldn't be a scene on the luxury liner when they handcuffed her?

She pulled her padded winter coat out of the wardrobe and slipped it on. Gloves, hat – not the pink beret, but a black knitted one – and carefully opened the door. The corridor was silent, the main lights out; just the soft white glow of the bulbs lined the hallway. As she strode towards the elevator, she heard the distinctive noise that signalled its arrival.

She flattened herself against the wall, looked left, right. Nowhere to go, nowhere to hide. Was it First Officer Patrick Duane, coming back for her, armed with evidence of her crime?

She pushed herself off the wall and stood straight as the elevator doors swished open and a man strolled out.

Tommy.

She smiled with relief. He looked at her, and his face lit up.

'Hi,' she said cautiously, in case Paula was in the lift.

'Anna, where are you going at this time of night?' he said.

He was slurring a little, but not too much. Just drunk enough, she thought.

'Thought I'd take a walk, see if the Northern Lights are on display,' she replied. 'Unless you want to join me for a drink in my suite?'

His eyes darted to the closed door of the Expedition Suite, and she caught his thought. Paula was in there, sleeping or, more likely, unable to sleep, waiting for the return of her wandering husband.

'Shall we go up on deck?' she said softly.

He nodded, reached back and pressed the button for the lift. A scratching noise came from one of the nearby rooms. The sound of a safety chain being released.

Anna slipped past Tommy, brushing his side as she walked smartly into the lift. With one last glance down the hallway, he followed her inside.

He was all over her as soon as the lift doors closed. Hands grabbing roughly at her shoulders, hips and waist. He was drunker than she'd thought, she acknowledged, as he shoved her hard against the mirrored wall.

She caught sight of her reflection, her cheeks flushed, hat askance, and she seemed so small in comparison to his big frame. She liked that, the sensation of being tiny, helpless, in need of a man like Tommy. It wasn't true, she'd never needed protecting in the physical sense, but it felt good to fool him.

The elevator juddered to a halt. Tommy pulled away from her, stabbed at the buttons, no doubt to keep the lift where it was so he could carry on pawing at her. But the doors opened, and Anna ducked under his arm and out onto the deck.

He stared at her, confused, before staggering out to join her.

She walked the length of the ship in the freezing night air, a few feet ahead of him, glancing back every so often to see if he was still following her. She paused, looking up, as a streak of white light raced across the sky, arcing over her head. A trail from the Leonids. As the shooting star blazed and faded where the sky met the sea, she recalled the notification that had pinged through on the app tonight. Behind her, Tommy's heavy tread sounded, announcing his approach, and she turned to watch him.

The bitter air seemed to sober him rapidly, leaving him blinking at her, his hand scratching his face as if he couldn't understand how he had come to be out here.

'I think you're really something,' he said, catching her up. He stood a few feet away, no longer buoyed by the shield of booze. He didn't look cautious, or shy. He looked like he had done this dozens of times before.

Like a fish, he was hooked. She grinned and shimmied her way over to him. She had to play it carefully now; she mustn't just hand it all over so he was sated. He needed to be left wanting more; he had to desire her in a way that was more than just a quick fumble.

She lowered her face coyly, buying time as she considered her next steps. They would get off the ship tomorrow in Iceland, and she still had things to think about apart from Tommy. Paula for one, and Patrick Duane, the officer who had questioned her about Mark.

Remembering the officer and his attitude towards her, she turned to the rail and climbed up, leaning over, scanning the ship for any sign of CCTV cameras. Because if Patrick came at her, that would be all he had apart from his suspicions, and if there was no security on the external parts of the ship, she was free and clear.

'You need to be careful,' said Tommy, alarmed.

His arms circled her upper body and with ease he plucked her off the railing and set her down.

'I'm just enjoying the view,' she said calmly, but her insides churned with anger at his macho heroics.

Then, behind him, it happened. The sky on the horizon changed, a gradual lightening above. It was like a sunrise, but the wrong colour. It burned emerald green, a glow that shimmered in the far distance, seemingly alive as it stretched upwards and outwards. It was growing, she saw, and even before it had really begun, she knew it was going to be a spectacular show.

She gripped Tommy's arm, pushing at him so he turned around. His breath caught in his throat as steadily the Northern Lights crawled towards them. Graphite and slate now, with piercing vibrations of fuchsia, and the whole thing suddenly pulsated, shooting across the previously black night sky.

In spite of the promise of the lights, that wasn't why Anna had come on this cruise. This was a business trip, another episode in a long line of getting to where she needed to be. But at the moment when the lights burst across the atmosphere, everything she had fought and killed for fell away. Beneath her coat, in between her thin ribs, she felt her heart hammering in her chest. It was awe but mixed with fear, she acknowledged. Because this show was out of this world, and just like in the elevator with Tommy, she was suddenly tiny and insignificant.

'Oh yes,' Tommy hissed the words from between clenched teeth. 'Yesss!'

She wanted to tell him to shut up, not to spoil it with speech, but as she glanced at him, something else overwhelmed her. He was like a child, she realised, and it didn't annoy or irritate her as she'd thought. It was actually quite endearing.

Another unfamiliar emotion.

She breathed in deeply, flicking her head from left to right and upwards, over to the horizon, determined to see it all, not to miss a single moment.

The door opened, and there were footsteps and excited chatter as more passengers flooded out. One of them could be Paula. It was a half-thought, not important, and a glance at Tommy's face told her he felt the same.

The guests streamed past them, exclamations of delight in their wake. Anna tilted her head back and stared and stared. She closed her eyes for a moment, and in the darkness she was delighted to find that the Northern Lights were imprinted inside her lids.

A hand brushed hers: Tommy. She let him take her fingers in his own, and tuned out everyone else on the deck. As they stood together, the freezing cold was no longer a factor. She was warm, she realised, inside and out, and everything else slipped away: the officer who was suspicious of her; Mark, for whom his colleagues were still searching; her photo in the paper, wanted in connection with William's death. And Paula. For however long this went on, none of it mattered.

She smiled.

As though the lights were a message just for her, she suddenly knew exactly how she was going to handle Paula.

-

Paula's plan had been to sit up and wait for Tommy to return. Regardless of what he had or hadn't done with Anna, she always felt safe with him. And knowing, or suspecting, that there was a killer next door was something that filled her with fear and dread.

She needed him here, in the suite, even if he wasn't speaking to her. Just the bulk of him would do. And she didn't want to go looking for him. He would return to the room when he was done drinking with his buddies.

Still in her coat and boots, she sat primly on the chair by the window. To pass the time, she pulled back the curtain and looked at the stars. It was a clear night, and maybe the Northern Lights would put in an appearance.

Letting the curtain fall, she rested her head against the back of the chair, allowed herself to close her eyes. Just for a minute, because she needed to stay alert, on guard...

–

The click of the door awoke her, sounding like a gunshot in the silence of the cruise ship. Gasping, she sat up straight, spinning around in her chair, her eyes seeking something, anything to use against the intruder. She snatched up the fruit bowl and raised it above her head as she pushed herself to a standing position to see...

Tommy.

He had his back to her as he held onto the door and removed his boots one by one. She put the fruit bowl back on the table before he could see it.

'You're awake,' he said as he turned around and took off his coat. 'Did you see them?'

She glanced at her watch and saw that it was almost five a.m. 'Did I see who?' she asked.

He grinned, and it took her aback. The years seemed to have fallen away from him; she hadn't seen him looking this way for a long time.

'The Northern Lights!' he exclaimed. He moved fast, covering the suite in a few strides, and threw back the curtains.

She stepped up beside him and peered out. The sky was dark, but the stars were bright. No lights.

'I didn't see them,' she said. She felt oddly disappointed.

'Oh, Paula, they were amazing,' he breathed. 'The colours... they started on the horizon, and then they were everywhere. They filled the whole sky.'

She sat back down in the chair. 'Who were you out there with?'

He was facing away from her, still gazing outside as though the lights were going to appear again at any minute. His back stiffened. 'The lads,' he said. 'Dermot and Angus and a few of the others were there.'

He threw her a look, and she saw she had ruined his high. She hadn't even mentioned Anna's name, but he knew that was what she was really asking him.

He went back across the suite and stooped to pick up his coat from the floor. Paula's breathing quickened. He had just got back, he couldn't leave her again. Not alone, not in this suite, not with *her* next door.

'Where are you going?' she asked, and then, in case he thought she was nagging, 'Can I come with you?'

He shrugged, and she took this as a yes as she pulled on her boots and grabbed her jacket from the peg. He was still in a mood, she saw, and he had been intending on going wherever he was headed alone. To see *her*?

She shivered, in spite of the warmth of the cabin, and followed him to the door.

Soon they would be in Iceland.

Soon she would have some sort of idea on how to go about reporting her suspicions about Anna to someone in authority.

And the sooner Anna was taken away, the sooner she would have Tommy back where he belonged. Until then, she would stick by his side.

Chapter 21

They walked around the upper deck twice, Tommy forging ahead, Paula a good two steps behind. In her haste to follow her husband, she had forgotten her gloves, and she shoved her hands deep in her pockets.

'No sign of the storm yet,' she called to him once the silence had gone on for too long.

Tommy stopped at the bow of the ship and leaned on the railing. She caught up with him and watched as he scanned the skies, his eyes glittering dark in the moonlight.

'It's coming,' he said.

She laughed and moved up to stand beside him. 'Can you smell it?' she asked.

He looked up and breathed in deeply. With an exaggerated glance at her, he nodded. 'I think I can.' Then he laughed too, and it was like a light being flipped. His mood had turned. She leaned into him and hooked her arm through his.

'What shall we do when we dock?' she asked as they began to walk again.

He looked down at her. 'What do you want to do?'

'I don't know, what are the options?'

She half listened as he reeled off the various excursions, and what Dermot and Angus had suggested, with them having been here before.

She knew how it would go anyway. This was how they worked. He appeared to offer her some suggestions; she knew well enough that the first things he mentioned were what *he* was keen to do. Then, when asked for her opinion, she would obediently go with what he wanted.

She slowed her step as she thought about it, this habit of their marriage. Julie's words spun in her head: *Don't lose yourself.* But she wasn't, was she? Surely she was just putting her husband first, like a good wife should?

But when do you get to be put first?

The thought popped into her head, unbidden. Uncomfortably, she pushed it away. She fixed a smile on her face as Tommy talked on. She should be happy; she should be relieved.

Her husband was back.

And all that with Anna, what she had seen in the casino… Anna was a slut, and Tommy had been drunk, but after this holiday was over, they would never have to see the wretched woman again. All Paula had to do was keep a close eye on Tommy, make sure she stayed close to him so he wouldn't be tempted. After all, he was only human.

But what about the other stuff? The old man who had died? No, not died – been killed! And the photo that looked so very much like Anna?

But the same thought came back to her: that after this trip they would never have to clap eyes on her again.

She nodded to herself and pulled Tommy closer.

'Shall we get some breakfast?' she said.

–

In her cabin, Anna pulled Mark's phone out of her bag and switched it on. The battery was still half full, and on

231

the locked screen a zigzagging pattern was visible, a greasy fingerprint track. She followed it with her own finger, allowing herself a smile as the phone unlocked.

Sipping at a glass of water, she scrolled through his texts. There was a string of them between himself and Patrick; the officer was in Mark's address book as Pat D. There was nothing friendly or sociable, she noted, just work instructions, rotas, destinations and times of departure.

She read through his previous messages, studying the tone he used, abbreviations – numbers used as words, which she personally hated – and when she was sure she had the inflection right, she typed out a text to Patrick.

> So sorry for leaving you in the lurch, i had 2 leave the ship 4 personal reasons. Sorry again, Pat, will call when i can.

She read through it and pressed the send key before she could change her mind. She was about to switch the phone off and put it away when she had another thought.

She put her own name in his phone and typed out another text.

> Annie thank u for being a gr8 friend. Cant go home yet but will text soon x

She sent it through, waiting until her own phone beeped before turning his off and pushing it deep into the bottom of her bag. When she got off the ship in Iceland, she would dump the phone, along with everything else incriminating. It would all be gone, buried in the snow, and none of it could ever be traced back to her.

Feeling better, she stood up and went in search of First Officer Patrick Duane.

—

She moved through the restaurant, recoiling at the stench of the buffet. The grease, the bacon, the eggs… it was like being back at William's house. In contrast to her disgust, her stomach growled noisily, betraying her.

Across the room she saw him, Tommy, alone with just a mug of coffee for company. She slowed down, smiling now, and considered diverting over to him.

Last night, or rather in the early hours of this morning, when the light show had finished, they had waited until the crowds had drifted away from the upper deck before parting ways.

'See you tomorrow?' he had asked hopefully, looking boyish and love-struck.

She had softened her eyes as she gazed at him, fully in character, and nodded.

Well, now it was tomorrow, and he was clearly alone. She thought of Paula in her suite, no doubt bouncing from teary and emotional to furious and hurt.

She took a step forward. Behind her, someone swished past. A murmured 'excuse me', and obediently, on reflex, Anna stepped out of the way. A waft of fried food trailed in the person's wake, and she breathed in sharply as the woman wove through the tables towards Tommy.

Paula.

She watched as Paula put a plate down in front of Tommy. He grinned up at his wife; in response, she plucked a piece of bacon from his plate. He snatched it back, laughing now, and she gave up the mock fight, sitting down next to him, so close their sides were touching.

What the fuck?! Anna knew her eyes were blazing, her stance stiff like ice.

She turned and fled before they could look up and see her, knowing that the ferocity showed in her face, her nails biting the skin of her palms as she hurried as fast as she could away from the restaurant.

–

'Officer... Patrick!'

She spotted him on the bottom deck, tall and authoritative in his heavy woollen coat, the gold insignia on his sleeve gleaming in the weak sunshine. He stooped slightly in order to hear what the passengers he was chatting to were saying.

The wind had picked up, she noted; the promised storm was coming. And Patrick hadn't heard her as he bade goodbye to the couple and walked on.

'Patrick!' She broke into a run, her breathing laboured as she charged on down the deck.

He'd heard her now, she knew that from the single moment of hesitation in his stride, but he kept on going anyway. She swore quietly, a stream of profanities, before realising it was making it even more difficult to run. She clamped her mouth closed, put her head down and thundered after him.

'Patrick.' She caught at his sleeve, panting, sweat running freely down her face, despite the harsh wind that whipped up around them.

He looked down at her, eyes penetrating, and she shivered. This man was so very different to all the others she had encountered. William, Tommy, Mark; a hint of bare flesh and a promise of what was to come and they were putty in her hands. Not this one. Not First Officer Patrick Duane.

'I–I got a text,' she wheezed, pulling her phone out of her pocket and waving it at him. 'I got a text from Mark.'

He regarded her steadily, much like he had in her cabin the other night. But then his eyes had been distrustful, knowing, triumphant. Now, they seemed resigned.

'Ah, Mark. Yes, I also got a text from him.'

She had ripped off a glove, holding it in her teeth as she stabbed at the phone buttons to bring up Mark's text message. At Patrick's words, she paused and looked up at him.

'Did you? What did he say to you?'

He jerked his head towards her phone, a silent instruction to show him the text. She obeyed, holding it up for him to see.

He read it once and nodded. 'I suppose I'll have to wait until he deigns to tell me when he's coming back to work,' he said.

Anna shrugged and kept her eyes on his. 'I'm sorry for any misunderstanding,' she said.

He didn't press her to elaborate, and for that, she was thankful. He had thought she was lying, back there in the Arctic Suite, and he had tricked her with a false name for Mark's wife. But now it seemed Mark had made contact, and Patrick seemed more irritated that he was a crew member short.

His exasperation had overridden his scepticism.

235

Anna smiled and lifted her hand in a wave as she walked slowly back the way she had come.

—

'It's barely even light yet,' said Paula as she stared out of the floor-to-ceiling window in the restaurant. She turned to Tommy. 'What time is it?'

He glanced at his watch. 'Nearly nine.'

She faced the window again. Outside, the waves crashed against the hull of the boat and spat up a spray of frothy white water. Beyond the glass, the sky was a strange greyish brown. Daytime had arrived, the frights of the night were gone, but here in this bizarre land it still seemed like twilight.

'They don't get many hours of daylight here, not at this time of year,' said Tommy as he edged his chair around to follow her gaze.

The tannoy played its familiar soothing tune, and Paula sat up straight.

'Not long now, fellow travellers, and we'll be docking in Skarfabakki. From here, you will have the day to explore whatever takes your fancy: the famous Blue Lagoon with its thermal pools; or if you're interested in Iceland's Viking roots, you can visit the National Museum or the Settlement Exhibition. If you are attracted by the epic nature and landscape that this magical land has to offer, why not try a day trip to the mighty Gullfoss waterfall, or the geothermal scenery near the Reykjanes Peninsula?

'Daylight fades quickly here, so please make sure you are back at the ship and on board on time. You know the rule: if you're late, the ship won't wait!'

The captain's cheery tones belied his warning, thought Paula. A heavy click that resounded around the ship signalled that his announcement was over. Beneath them, the *Ruby Spirit* juddered and whirred. Tommy stood up and moved across to the window.

'We're docking!' he cried.

Paula abandoned her coffee and went over to join him. Despite the gloom, her heart lifted. Tommy was right: she could see boats and buildings and cranes, and beyond them, lush green grass that poked up through a thin covering of snow.

'Thank goodness,' she murmured.

As they moved slowly closer to civilisation, she put a hand to her chest. She hadn't realised just how much she'd been suffering from cabin fever until she'd laid eyes on the land outside.

She touched Tommy's shoulder. 'How long until we can get off?'

He tilted his head towards her, one eyebrow raised. 'Someone's eager.'

She nodded. The ship was claustrophobic, stifling, and she wanted nothing more than to be outside, where she could just walk and walk, and not end up on the same deck or in the same room she'd spent the last few days in.

'Shouldn't be long now; look, the tugs are coming.'

She followed his finger to the tiny boats coming towards them in a V shape, six of them in all. They fanned out at the bow of the ship before vanishing from view.

'What are they for?' she asked. Surely the passengers weren't expected to disembark onto those fragile-looking vessels?

'They pull the ship in, guide it to the dock.' He looked down at her and let out a laugh, long and loud. 'Didn't you know that?'

She shook her head, allowing him to lead her across the restaurant towards the elevator. He was still chuckling at her naivety when they reached it. She took a deep breath. Things really were back to normal between them.

–

Apparently she wasn't the only one eager to disembark. In the lobby near the boarding doors, people stood in clusters. There was a hum of excited chatter and the rustle of maps, while phones lit up with routes and tour websites.

'Where are we going to go?' Paula raised her voice to be heard above the dozens of other conversations.

Tommy showed her his own phone: a photo of a lake with people in it, steam rising off the water.

'It's a thermal lake, naturally heated seawater.'

'I haven't got my swimming costume,' she said.

He huffed out a sigh. 'You knew I wanted to go and see the lakes,' he said. 'Hurry up and get it.'

'Sorry,' she said as she reached for the lanyard around her neck that held her key card. 'I'll be really quick.'

She ducked out of the crowd of people into the corridor just as the lift doors opened and another trickle of passengers came out. She drew in a sharp breath when Anna emerged.

But Anna hadn't seen her, and Paula turned her head away. To her left was a restroom, and on a whim, she pushed open the door and slipped inside, unwilling – *unable* – to walk past the woman and have to make eye contact with her. It had a porthole window, and she put her face up to it. The elevator crowd swept past, Anna among them. The hallway was narrow, and their bodies pressed against the toilet door as they crammed their way through to the large waiting area.

She might have missed it, but in the silence of the restroom there came a very definitive click. She gasped in fury, knowing instantly what had happened and who had done it. The times before, in the sauna, in her suite, she had been frightened. Anger was a welcome change.

She gripped the handle and pushed, knowing the door wouldn't budge, swearing anyway when she was proved right. She stood on tiptoes again, peering out of the porthole. Anna's blonde head bobbed through the throng of people, marking a trajectory towards… Tommy?

'Oh no, you don't,' hissed Paula. 'Not this time.'

She kicked the door, beat her hands against the glass. Toughened glass, she realised, and the noise of excited chatter in the waiting area drowned out her cries and the sound of her fists. All eyes were fixed on the doors that led out to Iceland. Nobody was even looking in her direction.

She knew what would happen: Anna would tag on to Tommy's group, they would leave without her, and she would miss out, stuck, imprisoned *again*. How had it even happened? One minute Anna had been exiting the elevator and Paula had ducked into the loo, certain that the other woman hadn't even seen her. But she clearly had. Anna had it in for her, was ready at every single opportunity. But why?

Tommy's fan club.

Paula stopped hammering on the door for a moment and narrowed her eyes. It had happened before. If she were honest, it happened all the time. Silly, pretty things, pound signs in their eyes as they looked at the self-made success in front of them. But usually a reminder that he was a married man was enough. A possessive hand on his arm, a glance that she had perfected did the trick.

But not in this case.

She returned her attention to the porthole. Down the hall, the elevator door was opening again, a fresh wave of day-trippers emerging. She waited until they drew level with the toilet door, then she curled her hands into fists and banged as hard as she could.

A middle-aged woman in the crowd jerked her head towards the door. Paula's heart leapt.

'I'm stuck!' she shouted, pointing to the handle. 'I'm locked in!'

The woman glanced over her shoulder, as if to check whether Paula was talking to someone else.

Paula slapped her hand on the glass. 'Help!' she mouthed.

Realisation dawned in the woman's eyes and she held up a hand in a 'wait' gesture. Paula pressed her face to the porthole, tracking her movements as she pushed her way to the front of the elevator group.

'*Yes,*' she whispered, as the woman located a staff member, talking to him and pointing back in the direction of the restroom.

The man followed her over, and selected a key from a bunch on his belt. He inserted it in a lock that was too low for Paula to see, and immediately the door sprang open.

Paula fell out into the hallway, profusely thanking both the stranger and the staff member. Then she darted off through the crowd, looking back only once. The woman had moved on; the man was holding the toilet door open now, peering at the lock, testing the handle.

She reached Tommy and opened her mouth to tell him her latest horror story.

'Did you get your swimming costume?' he asked.

Her swimming costume. That was where she'd been headed. She glanced around, trying to remain inconspicuous. There she was: Anna, moving towards the doors.

Fear shot through Paula at the sight of her, all the anger of moments ago gone. Terror, real and raw, at the thought of what this tiny woman was capable of. She blinked, and in her mind's eye she saw the body of the man Anna had been paid to care for, and the bruises on his face.

'You know what, I'm fine staying on dry land,' she said.

Tommy glanced at her. 'Well, I'm going in the water,' he replied.

'I'll watch.'

And watch she did, as Anna tracked a path across the lobby. She never had to say excuse me, Paula noticed, the crowds seeming to part for her.

As if sensing she was being scrutinised, Anna glanced over. Their eyes met, and Paula's heart thumped in her chest. Unconsciously, she edged closer to Tommy as the other woman's eyes burned into her own.

Anna smirked, hoisted her backpack off, and set it to rest on the floor.

Paula looked away.

'Mate, good to see you. Hi, Paula.' Angus, Tommy's pal, bounced up to them, Dermot hot on his heels.

Hands were shaken all round, and Paula tried to focus on the men's conversation.

'Did you see the lights last night?' Dermot asked.

Paula turned her attention to him. 'No, sadly I missed...' Her words trickled to a stop as she realised Dermot wasn't speaking to her, but to Tommy.

She blinked. Hadn't Tommy said he had watched the Northern Lights with Dermot and Angus?

'Yeah, I managed to catch them,' Tommy said weakly, his eyes sliding sideways, away from his wife.

A few feet away, Anna smiled serenely, showing small white teeth. Paula put her hand over her mouth at the same time as Tommy darted a look at her, a warning glance. His hand reached out, his eyes narrowed, a signal not to cause a scene, to let it go. At that moment, the doors swished open and the crowd surged. She jostled her arm free from his grip and let herself be taken, shoved and pushed towards the door. Tommy's face was flushed, his eyebrows knitted; his temper – no doubt at being caught out – was rising. Behind him, Anna had disappeared from Paula's view.

Paula turned around and let the mob sweep her out of the doors and down the walkway onto Icelandic soil.

Alone.

–

There was an expression in Paula's eyes that Anna hadn't known the other woman could pull off. If looks could kill…

She was tempted to laugh in Paula's face, to push her over the edge, but she held back. She couldn't be seen to be needling the woman, not if she wanted to get her hands on the final prize. Instead, she ducked down out of sight, pretending to fiddle with the zip on her backpack. When she stood up, she saw the back of Paula's head, a black hat in among all the others making their way off the cruise ship. Keeping enough people in between them, Anna put her own head down and blended into the middle of the crowd.

Tommy emerged minutes later, stationed in between Dermot and Angus. They were too far away for her to hear what he was saying, but she could give it a good guess. He gestured angrily with his hands, while his pals nodded sympathetically. He wasn't going after his wife, she noticed. Instead, the three men swung left and headed for the coaches that lined the dockside.

Without even glancing over his shoulder, Tommy climbed up into the first coach. Anna looked at the sign on the front: *Blue Lagoon Spa*. It was certainly the most popular option, she realised, as the majority of passengers followed suit.

Paula was still walking, moving with the serious hikers now, and Anna cocked her head in interest. She wasn't going to get on a coach then. Hanging back, Anna watched.

There were perhaps a dozen people near Paula. All were dressed in appropriate outerwear and sturdy hiking boots, most with crampons attached. Some even sported goggles and the majority of them had walking poles. They were grouped around a particular man, the trek leader, clearly, who waved his pole in the air, issuing instructions. Anna watched the spike at the end of the hiking stick; imagined felling Paula with a single blow and driving it through her neck.

The group began to move, the man in front and Paula – woefully unprepared Paula – bringing up the rear.

They were pros, Anna thought, smiling to herself. It wouldn't be long before Paula fell behind.

She shivered with anticipation.

Chapter 22

Before

'Are you cold?' my mother asked.

It was unlike her to enquire after my well-being. Ignoring her question, I wrapped my arms around myself in an attempt to stop the shivering. No, I wasn't cold. My tremors were of excitement, of anticipation.

Tomorrow I was going to Edinburgh.

The last couple of years had been far from easy. I had moved through my final school terms like I was swimming underwater. My body ached constantly with the effort, never having a chance to recover with sleep, because who had time to slumber, what with monitoring my mother's activities, keeping clear of Carl and his unwelcome advances, making the house as respectable as it could be with two addicts living in it and staying up to date with homework, coursework and exams…

It was all for the end game, the final prize. Edinburgh would lead to a career, and, later, a home that was always clean and neat as a pin, and maybe even a husband who was strong and handsome and able to provide for his family. The opposite of Carl, in other words. Sometimes I thought of Rebecca Lavery and the prize I had stolen from her. Each time I remembered what I had done, I was quick to reassure myself. She didn't need it. I had seen her

– the way she was dressed, the expensive aura she exuded. *She didn't need it.* It was my new mantra, to be repeated silently to myself until the guilt passed.

My case was packed. A single suitcase, reflecting eighteen years of living. Eighteen years of no friends, no family apart from my mother. No fun times or birthday parties or celebrations. No love, no tenderness.

I zipped up the case and glanced at my mother. She stood in the doorway to my bedroom, her thin frame supported by the wall she leaned against.

'Mum, do you want to come to Edinburgh with me?'

I tried to swallow back the words even as they were coming out of my mouth. I wondered why I had asked her that.

The answer was clear to me suddenly. If she stayed here with Carl, she would die.

'Nah,' she said. 'Carl likes it round here.'

I wasn't asking him, I thought. And there was a sense of hurt that shimmered inside me. Which was ridiculous in itself; she'd ceased to be able to hurt me many, many years ago.

I imagined it for a moment, taking her on the long train journey up north. It was seven hours, and she couldn't go half that time without taking a hit for her habit. And once we were there, what would happen then? Would she be out and about on the streets late at night, looking to score, seeking a replacement for Carl? I envisaged bumping into her late at night, leaving the bars and clubs that I would frequent in my new life as a normal eighteen-year-old. My friends would look on in horror, and I would be back at school all over again, shunned for being the person I really was.

No.

That *wasn't* the person I was. It was where I came from, and there was a big difference. I was shedding my old self and everything associated with it. That included my mother.

Downstairs, the front door slammed. I pulled my case off my bed and slid it underneath. Carl had said nothing about my leaving, and I didn't want to remind him that tonight would be my last night in this house. His heavy tread could be heard as he came up the stairs. I glanced at my mother, still leaning against the wall, swaying slightly, her eyes somewhere else entirely.

'My girls,' he said as he came into view.

With one hand he was unbuckling his belt, and now he tugged it free of the loops of his jeans. I sat with my hands primly in my lap, refusing to be intimidated by him, wondering what his actions were leading to.

He stopped in front of my mother, pulled a little foil package from his pocket.

Where she had been far away moments ago, she was suddenly eager, taking the belt from him and winding it around her scarred upper arm. He held the foil in his teeth as he plunged his hand into the front of her dressing gown. Roughly, he massaged her breasts and pushed himself against her. She paid no heed to his wandering hand, didn't seem to notice the knee that jerked and thrust against her crotch.

Eyes gleaming, moving as though they were one person, they stumbled out of my room.

–

I left in the middle of the night, even though my train wasn't due until seven a.m. I was frightened that when it came to morning and I tried to walk out of the door and into my future, I would be stopped. Carl might be an addict, but he was strong, and he would use that strength against me.

At one a.m., I held my little case close to me and slid out of the door. Pulling it gently closed behind me, I looked up at the house I'd lived in all my life.

Would this be the last time I was here?

I thought back to the little girl I once was, the girl who'd worked out at a young age that cutting herself was a sure-fire path to love and cuddles. That same girl who slept under a pink flowery duvet, oblivious to the man who pulled up her nightgown and photographed her body while she slept. I thought of the mother of that girl, who had never protected her from things she had seen too young, too early.

In the pitch-black of night-time, I promised myself that I would never return here.

–

At the station, I sat in the waiting room, surprised at the number of passengers who came and went in the middle of the night.

I didn't know much, I realised there in that cold, dank room. I knew very little of the world. The things I knew were unacceptable: the dosage of heroin and how pure it needed to be; the filler ingredients to look out for that would likely kill you. How to get blood and shit and vomit out of a carpet; how to dodge a man who seemed docile but could easily be violent and savage and sexually predatory.

My eyes were dry, but I was sad.

I picked myself up, like I always had. I didn't know nothing. I knew enough to get me into one of the top universities in the United Kingdom; I knew how to work my backside off while keeping a household running and a mother alive.

The 7:04 to Edinburgh rolled into the station. I raised my chin and tried to smile as I stepped onto the train that would take me to a new life.

–

I had a room in halls, sharing with two other girls. I forced myself to smile as they came in together, arms entwined, and threw me a friendly greeting.

My jaw hurt from the unnatural action. My muscles were rigid with tension, waiting for the attack. But none came; this wasn't school. These girls were older, *kinder*, here to get trashed for the next few years and have as much fun as they could.

I never went out with them, politely declining their offers to come and 'get wasted'. Instead, I took care of them when they returned in the early hours, vomiting after too much rum and Coke. In return for the care that I'd become accustomed to giving, they shared their food with me, and their clothes and shoes and make-up. It was a stunning way to live; being appreciated was a whole new world to me.

I got a job in the uni bar, and having my own money was another breathtaking experience. I didn't have to pay for heat or gas or electricity or water. I could buy food – and I didn't have to go to the supermarket near closing time to get the reduced stale bread or vegetables that were already on the turn. I could go to cafés and restaurants and eat freshly cooked hamburgers or melted cheese toasties.

My life and my body filled out to proportions I had never dared to dream of. I had spent so long living in a controlled environment that with no responsibilities, I went crazy. I wasn't accustomed to living this way, and it scared me as much as it thrilled me. I needed to claw back some control, starting with the way I looked.

I didn't have enough willpower to deny myself food, but I found how to purge it from my system. Soon enough, despite hating myself a little, I found a way to control one small area of my life.

For the first term, I kept mostly to myself. I observed this strange new world and the people who inhabited it: the goths with their dark clothes, studs and piercings; the artsy girls in their flowing bohemian dresses, the sexy, pouting students; the tomboys and the rockers. Back home, if you didn't have the right clothes or the newest brand of trainers, you were a loser. It didn't work that way at uni. Here, you could be anyone you wanted to be.

I looked at my own clothes, the jeans and unlabelled jerseys and jumpers, and thought about who *I* wanted to be. It wasn't a difficult decision. I wanted to be something that back home, could never, ever happen. I wanted to be sophisticated, classy and chic. A million miles away from the girl I actually was.

I scoured charity shops for cast-off clothes from the rich women of Edinburgh. I borrowed from my room-mates, who with their double-barrelled surnames never had to pretend. Time and time again I thought of Rebecca Lavery, the way she had escaped and rebranded herself into a poised, beautiful young woman. The way I had fought her – even without her knowledge – to take the place here that was rightfully mine. I remembered the way she walked, the way she wore her clothes, the glances she gave, the slightly snooty air. I put my mind to it; I became Rebecca.

I saw that the men here – well, they were boys, really – were nothing like those I had known in my life to date. I moved past my fear and I tried them all: the nerds, the bookish types, psychology students. On the plus side, they were attentive, kind and generous. But they were also inquisitive, nosy even. Where did I come from? What did my parents do? Could they meet my family?

I shuddered and gave them the cold shoulder. Why were my family so important? Why couldn't they just enjoy *me*? Would I ever be able to leave my past behind?

But then came the athletes. The ones who hung out in the bar I worked in, and who liked to talk about themselves rather than me. And there was one in particular.

He never asked about my past or my future. He told me all about his: the powerful father, the dutiful mother, the fact that he was adored above everything and anything. He talked about the future; he had it all mapped out. He was perfect.

And then one afternoon, the phone in my halls rang. There was one communal landline for the whole floor. I never answered it. I never got calls.

'It's for you.' Laurie, my roommate, put her head around the door. 'It's your dad.'

I didn't correct her assumption that I had a father. As I approached the phone, I felt like I was walking to my death. For a moment I thought about hanging up without speaking, but he would call again.

'Hello?'

I could hear him breathing, shallow whispers down the line.

'It's your mum,' he said. 'You need to come home.'

I clutched the receiver tightly and closed my eyes.

'Did you hear me? You need to come home.'

I breathed in and out slowly, in an effort to slow the build-up of panic in my chest.

'Okay,' I said.

I hung up the telephone and returned to my room to pack.

Chapter 23

Paula had no idea where she was headed when she found herself swept off the *Ruby Spirit*. All she knew was that she needed to get away from her husband and his lies. She knew him inside out, knew that he wouldn't come after her, that he would have enough confidence that she would be the one to give in, to return to him just as she always had in the past.

Things were changing, though, and she wasn't sure if it was him or them or just her.

She latched onto the outskirts of a small group of people from the ship. They smiled at her as they organised themselves, and she saw they were heading out for a walk.

Fine, she thought. *I'll walk with them.*

As they moved off and as she followed, she wondered what Anna was doing. She had looked ready for a professional hike, with her backpack and boots. Paula darted a glance at the people with her and relaxed slightly once she'd confirmed none of them were Anna.

But what if Anna went after Tommy?

She rolled her shoulders and forced her feet to keep walking. Let him do whatever he wanted with the skinny bitch. Clearly it didn't matter whether Paula stuck close to Tommy or not. Those two had a kind of feral magnetism to each other.

'I deserve better,' she whispered to herself, but her tone was doubtful, disbelieving.

She glanced up, hoping nobody had heard her talking to herself, and blinked in surprise as she saw that the group of hikers had moved a good couple of hundred yards in front of her.

Abandoned yet again.

She felt her face twisting in bitterness as she slowed to a stop. In front of her was a main road with three lanes. Beyond it she saw trees, greenery and hills that undulated up and down. The sky was slightly cloudy, but clear enough; no sign of that promised storm.

When the traffic came to a halt, Paula crossed over and stood beside the trees that lined the road. Then, taking a deep breath, and with a single lingering glance behind her, she batted aside the branches and stepped into the forest.

She didn't notice anyone watching her.

She didn't see anyone following her.

–

It seemed like hours later when Anna pulled a bottle of water from her backpack and drank greedily. Her breath came in short, uneven bursts and what felt like a lead weight had settled in her chest.

Never had she imagined that Paula would be able to walk this far, and at the speed she was going, she could easily have stuck with the professional hikers. The woman's stamina was disconcerting. Her own lack of it was worrying.

She paused at a rusted signpost and ran her fingers over the lettering.

Ellidavatn.

She removed her glove with her teeth and entered the place name into her phone. A lakeside town, she saw, part of the Heiðmörk nature reserve. It was seven miles away from the harbour.

Sunset was almost upon them now, and the sky was a strange yellow colour, with heavy hints of grey that held the promise of snow. The storm was brewing, and the captain of the *Ruby Spirit* had issued stern instructions to everyone that the ship must set sail no later than five p.m. or they would be stuck in the harbour overnight.

She dropped her backpack by the roadside and sat down heavily on it. Paula could be left out here; the ship might sail without her. And for Anna, that would mean a return journey with Tommy.

She shook her head. Tommy could be mean and nasty and was very good at belittling his wife, but surely he wouldn't let the *Ruby Spirit* commence its return journey without her?

No, Anna would push on; she would continue tracking Paula. And when she returned to the ship – alone – she would go back to England. If by some slim chance the ship had sailed, she would make her own way back and look Tommy up when she got there.

She locked her phone and pushed it into her backpack to nestle alongside the stolen waxed jacket. The pink beret caught her eye and she pulled it out. She needed to begin discarding the items that could be used as evidence against her. And not all in the same place.

Pulling out Mark's iPhone, she used it to dig a shallow hole and dropped the beret into it. She kicked snow over it until it had vanished.

When she was done, she hoisted the backpack onto her shoulders and began to walk.

At first, Paula thought it was a mirage, a shimmering, glittering pool of ice. She scrubbed at her head, at the pain that jangled at her temples. The throbbing intensified when she breathed in, and she closed her eyes.

Mirages only happened in the desert, or in really hot places, didn't they?

She opened her eyes. It was still there. And because she had no other options, she decided to walk towards it.

It was further away than she'd thought, and the condensation of her own breath and the snow that came in sideways obscured her vision. But it remained there, and didn't falter, and finally she came to a stop.

So, not a mirage, but a real lake, as wide and long as any she had ever seen. The bank was crusted with snow studded with gravel and sand. Bending down, she took her glove off, shoved it in her pocket and scooped up a handful of water. It burned her palm, and in some far-off part of her mind, she wondered if this was one of the thermal lakes Tommy had mentioned. But no, as the water trickled out between her fingers, she realised that it only felt warm because her skin was so cold.

She scooped up another handful, and raised it to her mouth, wondering if it was safe to drink, swearing a little at this fact being just one more thing she didn't know.

Tommy would have known.

She drank it anyway, then pulled out the almost-empty drinking bottle from her shoulder bag and filled it up. The world spun a little; she swayed, let the feeling take her and landed hard on her backside.

A half-hearted push in the snow with her hands behind her sent her staggering to her feet. Ahead, a solitary bird with a patch of red on its breast shrieked, shattering the silence, then took flight. Almost immediately the clouds opened up above her, and the sky shimmied, becoming lighter and darker all at once.

She held her breath, feeling the shift and the change, and kept her eyes focused on the sky. With a shudder it burst into life, and she released her breath in a long, drawn-out sigh.

A night-time rainbow. The Northern Lights. The reason for being here. Those magical elements that had so far eluded her. She drank them in, wondering what they meant.

A new beginning, perhaps. Or the end of something. Which made sense, because to have a new start, something had to come to an end.

The sound of footsteps had the same effect as shattering glass.

Reluctantly, she dropped her gaze from the sky and took a single step forward. The presence behind her mimicked her movement.

The rainbow flared, flickered and faded.

'Hi,' said a voice.

She ignored it at first. A part of her hoped it was a hallucination caused by dehydration and hypothermia. Her thoughts were very matter-of-fact, as though this was expected; what she deserved.

More footsteps now, crunching on gravel and snow.

Slowly, her body stiff now that she had stopped moving, she turned around.

Anna.

A flutter of fear, but so much less than she'd felt on the boat when she'd looked into her eyes. Just muscle memory, because the woman might have killed the man she was supposed to be looking after, but then again, perhaps it had been an accident.

Bruises on his face… airways blocked.

Paula nodded dully to herself. No accident.

'I'm lost.' Her voice had a strange echo. 'Are you lost too?'

'I'm not lost.' Anna smiled and moved closer.

Paula tried to back away as Anna approached, but there was something that made her freeze. Suddenly she was back on the deck of the cruise ship and someone was coming at her, and she couldn't move quickly enough, and that person was going to crash into her—

Instinctively she put her head down, flinching away from the oncoming figure.

But Anna moved on past and pointed out to the lake.

'The harbour is just there, do you think the ice will hold us?'

Paula looked at her incredulously. 'The harbour isn't there,' she said. 'That's a lake!'

'No, beyond it, look,' said Anna. 'I should know, I just came from there.'

Paula moved a few steps to the side. The wind flung the snow at her, and it stung now as it bounced off her face. The snow on the ground was whipped up into a circle that rose and fell. She watched it, fascinated, before looking across at Anna.

Anna shrugged. 'I'm going back anyway. The ship is due to sail soon and I don't want to miss it.'

With that, she began to walk, her boots splashing through the shallows before crunching as she moved through the snow and onto the ice-covered lake.

'Come back,' Paula called. 'It's too dangerous!'

But Anna paid no heed, and there was no sound from her footsteps now as they slid across the ice.

'Shit,' Paula swore. She squinted hard in the direction that Anna was walking. Were there lights there, twinkling across the icy lake?

She looked back the way she had come, remembering how long it had taken, battling through the pines, grabbed and scraped by their snow-covered branches. She was freezing now, desperate to get back to the *Ruby Spirit*. If she could take a shortcut, she wouldn't hesitate.

But she *was* hesitating. Did she really want to be trapped on an ice-covered lake with Anna?

No, but neither did she want to risk getting lost in the woods behind her and having the ship set sail without her on board.

She looked at the lake again. Making her mind up, she took two steps forward, the gravel crunching under her feet. With a gulp, she walked out onto the ice after Anna.

As she moved forward, she glanced up at the gloomy sky. The sun had been out earlier, making the temperature just about bearable. Surely the ice wasn't thick enough to walk on; wouldn't the sun's rays have weakened it? Beneath her, it shifted ever so slightly. She gasped and looked up again. She couldn't see the lights of the harbour, nor the shapes of ships. But it didn't mean they weren't there. Visibility was poor, that was all.

If she were to make this crossing, she needed a distraction. She sped up as much as she dared, and when she was within touching distance of Anna, she called out to her.

'What were you doing with Tommy last night?'

Anna turned, and regarded her with narrowed eyes. 'We watched the Northern Lights,' she said, her voice a thin whisper on the wind. 'You might as well know, Paula, I'm going to have him for myself.'

Paula barked out a laugh at the absolute nerve of the woman. But Anna's expression didn't change, and she wondered if she'd misheard her. Who would actually say that?

She coughed, feeling it deep down in her chest, and lights flared in her head as the motion sent another wave of pain through her temples.

'Excuse me?' she said, and her voice sounded weak and pathetic. 'I–I didn't hear you.'

Anna edged towards her until she was close enough to touch. Paula looked around, her mouth suddenly dry as she realised she couldn't see the shoreline any more than she could see evidence of the harbour. She swayed as the ice beneath her feet seemed to shift again, her arms automatically going out towards Anna for support. The other woman didn't move, and reluctantly she forced her hands down by her sides again.

'You heard what I said. And it means you'll have to go, of course.' Anna's eyes glinted dangerously in the twilight. 'There's not room for both of us.'

Run.

The instruction was brutally clear in Paula's mind, but her feet refused to move. She looked down at them, then across the lake, desperately seeking dry land, but her sense of direction had deserted her.

'You killed that man.' She didn't know why she said the words; it was as if she couldn't hold them back, but for some reason she wanted Anna to know that she knew exactly what she'd done.

'William, yes. And people before him, and after him, too.'

Paula was aware that her mouth was open, that her lips were flapping uselessly. Once again, she wondered if she had heard wrong.

'Who?' she breathed.

With a sudden motion that had her flinching, Anna whipped off her backpack and spun it around to clutch it in front of her. Pulling off a glove, she opened the zip and upended the bag. The contents toppled onto the ice. Paula flinched at the impact.

When she was sure the ice wasn't going to crack, she let her gaze land on the small pile of items. She drew in a sharp breath at the sight of the waxed jacket and lifted her eyes to meet Anna's.

'You,' she said. It wasn't a question, but Anna nodded anyway.

'I opened the gate. I saw it was unlatched the night before. I got the keys from Mark in case it had been locked. He was a crew member on the ship. Did you ever meet him?' Her eyes were far away, a smile in them that flickered for just a moment before fading. When she looked back at Paula, her gaze was blank and hard and... dead. 'That's his phone.' With the tip of her boot, she nudged the mobile. It slid soundlessly along the ice before coming to rest against the jacket. 'He won't be needing it any more.'

The words, loaded with hidden meaning, were more terrible than if Anna had described what she'd done with him.

'Wh–where is he?' But even as the question left Paula's mouth, she realised she didn't want to know.

Anna held out her arm in a sweeping gesture. 'He went into the sea,' she said matter-of-factly. 'Do you realise how easy it is to dismantle the railings on our balconies? I just rolled him straight into the water.'

Paula felt her body begin to quake with shock as finally, belatedly, she realised that she was in mortal danger. This woman would kill her, had killed before, two people that she had mentioned in as many minutes. She would not be telling Paula all this if she was planning to let her walk away. Paula had known people like this existed, but never, ever had she thought that in her adult life she would encounter such barbaric evil herself.

Run, she told herself again, and miraculously this time her body responded. She spun around to face away from Anna, her feet wheeling comically on the ice, and skidded away, running in a crouch, one hand trailing on the ice to stop herself from falling. Between the snowflakes that had thickened into a snowstorm, she saw tracks in the ice. Half of her brain wondered what they were, before realising they were not tracks; rather they were *cracks*. Spider webs of danger that even now were growing and multiplying. She changed direction, flashes of Anna in her peripheral vision to her right, and put her head down and urged her body along, sending up silent prayers that the ice would hold, that she could get back to the shore.

But what then? She chanced a look over her shoulder. Anna was moving fast, gaining on her, gliding along, and the sight made Paula slow down as she observed the other woman properly.

What could Anna do? Unless she had a gun concealed on her person, or a knife or some other weapon, what harm could this tiny, emaciated child-woman really do her?

She's killed men, a voice hissed in her ear. The man in the newspaper had been old, slightly infirm, but the other one, Mark, what about him? Paula looked down at herself. She was bigger than Anna, but she wasn't a fighter. She had never had a physical altercation in her life.

And then all her thoughts were shoved aside at the sight that suddenly appeared in front of her.

Through the snow that was coming down like tiny blades, she saw a dark hole open up in the ice a few metres ahead.

The shore!

The gravel, the sand and the sludgy ice – she had made it back to land!

She skidded to a stop just in time, and screamed, the sound ringing out, bouncing off the rocks that surrounded the lake, flinging her cry back at her in an echo.

It wasn't the shore at all; it was a hole. A great gaping breach in the ice. From here she could see the sides of it, the ice inches thick, and the jet-black water inside.

Her feet went out from under her, and she landed painfully on her knees.

Dead end! her brain was screaming. She scrabbled helplessly on the ice as she tried to stand.

Something, some piece of knowledge imparted by Tommy, came to her. Ice holes, drilled by fishermen to enable them to continue their trade while the lake or river was frozen. Too wide to jump, but no time to go around it.

She wasn't sure if she heard, felt or sensed Anna's presence, but there she was, gliding up behind Paula, the ice hole not frightening *her*.

No, for Anna, it was a perfect opportunity.

Her hands shot out, fingers roughly grabbing Paula's neck as she brought up her leg and jammed her knee into her back. Then she pulled Paula's head back and kicked it with all her might.

Paula's breath came out in a *whomph* sound, a sigh that seemed to draw every ounce of air from her lungs. There was no pain, not really, not yet. Just a deep sense of shock, dark and desolate as the hole in front of her.

The light, already fading from the day, dimmed rapidly, a vignette in her vision. She felt her head lolling and stupidly heavy, her chin nodding towards her chest.

She slumped backwards into the arms of her persecutor.

–

Anna worked quickly, down on her knees now, pushing the other woman across the ice. She had thought she was unconscious, but as they reached the lip of the hole, Paula's hands shot out to grip the edges of the ice, her fingers fluttering one minute, still the next.

Semi-conscious, Anna realised. She straddled Paula's back until she was kneeling on her shoulder blades, then raised her right leg again and this time stamped on Paula's hand.

Paula shrieked, her fingers splaying wide as she let go of the ice. With one hand free, it was easy to tug the other one away; then, in a single fluid motion, Anna leapt up and grabbed the back of Paula's coat, heaving her forward into the black water.

She wheezed as she tried to get her breath back, knowing she only had a few seconds before Paula's body would rise to the surface again. The shock of the water had temporarily revived her, she saw, and she came up kicking and screaming, arms flailing. Anna angled herself in preparation, and as Paula's face rose, mouth open as she sought air, she landed a boot on the crown of her head. Before Paula could recover, Anna went down on her knees and grabbed her hair, pushing her head down, down, down until no part of her was visible above the ice-cold water. Then, with the last of her strength, she shoved her backwards.

She stood up and shook her hands. Next time Paula came back up, she would hit the thick ice above her. No air, no escape hole.

She leaned over and put her hands on her knees, breathing hard.

Her job was done.

It was time to go back to the ship, and to Tommy.

Chapter 24

As Anna thrashed her way along the footpath that led back towards the harbour, she ripped the backpack off her shoulders. Anxiously, she glanced at her watch. It was well past the hour the *Ruby Spirit* should have left. She was short on time now, and though she was exhausted, and indeed felt rather faint, she pushed onwards.

She tore the zip open as she half ran, half stumbled through the densely packed pine trees. Out came Paula's iPhone, and she tossed it over her shoulder. It landed with a small thud on the path behind her, but she kept on going, no time to bury things now, but confident that nobody else was going to tread this path. The master keys were next, the ones she had taken from Mark. No need for them any longer. Over her shoulder they went too, along with the plastic sheeting, the spanner and the jacket that she had used to conceal her identity the time she had attacked Paula on deck, Mark's phone in the pocket.

With the bag now empty, she flung that aside too. There was nothing in it that would lead to her, nothing incriminating whatsoever.

She let out a rebel yell as she pushed onwards.

She was almost in the clear.

Practically home and dry.

On her way to start her new life.

On the main road, out of the woods and far enough away from Ellidavatn, Anna spotted a taxi rank. She hurried over to it, patting her pocket and pulling out a bundle of notes, relieved that they had not been lost in her day's adventures.

'Skarfabakki harbour, please,' she said.

The driver nodded at her in his rear-view mirror, and as he pulled away, she leaned back against the seat.

He didn't attempt conversation, and for that, she was grateful. She would have hated to have to be rude to him. If anyone asked questions later, people remembered things like that. In the back seat, she pulled up her scarf and covered her mouth with it, her hands going to her hat, ensuring her hair was concealed. Happy that she was unidentifiable, she lowered her eyes, and remained with her head down for the rest of the journey.

'Just here is fine,' she said when they pulled up on the main harbour road.

She handed over the fare, shook her head when he tried to give her the change. As he drove off, she walked the last few hundred yards to the harbour.

The *Ruby Spirit* was still there, a small cluster of people hanging around the walkway from which they had exited hours earlier.

Tommy, she saw, with growing excitement, was talking with the captain, and beside him… She heaved a sigh as she saw Patrick Duane.

She turned her back and fell in with a group standing around on the dock smoking, glancing continuously at their watches. She recognised some of them from the *Ruby Spirit*'s restaurant, and she shoved her hands in her pockets and attempted to look as bored and impatient as they did.

Every so often she would sneak a glance at the walkway. She couldn't go to Tommy while Patrick was with him. The officer was suspicious enough of her already, though she hoped the text message she'd shown him earlier had done enough to abate his distrust.

Discreetly, she examined herself for any signs of the misadventure that had taken place in Ellidavatn. Apart from wet patches on her knees and a body soaked in sweat, it wasn't apparent that she'd been doing anything but taking a leisurely stroll.

She looked again to the boat and saw Patrick speaking into a walkie-talkie. He cast a glance at Tommy and bent his head to the device in his hand. There was frustration on his face as the wind picked up, and with a gesture at Tommy, he moved inside the ship.

Taking her chance, Anna hurried onto the walkway and towards Tommy.

'What's the delay?' she asked as she reached him. 'The ship was supposed to leave an hour ago, wasn't it?'

He looked over at her, and even now, with his wife missing in a foreign land, she saw the desire in his eyes. Despicable, but flattering too, she supposed.

'I can't find Paula,' he muttered. His tone said it all. It wasn't worry that he felt, it was annoyance.

'I'm sure she's just lost track of time,' she said. 'Didn't she spend the day with you?'

He gave her a look, but said nothing. She reached out and put a hand on his arm. A comforting gesture. He looked down at it, then at her.

Above them, the Northern Lights appeared again, shimmering and flashing in bursts across a sky that had cleared after the storm passed.

It was freezing out on the front deck now, but Tommy showed no signs of leaving. Anna wrapped her arms around herself in an attempt to stop shivering and glanced up at his face.

'Can I get you a coffee?' she asked.

'No,' said Tommy. He looked at her properly, saw how utterly frozen she must look, and his face collapsed in a frown. 'You should go inside, though.'

Ah, but she couldn't. It was imperative that she remain by his side for the whole journey now. He needed to see her as a supporter, as someone who intended to take care of him, so that when they finally got back to Southampton, they would be so firmly entwined he wouldn't – couldn't – entertain the idea of her leaving him.

'I'm fine,' she said bravely.

'What is she playing at?' He shook his head, as if he were unable to believe his wife's selfish actions.

Anna stroked his arm again and gave his bicep a squeeze. 'I'm sure there's a reasonable explanation,' she murmured.

'They asked me to bring these out.' Dermot appeared, carrying an armful of flasks, sachets of milk and sugar spilling from the pockets of his parka. 'The officer is coming down soon.' At Tommy's sudden look, he pushed on hurriedly. 'I don't think he's got any news, though.'

Patrick was coming.

Anna rolled her eyes behind Dermot's back. She leaned in past him and addressed Tommy: 'I'm going to put on something warmer. I'll be right back, though,' she said.

He nodded, but didn't look at her, instead taking the tea that Dermot had poured for him. As the tall figure of Patrick Duane appeared on the bridge, Anna melted away.

Inside, she hurried into the elevator and impatiently stabbed at the button to her floor.

She didn't need to put on anything warmer, though she did need to fix her face and hair. She pulled off her hat and peered into the mirrored wall. Her skin was pale and dry, and her nose was so cold, it was red at the tip. She scowled at her reflection and lowered her chin, inhaling deeply.

She could smell herself, sweat that made her clothes cling to her skin. She wrinkled her nose and wiped her sleeve across her face. She was still sweating now, despite being out on the freezing deck.

It was the adrenaline, she thought, as well as the physical exertion. But the hard work was done now.

She swayed slightly as the lift doors opened and she moved down the hallway to her suite. At her door, she leaned on the wall as she pulled her key card out of her pocket. Thank goodness she was finished with the grind and the slog.

As she opened the door and stepped into the darkness, her world tilted again. She put a hand to her brow. Maybe she needed to eat an actual meal tonight. And perhaps she would; after all, she had worked hard today. She had earned it. A chicken salad, and it wouldn't be cheating; it would be like a prize or a reward.

Not yet, though. First, she had to make herself presentable.

She walked over to the bar and poured herself a half-measure of gin. Not too much, just enough to warm her. She sipped at it as she scrutinised herself in the mirror above the bar. She didn't like her reflection tonight, she decided. Being outside in the storm had ravaged her face. Still, she thought, as she raised her glass in a silent toast, she looked better than Paula did right now, of that she was sure.

She grinned, then paused, the glass halfway to her lips, as the curtain covering the doors to the balcony moved in the breeze. She put the glass down and walked across the room. She wouldn't have left the doors open; it was so cold, they were almost always closed anyway.

To the left of the door was a console table; on it was an iPhone, plugged into her own charger.

The pink trim of the case caught her eye, and a chill travelled up and down her spine.

Paula's phone. The one she had thrown away in the forest.

The curtain flapped again, making her jump, and an icy rush of wind blasted into the room.

Time hung, suspended, loaded, the tension palpable in the room. A second that stretched on. One sudden single movement, and then the attack came.

—

How long can you hold your breath?

Can you wake up now?

Do you see where you are?

Paula parted her lips and said, 'Are you talking to me?'

The words emerged in bubbles, and water streamed into her mouth and down her throat.

She screamed. It made it worse.

The voice that had spoken to her so urgently vanished as the last few moments crashed back at her.

She was under the ice; not just in the hole, but shoved under. The top of her head nudged it gently, and through the water she felt it burning her scalp. She raised her hands and her knuckles grazed something solid. She turned them palms up, hissing out more air as the ice above her held firm.

Air.

She was running out. She had wasted previous breaths. Her lungs juddered and burned, the feeling of a freight train within her.

How long did she have?

Not long enough, and the thought was strangely calming. She relaxed her shoulders and withdrew her hands. She had come in through a hole in the ice, and there were no tides here – this wasn't the ocean, it was a lake – so she couldn't have moved too far from there. The hole hadn't closed up in the last few seconds. It was here somewhere.

A shadow fell, and she tilted her head back. Terror ran through her veins, replacing the calm of just a moment before as a figure moved above her. Through the thick ice she saw the boots, the legs, the person they belonged to moving steadily over her. She curled her hand into a fist, but before she could smash it above her to get attention, she stopped.

Anna.

It took an astronomical effort to stem the panic, and even though time was against her, she remained motion-less. If Anna didn't think she was already dead, she would come back to finish the job.

It was an eternity, too long, and her lungs were burning, the air almost gone. Still, she stayed frozen, unmoving, and just as her eyes were rolling back in her head and her mouth was about to open, the shadow vanished.

No time, no time.

Thrashing now, she grappled at the ice above her, trying to claw her way to the right. If she wasn't correct, if she had lost all sense of direction and the exit hole wasn't over there, she wouldn't have time to go back the other way.

Too late.

Colours burst through the ice, the sky lightened to daytime and through the opaque ceiling overhead, she watched, quite unaware that she had stopped moving, stopped fighting, as green and blue flares lit up her under-water world.

Heaven, she thought, but then the colours changed to a bloody scarlet, with flashes of slate blue and frightening bolts of black. Her heart sank. Sadness hung suspended over her, covering her, like the water she was in.

Not heaven, but hell.

The intensity of the hues above her rippled and bled, and then she saw nothing at all.

–

Sight gone. Feeling nothing. But a sense that she was moving, a knowledge, a sensation almost akin to sleep-walking. And then... air. An icy blast that forced her eyes open, just narrow slits, but enough to see the lip of the ice, the new environment apparent as the last few flurries of snow landed on her lashes, obscuring her vision once again.

She drew breath, but the lower part of her face was still submerged, and the water burned down her throat. She shifted, throwing her weight up and forward, and then she felt it: cold wind on her face. Jagged inhalations, exhaled as part scream, part vomit. It floated past her, nestled against her neck, regurgitated food sticking to her sodden scarf. Tilting her face upwards, she laughed. It had a hysterical edge.

The colours were still there, those deep red and purple lights. Heavenly lights. Or hellish, maybe. She still wasn't sure.

She gulped and passed a wet hand across her eyes. Blinking hard, she looked again.

The Northern Lights.

Tipping her head back, she began to laugh again. All this time, all the money spent on the trip to see the lights, all the evenings of disappointment, of gazing fruitlessly at cloudy skies, and now, here on the brink of death, they had come out to play.

The laugh she heard coming from her frozen lips loosened something in her, a fear that had been settled in her soul for a long time now. Before this trip, before she'd ever clapped eyes on Anna. Even before Tommy. She had smothered it throughout the years, kept it hidden like a dirty secret.

She saw the error in that now, the mistake she had made. Because to conceal it meant hiding the person she was. Stifling it had led to her being careless. In turn, that had led to danger.

She stopped laughing and groaned instead, a long, guttural moan, like an animal. She was still in the ice hole, couldn't feel anything below her waist any more. She levered herself out with her arms, dragging her useless legs behind her, shuffling along like a commando until finally, after what seemed like hours, the texture beneath

273

her forearms turned from ice to the cold, hard gravel of the land.

Drowning had almost been the end of her, but now hypothermia was the very real risk. As if to cement this fact, her teeth began to chatter, her jaw working painfully no matter how hard she tried to clench it.

Warmth.

Her brain sent her a single instruction, and obediently she pushed herself into a crouch and tried to jog. Her movements were jerky and awkward, and time and time again she fell face forward into the snow. But by the time she reached the edge of the forest, she realised that her legs, only minutes ago numb and seemingly paralysed, were working again. She balled her hands into fists and punched at her thighs as she staggered through the trees.

On she went, not noticing the branches that reached out to grab her, paying little heed to the ground beneath her feet that dipped and rose. She moved unseeingly, and the landscape around her blended into nothingness.

A rucksack.

It dimly registered, the deep green material of the bag standing out against the crisp white snow.

Anna's bag.

She slowed and stooped to pick it up. The zip was open, and the bag was empty apart from a few euro notes in the bottom. With fingers that were increasingly stiff and painful, she grasped the money and shoved it in her pocket. Still holding the rucksack, she walked a few feet, scanning left and right now.

The waxed jacket.

It was caught on a low-hanging branch of a pine. She dropped the rucksack and ripped off her own sodden coat, putting the jacket on in its place. Even though her top and jeans were soaking wet, the single piece of dry material seemed to help.

She shook her head, droplets of water spraying around her, then tore her scarf off and draped it over the branch that she'd found the coat on. Above her, the Northern Lights seemed to be fading, and the forest around her settled into gloom. But before they disappeared completely, she saw the glint of metal a few feet off the path she had been following.

Keys.

The master keys to the *Ruby Spirit*, the ones Anna had stolen from someone called Mark. And… She pushed the leaves aside and picked up the next object. Her breathing sounded suddenly very loud in her ears.

Her own iPhone. The one that had gone missing.

She put it in her pocket to nestle alongside the money she had found in the bag, then stood up straight, rubbing at her breastbone as a strange ache began to spread and grow there.

Putting one foot in front of the other, she walked on.

–

'Just here is fine.' Paula leaned forward as the taxi rounded the corner of the harbour.

They were at the bow end of the ship, and the lights of the *Ruby Spirit* blazed out across the water.

She shoved some notes at the taxi driver and hauled herself out of the car.

She should find someone in authority, or ring the international number for the police. Or summon the captain. Tell him that one of his passengers had tried to kill her. She had to find Tommy, because Anna was after him now.

But not to kill him, though.

She nodded to herself. No, Tommy was safe for now.

The tips of her fingers itched. She rubbed them up and down the zip of the coat she wore, deep in thought.

Crowds of passengers stood in huddles on the deck at the top of the walkway. They parted for her, nobody looking at her, none of them realising that the person the ship was waiting for was in their midst.

In her pocket, she fingered the keys she had found in the forest.

Evidence.

'Yes.' She spoke the word quietly to herself, a confirmation that she knew what she had to do.

If she went to someone now and told them what had happened, Anna would be brought in and questioned. But she was clever, and everyone was charmed by her, and nobody would believe what she had done. Not even Paula's own husband.

Especially him.

Her lips curled into a scowl at the thought.

She pulled her hood up as she entered the corridor at the end of the ship and walked quickly along the hallway to the spiral stairs that would take her up to her suite. Her blood pumped freely now, and she patted at her face. She could feel both her fingers and her cheeks now, and she supposed the risk of hypothermia had passed.

On the floor where the first-class suites were, all was quiet. She walked past her own door, carried on until she came to the corner. She faced the door of the Arctic Suite and pulled the keys out of her pocket. Pushed one into the lock. A green light shone, a subtle click.

She put the keys away and slipped inside Anna's room.

A weight at Anna's back, crashing into her. Catching her foot on the step, she staggered out onto the balcony.

An attack, an intruder in her suite, and wasn't that just so ironic given all the things she had done herself? But whoever was behind her was still coming, up close, shoving at her now, a painful push in her spine.

The knife – the vegetable knife for the lemons that went into the gin – where had she left it? She had cleaned it after she had used it on Mark. If she could just make her way back inside and pick it up...

The thoughts ran through her mind in a millisecond, and she put her hands out, an instinctive gesture to catch at the railing of the balcony and steady herself so she could turn and confront her attacker, dodge past and get back inside.

But something wasn't right, and it took her precious seconds to realise as her hands searched blindly for support that *the railing wasn't there.*

She threw her arms back, hands up, staring at the gaping hole in front of her. The pressure on her back lessened for a second before the intruder came at her again. This time the hands were on her shoulders, moving up to grip the back of her neck. She gasped as her head was pulled back, her body almost bent in two... and she found herself staring into Paula's face.

The world tilted strangely, and for a moment she wondered if this was a hallucination. How could Paula be here, in her suite? She was back in Ellidavatn, in the lake, frozen and dead under the ice.

Was it possible she had underestimated this woman?

'Did you think you could take my life?' Paula hissed in Anna's face, and even now there was minimal anger showing; just what appeared to be a regretful mask of sadness.

She shook her, and an involuntary groan emerged as Anna's bones seemed to rattle in her body. There, there was the fury. Not in Paula's face, but in her body, in her strength.

Anna tried to still herself, to think clearly, to remember who this woman was in comparison to herself. She was nobody.

And in spite of the pain, she laughed. 'You can't hurt me,' she said, a little of her old self coming back as she taunted her. 'You're not built for it. It's not you. It's not *in* you.'

Paula narrowed her eyes. Still, she spoke softly, quietly, almost conversationally. 'You have no idea of who I am or what I can do.'

Anna felt herself shifting as Paula moved her arms. Suddenly that gap in the railing was an awful lot closer. She eyed it, uneasy now. Her hands crawled along the floor, seeking something – anything – that she could use to defend herself. Above her, Paula spotted the movement. She lifted her again, oh so easily, and Anna felt herself falling backwards, the world now upside down, the white-painted concrete floor rising up to meet her.

Her breath heaved out of her body as her head made contact with the ground. Something in her neck snagged and tore. Beyond the balcony, in the sky above the sea, she watched as the Northern Lights once more came out to play. No colours this time, just white flashes that zigzagged their way across the cloudless landscape.

Not the Northern Lights, she realised dimly. Nor was it the Leonid meteor shower. Rather, damage inside her own head, her own body. On the brink of unconsciousness, she tore her eyes away from the outside world and forced herself to look at Paula.

Yes, she thought. She had underestimated this woman.

And then Paula began to talk, and Anna listened as best she could.

Chapter 25

Before

On the doorstep of the house I'd hoped never to see again, I took a deep breath as I dug my key out of my pocket.

I'd not told anyone in Edinburgh that I had to return home. I'd not mentioned the phone call from Carl. I didn't tell the girls I roomed with, not the boy I'd met, who I thought I could love, nor any of the teachers or staff.

In the dark hallway, I flicked the switch as I closed the front door softly behind me. I almost turned it off again straight away, wishing I didn't have to see that no housework had been done since I'd left.

All was quiet, and there was an impending sense of something twisted and wrong as I took my coat off and hung it on the banister. Carl hadn't said why I needed to come back. Just that it was my mother.

I took another deep breath and trudged slowly up the stairs.

They were in her room, my mother propped up on the floor with her back against the bed, her head hanging low. She wore just her underwear, and without the ever-present dressing gown, I was shocked to see how thin she was. I thought of my own new-found purging routine, and it was something of a wake-up call. I vowed that I would stop before I ever got to look like the emaciated woman in front of me.

Carl was in the bed, the dirty sheet pulled up to his chin, the telephone beside him. In the gloom of the room, the whites of his eyes watched me carefully.

'Mum?' I said, and when there was no response, I repeated it louder. 'Mum.'

'I don't know what happened.' Carl spoke for the first time.

'What do you mean?' I looked at him, because it was easier than looking at her.

He shrugged, his mouth downturned and sulky.

My heart began to beat faster. I put a hand on my chest, hoping to steady it, but already my body was preparing me for the blow that I didn't even know had landed.

I went down on my knees next to her, scanning the floor first for stains or needles. In a dim part of my mind it registered that I was wearing my newest jeans and I didn't want them ruined.

I put my hands on her shoulders, ready to get her up and onto the bed, where she could sleep it off. The same way I had done hundreds of times in the past.

Her skin was like marble; cold and unyielding. I snatched my hands away before forcing them back, my fingers working upwards to the side of her neck.

I knew there would be no pulse; I knew she was dead.

I'd known it, deep inside, when I got the phone call from Carl, though I hadn't admitted it.

'How long has she been like this?' My voice was a breathy whisper, filled with the horror of what was in front of me.

Carl shifted in the bed. I looked up at him, at this pathetic man. The sheet slipped down, and he grabbed at it.

'I don't remember,' he said. His voice was dull and heavy. He looked at me suddenly, a frown crossing his face. 'When did I call you?'

I didn't answer him. I turned my attention back to my mother. I had known that one day this would happen, I'd imagined it and, horribly, sometimes I had wished for it. But now that time had come, I found myself beset with a deep, dark sadness.

I tilted her face so she was looking at me. Her eyes were cloudy, unseeing, and her mouth was partially open in a painful grimace. What had her last words been? What had she thought about as she slipped away?

Could I have done more?

I clapped my hand to my mouth. At eighteen years old, kneeling next to my mother's corpse in that filthy house where I had grown up, I knew that question had the potential to haunt me for the rest of my life.

I couldn't let it. I *wouldn't*. I had only just begun to live. I was starting to find out who I was. People in Edinburgh liked me. And yet it all came back to this.

Around her left arm was that old pink belt that used to belong to me. It was a brownish-grey now, years old, and it made me even sadder to look at it. Why was she still using it? In some warped, horrible way, did it remind her of me? Or had it originally just been the closest thing to hand and was simply now a habit, part of her kit, like the tablespoon she favoured?

Gently, I unclasped the buckle and removed it from her arm.

Behind me, Carl shifted. As if the belt had awoken something in him, he shuffled to sit on the edge of the bed.

'I need my stuff,' he said.

In an instant, my strange sadness turned to hate and anger. It felt pure as it ran through me, cold as ice in my veins, like the brown stuff was in theirs.

Him.

It had always been him who was to blame.

I looked around the room, my eyes landing on their paraphernalia. Why had this happened now? Despite what people thought, it was difficult to overdose from heroin if you were a long-term continuous user. Something must have happened. Had they mixed it with alcohol or another drug? I could ask him, I supposed, but I'd never get the truth.

'Stay there,' I instructed him.

He looked resigned, weary and shattered as he leaned back on the pillow.

Downstairs, I moved around the kitchen. I touched nothing but looked carefully at the boxes and bowls and needles that covered the worktop.

I peered closely at a box. Fentanyl. I knew about this. I'd read an article only last week about heroin users in Glasgow dropping dead after using this opioid painkiller to cut their powder.

I looked in the dining room. I recalled the time I had orchestrated the meeting between my teacher and my mother, and the hope that had bloomed in me when I realised how close I was to getting out. Mum had been proud of me, and had tried to behave and present herself as a normal mother living in a clean and tidy house. All under my instruction. Then there was the deceit. The words I had spoken to Miss Hayle about Rebecca Lavery, my scholarship competitor. My lie had been bad and wrong, and though I had justified it for my own means, was this my punishment?

Outside, the garden seemed lighter than normal. I glanced up and a smile almost reached my face at the sight of the white and blue tail in the sky. The Hale-Bopp comet. We had been taught about it in school, a full year before it arrived in the sky visible to our naked eyes. I had loved hearing about it; it was even better the few times I had seen it. One night, Carl had come to find out why I was in the garden so late. I told him about the comet as I strained to see it through the clouds. For a moment we observed it in silence, and I wondered if it could be a starting point for the two of us.

Seconds later, he broke the companionable silence with a laugh, a rasping, wheezing sound. Then he told me about a group in America called Heaven's Gate. Thirty-nine people had believed that the Hale-Bopp was actually a UFO; they had killed themselves in a mass suicide, believing their souls would enter the craft as a direct link to God.

He sneered as he left me in the dark of the garden. I sat for a little while longer before returning inside.

He had ruined it for me; the magic was gone.

I had never looked at the skies again, until now.

During that small, seemingly insignificant episode that lasted no longer than a few minutes, my mother had been elsewhere.

Like she always was.

I closed my eyes and remembered her. I thought of what she could have been.

Upstairs, Carl hadn't moved. He didn't look at my mother. He scratched at the side of his face and I heard his long nails as they rubbed over the coarse unshaven hair on his cheeks. He needed the stuff.

'Do you want me to…?' I trailed off, holding up the syringe I had prepared.

His dark eyes flashed briefly, and he stretched out his arm.

I shook my head and gestured. 'No, that one.'

He looked at his tattoo. 'It's got scar tissue. I had an accident; it's why I got the tat, to cover it, see? It's not as good for me in that arm. It's not got as much sensitivity.'

I listened to him prattling on. It was the most he'd ever spoken to me since the Heaven's Gate conversation. Like now, that too had been one-sided. Outwardly, I nodded, but inwardly, I seethed. My mother's dead body was two feet away, and still it was all about him. As if sensing what I was thinking, he stopped talking and rested his arm on a pillow.

It was strange to touch that mottled, patterned limb. Up close, the scar tissue was clear to see and feel.

Deftly and with such efficiency you would have thought I was a user myself, I wrapped my old belt around the top of his arm. I lifted the end close to his wet mouth.

'Hold it,' I instructed.

He did as I asked, biting down on it.

I waited until the veins stood up. I pushed the needle in at an angle.

He watched me, half smiling, his inflated ego apparent on his face. He thought he had me. An easy replacement for my mother. The arrogance. The self-entitled nature of this beast.

As the liquid flowed into him, I saw the moment of change. His eyes widened to large black pools, and for the first time, the only time, the last time ever, I saw fear in them. He knew what I had done; he knew I'd massively overused the fentanyl.

His lower lip trembled, and with all the strength left in him, he ripped his arm from my grasp. His face was a world of shock, of horror and disbelief.

I had hurt his feelings. I uttered a laugh, but it was shaky, bordering on hysterical.

'Why?' he bleated, and his words trickled away to a whisper.

I glanced at my mother, at the mess he had made of her over the years. That was why.

He drew a breath, shallow and thin. We watched each other for a while. He blinked rapidly, and a tear trickled out of his left eye.

His next exhalation would be his last, and we both knew it. As it puffed out of him, he spoke my name. It was the first time I could ever remember him saying it. And it would be the last.

'Paula,' he breathed.

Chapter 26

Anna kept her eyes closed the whole time Paula was speaking. She didn't struggle, didn't attempt to shout.

'Did you hear me?' Paula asked when the silence had stretched on for too long. 'Did you hear what I'm capable of, what I've done in the past?'

Anna opened her eyes suddenly, and Paula drew in a sharp breath. Her left pupil was blown; so large that the black covered the blue iris entirely.

She gurgled, and Paula glanced away. It was hard to look at her.

She wondered if Anna would say her name, like Carl had. Suddenly she felt desperately sad.

Why me?

And with that thought, the fury came, just a small wave upon a shore, fluttering inside her in little flashes. Outside, the sky mimicked her emotions and the colours came out again.

'Look,' she said. 'The Northern Lights are back.'

She hefted Anna up and around so the woman was facing the sea, then went down on her knees beside her.

'They're really something, aren't they?' she said.

Beside her, Anna twitched.

–

On the frozen balcony of Anna's suite, Paula waited. Next to her, Anna sat docile, quiet, still. After a while, the Northern Lights flashed for one last time and dimmed. Beside her, Paula felt Anna stiffen.

She knew it was over.

There was no need to prolong it.

Paula wasn't a psychopath, after all. This was just like Carl; someone who had done wrong and had to be dealt with. Not a punishment; it wasn't teaching her a lesson. It was simply the knowledge that the person on the floor in front of her was very, very dangerous and needed to not be here any longer.

Just like Carl.

She braced herself and put out her hand. For a moment it rested lightly on Anna's wrist before she gripped tightly and rose at the same time.

The smaller woman made no sound as Paula hauled her across the floor in the dim light that glowed from the lamp inside. As she did so, there was a cracking noise, and the strange feeling of Anna's arm extending further than it should have in Paula's grip. Paula paused, looked down at her.

Anna's eye, the one that didn't have the blown pupil, shimmered in the moonlight.

Paula went down on her knees and pushed at the tiny form in front of her until Anna was balanced on the edge.

I'm sorry. She bit at her lip to stop herself saying the words out loud. The woman didn't deserve an apology, but the social norms were so deeply ingrained in her that it was habit.

The absurdity of the situation hit her, and now she was biting at her lip to stop herself from laughing.

Don't get hysterical, she warned herself.

One last push, and Anna's lower half was dangling overboard.

The broken woman came to life then. With her damaged arm she caught at Paula's wrist. The pain hissed out from between her teeth. Her body juddered and she slipped further over the edge.

Paula flicked her hand back and forth, trying to shake the woman from her grip. She gritted her teeth and tried to yank her arm free, but Anna held on stubbornly.

No words were spoken; a silent struggle. Paula lay flat on the ground, the cold of the balcony sinking into the front of her body.

Their eyes met, and the stillness of the night was heightened.

Something pushed at the inside of Paula's mind. The memories of her youth, freed from their self-imposed prison by telling the story of Carl's death, sprang at her, as bright and vivid as the Northern Lights had been.

'Oh my God...' she stuttered. 'I-I know you.'

Anna's one good eye, previously sullen, widened in fear.

Paula looked at her properly, amazed that she hadn't seen it from the start. The woman she'd thought about so much over the years of her childhood, the girl whose life she had coveted. The girl whose life she had stolen with a lie.

Look at her now.

'Rebecca.'

She said her name, and even though she knew she was right, the expression on Anna's face verified it.

'You're Rebecca,' she said again, almost shouting now, strangely furious, absurdly let down. 'I envied you!'

Anna opened her mouth. Her front tooth was chipped, and vaguely Paula wondered when that had happened.

She hauled her up, clenching her jaw with the exertion. Anna flapped across the ground, a fish out of water, her head at an angle, her one good eye staring balefully, accusingly at Paula.

And now I'm the broken one, thought Paula.

Anna shuffled to a sitting position. She cradled her bad arm, inspecting it for outward signs of damage.

'What happened to you?' Paula whispered. She remembered the night she'd gone out on the streets to buy heroin for her mother, seeing Rebecca wearing that dress, those heels, looking utterly beautiful, but still oh-so-sad.

Anna lowered her head, her chin to her chest. A child-like gesture, and with that one movement, she told Paula everything she wanted to know.

'You were still being abused.' It wasn't a question, and Paula inhaled sharply at the realisation.

Slowly, Anna pulled herself to a standing position. Paula cringed back against the cold white wall of the balcony. The exertion it must have taken, the strength… Beneath her coat, she felt her heart thumping. Now it was the end, because this woman's strength was superhuman, ongoing. Nothing could destroy it, not a broken arm, not being blinded in one eye, not half starving herself to the point of collapse.

The tables had turned, suddenly, without warning. And Paula was weary now, so she closed her eyes and waited.

A clang of metal on metal. She opened her eyes. Anna was holding onto the railing to her left, her bracelet making contact with the frame. She stood in the gap, and she smiled now, and Paula saw what she was going to do.

She understood. Anna – Rebecca – couldn't stand to have someone know that the front she had put up was just that. Pretence, a fake life.

Paula shrieked, some part of her still obsessed with the young girl she'd never actually known. Because she understood, *she'd been there too.*

She darted forward, hands out, fingers grasping at air, staring in horror at Anna's pale bone-china face, her eyes closed, her expression no longer hard, no longer falsely friendly, no longer calculating or plotting or deceiving.

She was serene.

The splash was minuscule and the pale face remained, tilted upwards, just for a second or two, before it was swallowed by the black water.

–

Later, freshly showered and dry and warm, wearing her own coat now, Paula stood in the doorway where hours earlier, she had prepared to alight the ship for a day in Iceland.

How things can change in a few hours, she thought as she watched the staff and the police milling around.

Beyond them, torchlight bobbed on the edge of the forest. She heard her own name called, far in the distance, and smiled to herself.

This is it.

She pushed herself off the door frame and strode out onto the deck.

He was on his own. Clusters of people stood near him but kept a good distance away. Dermot was there, one hand on the rail, speaking into his mobile phone, casting anxious glances across the landscape, where the police and the public searched diligently.

Tommy looked lost, and she slowed her step. It was interesting, watching him like this. He must have been freezing cold, but he didn't move like the others. They switched from one foot to the other, cuffs pulled over hands, arms wrapped around themselves. He didn't move a muscle. He stood immobile, staring out, his face dragging seemingly with sadness.

She moved up behind him and put her hand on his arm.

'What's the hold-up?' she asked, striving for impatience in her tone. 'Shouldn't we have set sail by now?'

He stared at her for long moments. His eyes widened, his hand went haltingly to his mouth, where it hesitated, suspended in mid-air, before darting out and gripping her shoulder.

'Where have you been?' he hissed.

He grabbed her other shoulder with his left hand, and his fingers dug in painfully. She felt her sadness go up a notch. Anyone else's husband would have wrapped them in a bear hug, but his reaction seemed to be one of anger.

'Jesus, Paula!' Dermot stepped up and laid a hand on the back of her neck.

A different touch to that of her husband, she realised. She wriggled out of the grip of both men. The contrasting contacts were a reminder of what she had and what she was missing.

'What's going on?' she asked.

Tommy's mouth worked, but words seemed to escape him.

Dermot cleared his throat. 'We thought you'd got lost. Everyone's out looking for you.'

She frowned and tilted her head to one side. 'How could I get lost,' she asked, 'when I never even left the ship?' It was a risky statement; after all, there had been the group of walkers she had originally set out with. They hadn't paid much attention to her, though, and she could always say she'd changed her mind and come straight back.

'You didn't leave the ship?' Tommy spoke between gritted teeth.

She shook her head and glanced at her watch. 'No, too cold.' She smiled brightly at him. 'Did you have a good time? Did you go to the thermal lake? Hey, did you see the Northern Lights? They were fantastic!'

He took her arm and squeezed it. 'I don't think you realise the trouble you've caused,' he said, his words sharp and clipped. 'The police have been called.'

She barked out a laugh and looked around at the people who had gathered beside them, all wanting to catch a glimpse of the woman who had walked into the wilderness and come back seemingly unscathed.

'Who on earth called the police?' she asked, feigning amazement.

'I did.' His jaw was clenched, and his face, only moments ago sagging with sadness, was now stony.

'You reported me missing to the police and held up everyone's journey home?' she asked, incredulous. 'And all that time I've been on board!'

His nostrils flared. She pressed on, the desire to see him look small and stupid growing by the second. The sudden power she held was intoxicating. 'You must feel so silly!'

It was the very first time in their relationship that she thought he might hit her. She locked eyes with him. Did he see her now? Did he see the person she had suppressed for all of her adult life?

The captain appeared, and Dermot hurried over to him. She watched him duck his head as he spoke to him. The police came on board not long afterwards. She listened as Tommy explained to them haltingly that she had been located safe and sound.

'I haven't actually been off the ship,' she chipped in. 'I came out here earlier, but it was too cold for me.'

Their gazes lingered not on her, but on Tommy, expressions of quiet fury on their faces at the time he had caused them to waste. Tommy's face blazed bright red.

Satisfied, she wandered back through the doors. He fell into step beside her. At the elevator, she pressed the down button.

'What're you doing?' he asked.

'I'm going to get some dinner,' she replied. 'It's been a long time since lunch.'

His lips flapped uselessly as he fought for words. 'Don't you think you should tell me what happened? Where you've been?' he asked roughly, his voice granite and steel, cold and black.

She sighed. 'You made an error, Tommy. I'm sorry if you feel stupid, but that's not my fault.'

He blinked at her, speechless.

The lift doors swished open. She went inside and pressed the button for the restaurant, leaving him outside in the hallway, something else on his face now as he gazed in disbelief at the stranger in front of him.

–

She piled her plate high from the buffet and took a seat in the corner of the restaurant. It was late, and there were not many other people in there. Those who were finishing their meals cast glances at her, but nobody approached her table.

The tannoy crackled and sparked into life. Paula paused and lifted her head to listen.

'Good evening, fellow passengers, we are truly sorry for the delay in setting sail this evening, and we thank you for your patience. The Ruby Spirit *is now ready to leave…'* A pause, as though the captain expected a cheer or a rapturous round of applause. *'We will be easing out of Skarfabakki harbour and travelling at a rate of around eighteen to twenty knots.*

'Our next sky-bound adventure will be seen in the early hours of tomorrow morning, when Jupiter and Venus will be visible in conjunction. This usually takes place roughly once a year, but tomorrow will be your second chance this year to witness this special event.

'These two planets are actually millions of miles apart from each other, but to the naked eye, they will appear to be as close as you can get.'

Paula let out an ironic laugh. The captain could have been describing her and Tommy. To the outside world, they were in perfect sync. Reality was another matter.

Stabbing her fork into her plate of food, she ate ravenously, unable to remember the last time she had let herself enjoy a meal with such abandon. What a waste, she thought, to deprive herself of something so wonderful for so long. And what had it been for?

No, not what, but who?

She thought of Anna, how rarely she had eaten, and how small and brittle her body had been. Who had she been dieting for?

That wasn't a diet, though, what Anna had been doing. It was a whole other ball game.

A memory, a recent one, flickered in Paula. Heaving Anna across the balcony, feeling the snap of her arm. The tears had sprung to Anna's one good eye then, and Paula had watched, mesmerised, knowing that the broken woman on the ground in front of her probably hadn't cried real tears in an awfully long time.

Her stomach turned over. The last of the lasagne refused to be swallowed. She chugged back a glass of water and put her fork down.

She tried to push the thought away, dismiss the recollection that quite suddenly threatened to overwhelm her. But that was what she had done with Carl, and it had been an error.

She swivelled in her chair and looked out to the dark black sea. She lowered her head and let the awareness in.

Chapter 27

Before

I never told anyone what really happened the night I found my mother dead in our house. Of course, some of it was known. Once Carl was dead, I dialled 999, stuttering over whether I needed the police or an ambulance.

'I found them like that,' I told the policemen as they surveyed the two dead people in my mother's bedroom.

Most of it was true. I hadn't moved my mother, and Carl remained where he had died. The only anomaly was the needle, now resting in his cold, stiff fingers instead of where it had been.

In mine.

'What time did you arrive?' they asked me.

'Just before I called you,' I replied.

I thought of the neighbours, but didn't worry that they had seen me. Nobody saw me. Nobody ever had.

I watched them take my mother and Carl out. They loaded them into a private ambulance. I felt an absurd need to wave. At the last moment, I saw Kevin smoking in his front garden.

He locked eyes with me, just for a moment. I nodded to him. He tilted his cigarette in return.

'Sorry,' he mouthed.

I nodded again, slipped inside and closed the door behind me.

–

Later, after the funeral, I returned to Edinburgh.

He was there, the boy I had been dating. We spent the night in his room, in an apartment off-campus.

He didn't ask where I had been. I felt no need to tell him. Later, when things were serious, I would say my mother had died, and I'd never known my father. Later, I would tell many people this fact. It covered my history nicely, and it was rare that anybody probed further.

That night, that first night back, we ate pizza like we had a dozen times before, and watched a film. He had his hand on my knee, and it was comfortable, and lovely, and for a time I forgot about what had happened at home and thought about my life from now on.

When the pizza was finished, I went to the bathroom and purged it quietly. When I emerged, he was there, in the hallway, looking at me.

'Don't do that, Paula,' he said, and his lip curled as he spoke, his words clipped and tinted with disgust. 'It's such a cliché, I don't want to see or hear that.' He looked me up and down, his eyes probing, reflecting, judging. 'There's nothing wrong with you that can't be fixed in the gym. I'll take you along with me one day.'

I tried for a smile. I looked for the words that would convey how grateful I was that somebody cared about me and what I did to myself. Back then, it never occurred to me that he should have told me I was beautiful the way I was.

I nodded at him, and just like that my purging days were over. 'Okay,' I said, and as an afterthought, I added, 'Thank you, Tommy.'

Chapter 28

She was still there, at the same table, looking out of the same floor-to-ceiling window at the same black night.

The *Ruby Spirit* had set sail an hour ago. Paula had sat stiffly in the chair, the half-finished plate in front of her. She'd anticipated shouts; maybe the ship would come to an abrupt stop when somebody spotted the small, pale, blonde form floating in the harbour.

But there had been nothing.

She began to relax, feeling her ramrod-straight spine loosen.

There would be something. When the boat docked, and the cabins came to be cleaned, they would find Anna's with all her possessions inside.

She patted her pocket where her iPhone sat. She had swept the suite, taken the phone once she had charged it. In the bathroom, she had looked for a long time at the box of condoms in the small cabinet over the sink. The same brand that she had found in Tommy's wash bag, planted there, she saw now, by Anna.

The threat was gone now, laid to rest, never to return. Of course, there would be others; silly little girls with designs on Tommy. There always had been. That wouldn't change. But there would never be another threat quite like Anna. Of that, Paula was sure.

Here he was now. Her husband, hesitant by the lift doors, observing her from across the room. She lifted her chin and met his gaze straight on.

Tommy looked away first.

Paula smothered a smile.

How liberating it was, to release this power, leashed and controlled and... *hidden* for so long.

Paula remained seated. Eventually Tommy made his way over, weaving his way through the tables.

'You all right?' he asked as he reached her.

She watched him, standing awkwardly in front of her.

All their history there, in the small gap between them. She liked knowing someone so well. She liked that she still had the ability to surprise him. She liked that she had spoken up against him.

'Do you want to go for a walk round the deck?' he asked. He shuffled his feet. 'It seems a bit milder.'

She felt a smile rise inside, but she didn't allow it to show on her face.

Knowledge nestled in her gut, that if he were ever lost to her, she would be just fine.

He reached out a gloved hand, a nice gesture, so simple, yet it had been missing for quite some time.

She took his hand, let him haul her up. He stayed close as they walked to the elevators. Inside, she leaned forward and pressed the button for the top deck.

She felt movement at her back. A sudden warmth as Tommy removed his scarf and placed it around her neck.

'It's a bit milder, but still cold out there,' he murmured.

She didn't thank him. Instead, she nodded, touched the woollen scarf and raised her chin.

Her thoughts were elsewhere now, on what came next, on where to go now, on *herself* for maybe the first time since she'd escaped her childhood.

On her own future.

A Letter from J. M. Hewitt

Thank you so much for reading *The Life She Wants*. I hope you enjoyed reading it as much as I enjoyed writing it! If you'd like to keep up to date with any of my new releases, please follow the link below to sign up for my newsletter. Your e-mail will never be shared, and I'll only contact you when I have news about a new release.

www.jmhewitt.net/newsletter

If you have the time to leave me a short, honest review on Amazon, Goodreads, or wherever you purchased the book, I'd very much appreciate it. I love hearing what you think, and your reviews help me reach new readers— which allows me to bring you more books! If you know of friends or family that would enjoy the book, please recommend my novel to them, too.

You can also connect with me via my website, Facebook, Goodreads, and Twitter. I'd love to hear from you.

Website: www.jmhewitt.net

Facebook: J.MHewittauthor

Twitter: @jmhewitt

Goodreads: www.goodreads.com/author/show/2972605
.J_M_Hewitt

I wrote *The Life She Wants* during the first lockdown in 2020. Collectively, we were all confined to our houses, and I don't think I was alone in finding activities closer to home. For me, it was stargazing, and the night sky. The International Space Station was passing over frequently, and Space-X launched into orbit on 30th May 2020. It was a clear evening, and late that night I found myself in my garden, with my neighbour on the other side of the fence, and we watched both the rocket looping and the space station circuiting in awe.

Later that year, I was lucky enough between lockdowns to take a holiday with family in Norfolk. The light pollution there is minimal, and we stood outside and watched the bats swooping and the stars gleaming. The Northern Lights are something I'm hugely interested in also, and all of these elements led to the scenic parts of *The Life She Wants*, when Paula and Tommy go on what should be a once-in-a-lifetime Scandinavian cruise to view the lights. The lights, the sea, and the skies can be malevolent as well as magnificent, and I hope this shines through in the atmosphere of *The Life She Wants*.

Thank you again, so very much, for your support of my books. It means the world to me!

J. M. Hewitt

Acknowledgements

Novel writing is very much a team effort, and I'm so grateful to have so much support. Firstly, as always, so much love and so many thanks to my parents, Janet and Keith Hewitt. Thanks also to my family: Darren, Jordan, Liv and Eloise, Emily and Dawson and the newest addition, baby Emma Rose. I also wish to thank John and Joan Daly – I hope to deliver a copy of this book to you personally this year! A special thanks also goes out to my little Marley, unconditional friend, and constant writing companion.

Many thanks to my wonderful agent, Laetitia Rutherford of Watson, Little, for consistent support and championing my books. And thanks to my gorgeous editor, Leodora Darlington, I'm loving working alongside you! Copyeditor Jane, thank you for a tremendously thorough job – your work is hugely appreciated.

All my girls, Heidi, Tracey Jordan, Kim, Lou and Lisa, thank you for the regular calls, messages, lunch dates and catch-ups. Special thank you to Victoria Hill, photographer and artist extraordinaire and a wonderful friend. Big thanks to Corrie, continuous supporter and reader of my books, giver of treats and cakes, and generally the best neighbour for sure.

I would also like to thank the crime fiction community. The writers, bloggers, publishers, book club admins (Tracy Fenton #TBConFB). You all rock and I hope to see more of you this year.

Finally, a huge thanks to you, the reader, and as always, as long as you keep on enjoying my books, I'll keep on writing them.